WHAT WE ARE MADE OF

Thomas Hettche studied philosophy and modern languages in Frankfurt. After prolonged stays in Kraków, Venice, Rome and Los Angeles, he moved to Berlin with his family. Hettche has written numerous literary essays, and his previous novels have been translated into ten languages and won several awards.

WHAT WE ARE MADE OF

Thomas Hettche

Translated from the German by
Shaun Whiteside

PICADOR

The work on this novel was funded by the Deutsche Literaturfonds e. V.
The translation of this work was supported by a grant from the
Goethe-Institut that is funded by the Ministry of Foreign Affairs.
My thanks to the *Villa Aurora* in Los Angeles, the *Casa Baldi* in
Olevano Romano, the *kunst:raum sylt quelle* in Rantum and
the *Stiftung Schloss Leuk* for their hospitality

First published 2008 by Picador
an imprint of Pan Macmillan Ltd
Pan Macmillan, 20 New Wharf Road, London N1 9RR
Basingstoke and Oxford
Associated companies throughout the world
www.panmacmillan.com

ISBN 978-0330-45208-3

Originally published as *Woraus Wir Gemacht Sind*
by Kiepenheuer & Witsch, Cologne 2006.

The publishers gratefully acknowledge Suhrkamp Verlag for
permission to reproduce an extract from 'Die Bäume verneigen sich'
by Heiner Müller, from *Werke, Die Gedichte*, Band 1.

9 8 7 6 5 4 3 2 1

A CIP catalogue record for this book is available from
the British Library.

Typeset by Set Systems Ltd, Saffron Walden, Essex
Printed and bound in the UK by
CPI Mackays, Chatham ME5 8TD

For Friederike

CHAPTER ONE

Engel

They were late. They had no idea how long the taxi ride would take from the hotel down to 29th Street. They just wished, jet-lagged, exhausted, that the hot summer city would keep on passing by the car windows, while they slid towards each other on the soft back seat of the car, into the blast of air conditioning that dried their sweat until they started shivering. With exhaustion, he said. With excitement, said Liz. They kissed, stared outside, and then they were there. Just three steps through the evening, its air damp and heavy, and they were standing in the agreeably metallic chill of a restaurant whose French name Niklas Kalf had quickly memorized and, as they entered, promptly forgotten.

Businessmen with braces, their jackets over their arms, jostled noisily at the bar by the door, women in linen suits held cocktail glasses, the barkeepers behind the counter had a lot to do and didn't smile. The restaurant itself was so dark that only the candles and the white tablecloths gleamed coldly, gold-framed mirrors and high-backed leather benches by the walls, bistro tables in front of them in a narrow line.

Kalf recognized Albert Snowe immediately. Late forties, white shirt, red tie, and distinct stubble. He was constantly rocking from his toes to the balls of his feet, his beefy torso bobbing back and forth as he did so. His companion must have been Lavinia Sims, the translator. When she had told him that his editor at Crowdon Myers & Trax wanted to meet him for dinner, Niklas Kalf had been very surprised. He blinked, as he often did when he was nervous, and the bright pupils of his blue eyes were watery and transparent. Since childhood he had worn his pale blond hair short. It lay fine and thin on his head, and his bright, freckled skin also contributed to the impression of strange transparency that emanated from him. Usually, when he was interviewing, it helped that he seemed to disappear. Another ability that he had nurtured since his childhood days.

Just as Liz touched her husband's arm, Albert Snowe spotted his guests and waved, and they pushed their way through the crowd. They greeted each other, and the waiter led them to a big, round table. They sat down in the light of the candles that ringed the white circle of the tablecloth and shone for a brief moment in the pupils of all four of them, with a strange technoid shimmer that flashed and vanished like the trembling light from a diode.

Two tall waitresses who looked like sisters handed out large menus. It'll be a pleasure to serve you. A waiter, skilfully measuring out the number of ice cubes by tipping the pitcher over the back of his hand with a motion the newcomers had never seen before, poured iced water into very big glasses. Snowe had a massive head and strong jaws. Deep wrinkles dug into the dark, leathery skin on either side of his mouth. He took his glass and tinkled the ice in it before he drank, washing into his mouth an ice cube that he slowly crunched.

'How was the flight?'

Niklas Kalf saw the gaping door to the kitchen, its neon-white tiles gleaming like the entrance to some unimaginable subterranean system of cellars, and nodded. The flight, he thought. It took only Snowe's question for the LCD screens above the seats to whirr back into place, and for everything, for that very long moment, to be quite still. And again he remembered what he had been thinking.

Nothing, he thought, has any existence compared to the cascade of effects that will be unleashed when the plane takes off. Nothing about the whole routine is to be trusted, not the safety instructions, the friendliness of the flight attendants or the boarding card or the smooth lines of the plastic-covered cabin. One last seat belt engaged with a click. Then the plane's thrust drove heads back into seatbacks, something rattled, stopped rattling, and Lufthansa flight 340 from Frankfurt to New York City was, after a slight delay, in the air at one thirty-five p.m.

The stewardesses immediately began distributing food. Relieved, the passengers rummaged in their hand luggage, bags and jackets, books and CDs were passed across the seats. Liz unpacked her pale blue mohair knitted jacket and a magazine, and began evenly flicking through it with great concentration, not stopping to read. Every now and again she pushed her curls back behind her ear. Since she had fallen pregnant, her hair, the same colour as his own, seemed even thicker and heavier than before. He watched the way she rested her hand on her high-arched belly. The shiny paper pages flashed regularly in the beam of the overhead light. Women and houses, clocks and big, made-up eyes. Again and again, the sea. He looked at his wife, calmed by the evenness of her movements, and growing increasingly tired, as killingly cold air streamed uninterruptedly into the turbines and burned unimaginably hot in a fine kerosene mist.

The display on the screens above the rows of seats changed in a silent, monotonous sequence. Time to destination, local time at origin, local time at destination, estimated arrival time, metres and feet, Celsius and Fahrenheit, kilometres and miles. Ground speed 448 m.p.h., altitude 31,000 feet, outside air temperature – 51 F. And a small dot on the screen, the tiny depiction of them, moved very slowly across the dark blue Atlantic to the coast of North America, which waited on the left-hand edge of the screen.

Kalf cleared his throat. The small, wandering dot in front of his eyes wouldn't disappear. Snowe laughed and crunched up another ice cube when he didn't reply. Kalf must be delighted, he said, to have the chance to be in New York. And as an author, too.

Yes, of course. Particularly since they were both, he and Liz, visiting the United States for the first time. But he wasn't an author.

The editor raised his eyebrows in surprise.

'A biographer,' said Kalf.

'So is a biographer something different?'

'Niklas is a bit awkward where his own life is concerned,' Liz explained apologetically.

Snowe looked at her. He understood that, he said. Very well, in fact. He himself was exceptionally interested in the life stories of strangers. Perhaps that was why he had become an editor. 'And sometimes a strange life can contract to a single moment.'

Kalf nodded. 'A secret.'

'Yes,' said Albert Snowe.

And after watching him quietly for a moment, he leaned forward, looked at him intently over the candles and the little bouquet of blue and white orchids and asked, 'Have you ever heard of Imogen Engel?'

Kalf shook his head, and time stood still. Imogen Engel, he repeated in his mind, suddenly no longer tense and tired, out of his jet-lag bubble of dream and half-sleep, but awake, now, and curious about the story that might lurk behind that strange-sounding name, which had immediately cast him under its spell. But first the two waitresses came into the circle of candles to take their orders, and when one of them bent down between Lavinia and Kalf, he was surprised to register the tiny image of a Madonna on each of her long fingernails. Blue Cheese, Thousand Island, Vinaigrette, French, Italian, Caesar, Ranch, Russian, Dijon, she listed the salad dressings, and only the ring finger of the left hand with which she held the pad quivered. Snowe ordered red wine for everyone.

'Who is Imogen Engel?' Niklas Kalf asked impatiently.

Lavinia Sims pacified him. The translator was a tall woman, a few years younger than Kalf, with long, dark hair and clear features. 'An old New York story. It must be seven years ago.'

'So?' Kalf asked.

'What happened?' Snowe replied in English, as if he hadn't even noticed that they were speaking German.

'Well, back in May of '95 early one morning a man was found floating in the lake in Central Park. His torso was slashed open. The police said they found something like a dozen stab wounds.'

Kalf wasn't quite sure what stab wounds were. 'And?'

'Imogen Engel was the perpetrator,' said Lavinia. 'And the most important thing is: the girl was thirteen years old.'

He immediately imagined the lake, which he'd never visited, but which he'd seen on television. A figure in it, heavy and dark and faceless as the girl whose name was enough to throw a hand in horror over a face in his imagination. Oh, yes, stab wounds: *Stichwunde* was the word he'd been looking for. They brought the wine. Snowe tasted it and nodded to the waitress, and she poured for each of them in turn, except for Liz, who kept her hand over her glass.

The girl, said Snowe, picking up his thread, stabbed the man in the belly until he was dead. Then she rolled him into the lake. 'Listen, Nick: she was a child! And she led an affluent lifestyle with her family on Central Park West.'

'Affluent?'

'She was rich, Nico,' said Liz, helping him out.

Kalf looked at her with surprise, as if they hadn't seen each other for ages. He thought again of how they had come from the airport into the city, still trembling from the night and suddenly plunged back into reality. The way the taxi bobbed up and down over the bumps of the New Jersey Turnpike, as though breathing in and out, until the tips of the skyscrapers had appeared off to one side. Straight away they had eagerly begun to decipher the familiar, but just as they had recognized the Chrysler Building and the Empire State Building and wondered where the World Trade Center might have stood, the strip of highway plunged between graffiti-strewn cliffs into a dip in which a toll gate held up the car for a moment, before the tiled Lincoln Tunnel sucked it into its endless dirty white, and the storm in front of their eyes stopped for a moment.

Perhaps because they couldn't bear the strangeness of it all, at that instant they had kissed, and he had laid his hand on Liz's belly, and then what Brecht called the Isle of Manhattan had risen breathtakingly quickly behind the high walls of its towers, as immeasurably high and coldly strange as the Aurelian Walls around Rome.

Jet lag, he thought in amazement, when he saw Liz already setting her cutlery back down in what was left of the shimmering, oily vinaigrette. He had no idea how long he had been inattentive, his salad dish was empty, too, and they were already clearing the plates. Then the waitresses stepped out of the darkness up to the table, and very slowly and with strange, submissive care, handed out large plates. Everyone but Liz had ordered the entrecôte. The rest of them waited till her fish was brought.

'What about Imogen Engel? What was she like?'

'She had short, cropped black hair, I think. She looked a bit like a punk.' Lavinia rummaged through her memory, while the waitress pushed open the swing door to the kitchen with her back and quickly dabbed a smudge of sauce from the edge of the plate with the tip of her apron, before stepping to the table and, in the candlelight, handing Liz her very pale fillet of catfish.

'I remember she'd been medicated for years,' said Lavinia Sims, speaking in English now, more to him than the others.

Snowe nodded. 'Zoloft.'

As if talking about a book to which he had just bought the rights, he didn't have to think for a second before mentioning the name. Then no one said anything until Snowe raised his glass with a smile. It's great that we've finally met up!

What sort of deal, Kalf wondered, have we travelled all this way to negotiate?

Snowe was, he said, really excited about the book. And of course he was interested in how Kalf had ended up writing about Eugen Meerkaz, of all people, a German immigrant who was almost as forgotten in the USA as he was in his homeland.

'Quite simple – his widow rang me up one day.'

'Elsa?'

'Yes, Elsa Meerkaz. She asked me to write up her husband's life.'

Albert Snowe nodded. So? All secrets out in the open? Snowe put his water glass back to his lips and let an ice cube slide into his wide-open mouth.

That depended, Kalf said, what Snowe meant by secrets. He didn't know what the publisher meant, and talked about the agreement he had made with Elsa Meerkaz in Los Angeles. 'Do you know her?'

'A little,' said Snowe slowly, chewing the ice. It had all been very strange. All those suspicions and then Eugen Meerkaz's sudden death.

A waiter whose pectoral and abdominal muscles stood out clearly beneath his white T-shirt began clearing the plates away. Kalf had no idea what Snowe was referring to. The life of the physicist Eugen Meerkaz struck him as a typical immigrant's tale. And he didn't actually understand why his widow wanted a book about her husband. In her letters and occasional phone calls, the widow didn't seem particularly vain, in fact she didn't even seem particularly interested in what he wrote. Only the fact that she was paying him very well consoled him for her lack of interest.

A new bottle of wine was brought, and Snowe raised a glass to the book. Niklas Kalf felt as if he had long ago started playing a part in a story that he knew nothing about. He remembered that at some point in the flight he had found himself thinking about the *Macao*, that Portuguese ship on which Elsa and Eugen Meerkaz had fled Lisbon in 1941. Now we're flying over their heads, he had thought. And over all the others, slaves and immigrants, exiles and businesspeople who had set off over the centuries from all the countries and cities of Europe, their goal that harbour on the other side of the Atlantic.

'Now we're flying over their heads,' he had whispered to Liz.

'Whose heads?'

'Meerkaz and his wife.'

Liz had smiled and put her hand on his knee. Then he had stared sleepily at the dot of light on the screens above the rows of seats, which had wandered further and further across the world, while names flashed up on the left-hand edge of the picture before disappearing again on the right. Galway, Reykjavik, Shannon, Godthab, St John's, Gander, Halifax, and all of a sudden at some point the outline of a figure had slipped into his perception, vaguely, intangibly at first, but more and more clearly the longer he yielded to his dimming wakefulness. Visible for a moment, then vanishing again, then clearly recognizable once more like the figure of the Saviour in the coral, face in the root, the marble hand of a forgotten stone god.

He clearly recognized a sleeping boy, his head Europe, lying dreaming on his arm, his hand lying slackly in the Holy Land while his cool nape, the vertebrae standing out beneath the evenly suntanned skin, stretched across the cold sea to America, which was his body. The boy's bony hip bent away where the continent ended at the great Pacific Ocean, and the youthful feet with the beautifully shaped toes stretched all the way to Asia. We set off, Niklas Kalf had thought, from one of his eyebrows.

'But what I still don't understand,' he said, changing the subject, 'what was the girl actually doing in the park so late?'

Snowe stared at him across the table and started talking about Sheep Meadow and Strawberry Fields, the twisting paths by the lake and the grassy slopes by the Metropolitan Museum of Art. It wasn't just the front garden of the skyscrapers, a strip of green amongst the main roads, Central Park was really a world of its own within the city. Particularly when at night the park dimmed its lights, and the noisy metropolis seemed almost small.

'It's a place where a secret world unfolds on its grassy fields and beside its still waters. It's very Whitmanesque, Nick!'

It was the second time he had called him that. Niklas

Kalf stared into his eyes for a moment, before the publisher looked down and started engraving patterns in the tablecloth with his fingernail, as if he was only waiting to hear what Kalf thought of his story. And reluctantly at first he imagined the lights of the park making creamy circles on the dead water of the lake, the trees behind them a black palisade wall, and above them the silhouette of the smiling buildings that stand attentively around the park. How quiet it must have been!

They'd found the body at a point on a level with Seventieth Street. It was floating in the water about a hundred yards north-west of the terrace near the Bethesda Fountain. The police had found Imogen not far away, on the shore, sitting under a tree and staring fixedly at the water.

Kalf nodded. He could tell there was something about the murderess's story that interested Snowe, something he hadn't understood.

'I'd like to see a picture of her.'

Snowe shook his head, as if her appearance was unimportant. A young woman with rich parents, who found comfort crossing the borders of class. One of the waitresses asked if any of them wanted a dessert. Cheesecake, German chocolate cake, chocolate layer cake, strawberry shortcake, lemon meringue, Mississippi mud pie, pecan pie, cherry pie, sherbet, ice-cream sundae. No one made a move to order anything.

'And what about the victim?'

'His name was Lester Mahoney,' said Snowe. 'He grew up in the Bronx.'

A sales assistant at Macy's, in his mid-forties, who lived alone. In the summer he played softball in the park.

THOMAS HETTCHE

And he drank. Niklas Kalf nodded again. He was already settling into this stranger's life. That was his job. Like an innate quality that can't be changed, squinting, say, or having a particular memory for numbers, he could rely on that strange life suddenly being familiar and very close to him. The heat that fades so hesitantly in the park in summer that you're left gasping for breath. That strange atmosphere in which the present won't burn out and in which a lonely man in his mid-forties, who drinks too much, falls into conversation with a young girl at night, as if it was the most natural thing in the world. As if the park was a neutral zone in which Lester Mahoney, from the north, from the Bronx, was watching the sun sinking behind the block where Imogen lives. Imogen Engel, who is thirteen and rich.

He still didn't have the sound of their language in his ears, and didn't know what she asked Mahoney. He still couldn't imagine those sounds that exist in every language when you're sitting close together and it's getting dark. He struggled to imagine what it smelled like that evening, in the park that he knew only from the movies.

'What sentence did she get?'

Snowe grinned, as though that was the first question aimed at the heart of the story.

'Imogen pleaded guilty to first-degree murder,' he said without a moment's hesitation, keeping his eyes fixed on Kalf.

First degree murder, that is: deliberate, malicious, cruel. As a juvenile she was only sentenced to seven years. That was in 1995. 'So she could be free right now?'

'You're right!'

Snowe slowly lowered his head, and the smile lay soft and dark on his face. He looked at the German for a long time, as if he wanted to add something, but he didn't.

Had he known her, Kalf wondered, having noticed Snowe's expression.

'What really happened that night?'

It's almost midnight, Snowe said quietly. Imogen Engel walks slowly from the brightly lit path and across the dark grass, holding a paper bag full of beer cans. She's wearing a loose black shirt with a worn-out collar, and a leather thong around her neck. She willingly hands out the beers. One member of the group, Lester Mahoney, is the same age as her father. He's so thin that he looks almost ill, and the insecurity in his face is apparent even to a teenager. But perhaps it's precisely this embarrassed hesitation that attracts her or irritates her, or perhaps both at the same time.

'She had met him in the park several weeks before and they'd chatted about the Oklahoma City bombing. "Hi, you remember me?" she asked.'

Kalf knew what Snowe meant. Now at last he could hear her voice. And the voices of the others, too. He nodded to the publisher and continued the dialogue. '"Yeah," says Lester Mahoney, looks up at her and opens the beer can.'

Snowe replied, ' "I'm Imogen from Oklahoma." '

' "Yeah," Lester says again,' Kalf continued, 'and repeats with a grin, "Imogen from Oklahoma." '

At around this time, Snowe explained, a police patrol goes by, they catch the group in the dark with their searchlight and tell everyone to leave the park. They complain, but the officer won't budge, so the drinkers head off in all directions.

'Lester Mahoney, beer can in hand, was seen rambling north.'

First of all he heads towards the lake, but then he suddenly changes direction and takes a wider path through rose bushes and hazel trees, Imogen close behind him, the brown paper bag in her hand, still with a few cans in it. For Kalf, now, it was as if he were there, that night in the park, watching after her. As precisely as possible he memorized her gait, and the way her thin, girlish arm dangles by her hip, her black hair and her childish face, purse-mouthed in the flashing red and blue light of the police car, wide-eyed like an animal taking refuge, silent and sniffing, in the undergrowth of the park.

The table was empty and the evening was over. Once more one of the two waitresses appeared and brought the bill. The publisher looked at the total, dropped a credit card on the long, thin book and clapped it shut, as if finishing a novel. Everyone was waiting to go. Not yet, thought Niklas Kalf, and Snowe hesitated and stared at the table again, as if wondering what might still be missing from the murderess's story. And as Kalf watched his fingernails drawing lines on the tablecloth again, he suddenly realized how he knew the name of that fountain in the park, the one where the sales assistant's corpse had been found. Bethesda: a healing pool near Jerusalem. *Krank, Blinde, Lahme, Dürre,** according the Gospel of John, waited there for the moving of the water. *Denn ein Engel fuhr herab zu seiner Zeit in den Teich, und bewe-*

*gete das Wasser. Welcher nun der erste, nachdem das Wasser beweget war, hinein stieg, der ward gesund, mit welcher Seuche er behaftet war.*** It's an illusion to believe we know when a story is over. We barely sense its beginning.

CHAPTER TWO

'Liz?'

Niklas Kalf snuggled against Liz from behind and slowly stroked her shoulders and the back of her neck. Resting his head in his other hand, he looked out into the night. The Excelsior, an old immigrants' hotel with narrow, winding corridors whose deep carpets absorb every sound, is just by Central Park, and their room on the ninth floor faced the back, towards West 82nd Street. From their bed they looked out over several blocks of low town houses, most of them with roof terraces, with plants in tubs and low wooden palisades, tables and chairs. Behind them, wooden water tanks jutted into the sky. In the air-conditioning unit below the window, the rotor turned with a metallic, grating noise. It was as if the tension that had lain over the city all day were finally relaxing.

Before they booked the flight, Liz had hesitated for a long time about whether she really wanted to be in New York. It's a magic date, she had said, whatever happens. There are no magic dates, he had replied, although that was, as he knew, untrue. In the morning they decided to spend the day in bed, except when he got up to fetch pastrami sandwiches and beer from the deli around the corner. He had been crazy about Liz since she had fallen pregnant, and again and again they acted that day as if they were making a child.

Liz turned to face him and ran her hand through his short hair. For a moment she seemed to study him very closely, before a smile spread across her face.

'Nothing has happened,' she said with a grin.

'I disagree,' he grinned back.

'Kiss me, Nico!'

She closed her eyes. Her mouth was rather small, and even after all that time rather shy. They had been together for fourteen years, and Niklas Kalf had watched the network of little wrinkles spreading around her eyes over that time. Her tongue felt carefully for his.

Apart from that dinner with Snowe, they had spent the four days that they had so far had in New York on their own, doing nothing but walk around, once all the way down Broadway and back up Park Avenue. They'd strolled across Brooklyn Bridge and through Chinatown and taken the ferry across to Staten Island. They had soon got used to the vibrant heat of the city and, sweaty and tired, they had barely paused in their forays.

My Big Fat Greek Wedding and *Blood Work* were on at the cinema, and Liz had allowed herself to be persuaded to see *One Hour Photo*. In the *New York Times* Niklas Kalf had read the obituary of Kim Hunter, who had died in the city at the age of seventy-nine. The picture beside the text showed her as Stella in *A Streetcar Named Desire* with Marlon Brando, for which she had won an Oscar. Aldrin, the Apollo 11 astronaut and the second man on the moon, had been attacked in Los Angeles while leaving the Beverly Hills Hotel. A film-maker who had been trying for years to prove that the moon landings had never happened had challenged Aldrin to swear on the Bible that they had, and then attacked him with the Bible.

Preparations were going on everywhere, both for the memorial celebrations and for a possible threat. There were a lot of police in the streets, while the subways were emptier and emptier. It was as though everyone who could was leaving the city before the eleventh of September. Something like the smell of silence had entered Manhattan, and when bagpipers from all five boroughs set off on their long walk to Ground Zero, their music could be heard everywhere in the city. It even entered their dreams, because the Excelsior was no distance from Broadway, which the bagpipers walked down, but not until the Memorial Minute at 8.46, when the first plane had hit the Twin Towers a year previously, that sudden, weird interruption of life, when SILENCE SETTLED OVER LOWER MANHATTAN, did they wake up. For a moment they both thought the city had disappeared from outside their windows.

Later they heard the bells recalling the impact of the second plane, then the foghorns of the ships on the Hudson, when the second tower had collapsed at 10.29. All day they listened to the screaming, wailing, throat-clearing sirens that were constantly sounding and fading in the streets below them. And when Liz had been asleep for ages, Kalf stared beyond her into the pink-black sky with the old water tanks standing out against them, wooden barrels on three-legged iron structures anchored high on the roofs of former factory buildings.

Imogen Engel, he said, repeating the name of the young murderess that Albert Snowe had talked about. In a curious way, her story now connected him with New York, and he imagined taking what he knew about that young woman back to Germany a few days later. And he couldn't help thinking about how Liz had looked at him, when she had read the manuscript of his first book, and then said something that had struck home, as though she had read the irrefutable future in his hand. 'You're a biographer, Nico!' And she'd been right, even if he hadn't replied at first, and had only looked at her, blinking, as though trying out the idea for the first time. But the subject of his second book had turned out to be a stranger's life, too. Now, at the age of forty, his PhD was forgotten and he was working on his third biography. Imogen Engel, he thought, even though he was half awake, then went to the bathroom, lay back down next to Liz as she slept deeply and evenly, and long after midnight he himself had finally gone to sleep.

Once, when dawn was already breaking and the hotel room was full of cool grey light, he felt her arm on his belly, but when he woke up in the morning, very late but still tired, Liz was no longer lying next to him. The radio alarm clock beside the bed showed 10.39, and the television was murmuring quietly, although he was sure he hadn't switched it on. And as he looked around sleepily and unsuspectingly for Liz, he registered on the screen the American President climbing the steps to a podium, with a high wall of black porphyry behind it. In the spotlight over Bush there gleamed the white hair of Kofi Annan, who folded his hands without taking his eyes off the President.

'Mr Secretary General, Mr President, distinguished delegates, ladies and gentlemen: we meet one year and *one day after a terrorist attack brought grief to my country, and brought grief to many citizens of our world.'*

That's here! The thought darted through his head. That's the UN. And it's happening right now. And as he listened to Bush, he waited for Liz to come out of the bathroom. But she didn't come.

After a few minutes he turned off the sound and went to check. Then he stood helplessly in the middle of the room and looked thoroughly about for any sign of her, studied bags and clothes to see if anything had changed, but everything was in its place. Except Liz wasn't there.

Although he told himself that she would knock at the door at any moment with lattes and muffins, he considered asking at reception whether she'd gone out. Or should he go straight down and out into the street to look for her? He decided to wait for a while, and switched the sound of the television back on. *'In cells and camps, terrorists are plotting further destruction, and building new bases for their war against civilization.'*

The text of the speech was shown on teleprompters on either side of the podium. Not for a moment did Bush take his eyes off the delegates, his eyes sweeping from left to right and back again, like those of a watchful animal. Like the yellow eyes of a wolf, Kalf thought, noticing for the first time that tiny, panting, teeth-baring smile that accompanied everything Bush said. How complacent he was. *'And our greatest fear is that terrorists will find a short cut to their mad ambitions when an outlaw regime supplies them with the technology to kill on a massive scale.'*

At that sentence the phone began to ring. He was sure

it couldn't be Liz, and hesitated for one more ring, the way you move in a dream, and only then picked up the receiver, and a soft voice asked, 'Nick?'

'The United States has no quarrel with the Iraqi people!'

'Yes? Who is it?'

A woman's voice.

'A regime that has lost its legitimacy will also lose its power.' A war, he thought, is being decided upon. Right here, where I am.

'Liz is fine. You can stay completely calm. Everything else depends on you.'

A shock of horror ran through Niklas Kalf. 'What do you mean? Who are you? And where's Liz? And what depends on me?'

'No police. Tonight, just act as if nothing has happened. Then everything will sort itself out.'

'What's going on? I don't understand.'

'It all depends on you,' the soft voice said again, before hanging up.

'We must choose between a world of fear and a world of progress.'

He held the receiver to his ear a moment longer, and waited for the voice to come back. The President's wolfish little smile panned through the auditorium. Kofi Annan had put the tips of his long, thin fingers together in front of his face, and held his head, with its big, tired eyes, at a slight angle.

'We must stand up for our security, and for the permanent rights and the hopes of mankind. By heritage and by choice, the United States of America will make that stand.'

The President paused and pursed his small mouth as though to blow a kiss. War surrounded him like immortality. Once again he cast his eye across the room, which he was about to leave, although no longer as a politician. *'And, delegates to the United Nations, you have the power to make that stand as well. Thank you very much.'*

The red figures of the digital alarm clock by the bed showed exactly four minutes past eleven. Only now did Niklas Kalf fully realize that Liz had disappeared, and that knowledge flooded through him, cold and black it foamed through all the spaces of his memory and self-certainty, nothing but brackish, oily fear which paralysed him, and in which he drowned unresisting and silent, until that fine, gleaming point at the tip of his tongue, the one with which we say 'I', was finally extinguished. His hand stroked her pillow until nothing remained in it of the impression of her body.

CHAPTER THREE

Bodies everywhere

The walls of the big hall of the Museum of Natural History consist of dioramas, big windows onto artificial worlds, from which countless animals stare out. There is no daylight, and yet the hall isn't dark, it gleams with the colours of all the places that open up into it. You immediately grasp the rigidity with which the animals are captured, as though their actions had frozen at the very moment you entered the space. And from all of these deep-frozen movements there drips dead, thick, viscous silence.

Instinctively, Niklas Kalf stopped dead and held his breath. An unreal aquarium light, cold and green, filled the high-ceilinged, three-storey room, and with a glance at the skylight he saw that down below, on the ground floor, a whole herd of elephants was solemnly walking on the spot. The rigor-mortis light touched him, seeped into him and finally dissolved the spell that had held him prisoner since Liz's disappearance that morning. He stood at the balustrade for a long time, looking down at the elephants. He remembered a newspaper report that he had read a few days previously, still in Germany, and started to tell Lavinia Sims about it, as if nothing had happened. It was about the gorilla in Prague Zoo, which had drowned in its cage.

'I think his name was Pong.'

'I don't understand.' Lavinia looked at him sideways.

'Half of Europe is flooded at the moment. The rivers are bursting their banks, even the Moldau.'

He became aware that tears were starting to run down his cheeks, turned away and walked over to one of the dioramas. In the mild light of a sand dune in the evening, with desert jumping mice and the winding trail of a lizard, he stopped and wept. He remembered the untiring, continuous tone of the telephone, which had forced its way painfully deep into his head, until he had finally hung up and turned off the television. Then he had picked up the receiver again and phoned Lavinia Sims, the translator. It had been his idea to go to the museum, when they were standing outside the hotel, and on the way here he had tried to explain to her what had happened.

'What's it got to do with the book?' She was standing a few feet behind him.

'It's all about the book!'

'And who rang you?'

He shrugged. 'I don't know.'

His anxiety about Liz, which had frozen into a strange kind of numbness since he had hung up the phone, welled back up in him and took his breath away.

'I'll ask Snowe what we should do.' Lavinia took a mobile phone from the inside pocket of her tweed jacket.

He didn't like the idea of telling the publisher, but on the other hand he didn't know what else they were supposed to do, so he just nodded and, as she made the call, walked slowly from one diorama to the next, looking at the animals in them.

'The Moldau in Prague, you know,' he murmured to

himself in a tear-choked voice, as Lavinia Sims pressed her phone to her ear. 'The zoo is right on the bank. The whole monkey house was under water.'

He didn't actually care whether Lavinia was listening to him. But as he spoke, he was calmed by whatever it was that wept within him, and slowly the numbing effect of the soft voice ebbed away. He cleared his throat. 'The seals took flight. One of them, I read, later came back to the pool of its own accord. A second one was caught somewhere in the north of the city. They never found the others.'

Now he was standing by a window from which fell a cool, clear northern light. An elk among birch trees. Far off in the hazy sky, a few thin cirrostratus clouds. In the foreground, in a puddle in the boggy ground, which looked like meat in aspic, three woodcock were bathing. Liz, he thought, nothing but her name: Liz.

'The elephant, I think it was an Indian elephant, they shot it.' He noticed his voice becoming firmer, and then the tears stopped coming, too. He turned round and walked back to Lavinia. 'He refused to leave his cage, although the water was up to his ears.' The idea made him grin. 'They also killed a bear and a lion. Two rhino-ceroses escaped.'

Lavinia snapped her cellphone shut and waited for him to stop talking.

'I talked to Snowe,' she said. 'He thinks we really shouldn't go to the police right now. It still isn't clear what's actually happened. And there's too much risk of harming Liz.'

Kalf looked at her, shocked. 'But we've got to go to the police.'

'Snowe suggests we wait for the reading first.'

She ran her fingertips very carefully across his cheek, as though checking whether there really were any tears, even though she could see them. Then she hugged him, and her closeness felt so good that he completely forgot how little they really knew one another.

'I think Snowe's right,' she murmured after a while. 'You can't cancel your reading.'

He closed his eyes again, before the hug was over. Then they pulled apart. Lavinia smiled at him rather uncertainly.

'Snowe said you'd be best off doing what people expect of you.'

'But I haven't the faintest idea what people expect of me.'

'There must be something weird about this guy Eugen Meerkaz.'

'I don't know. I really don't know.'

Niklas Kalf turned away. He stopped by a cliff in the mountains. A rough nest of bare branches, a golden eagle, wings spread wide, landing on its rim. Two chicks squawked at it inaudibly. Down below, an ibex prepared to leap from one rock to another. Tears welled up in him again, and he realized that he felt sick to his stomach.

'I can't do a reading today.'

'You've got to.'

He looked at Lavinia. What he felt was that Liz seemed still to be very near. The inexplicability of her disappearance meant that she was somewhere nearby, as if it would take only a quick movement of the head for him to see her again. Like a ghost standing behind him. Like these animals here. Corpses everywhere. If you bend over them from close to, you can see the badly hidden stitches, the bald patches and the dusty bits of fluff between the tufts of hair. But the looks from the glass eyes still follow you, and their noses sniff at you, their lips glisten, and they scrape their hoofs.

'I always go to natural history museums,' he said, looking round again.

He pushed open the heavy door, they left the room, and as they walked along the corridors and back down the stairs, on which they didn't meet a single other person, he told Lavinia about the giraffe in the Natural History Museum in Basle, which stretches its neck through two storeys, and about the Museo de Zoologia in Barcelona. On the ground floor of that one, the skeleton of a whale flies beneath the ceiling and on the first floor, in an old wooden display cabinet, tiger, wolf and hyena are brought together. In the staircase is a small elephant. He heard himself talking, and felt his own loneliness, and the thought flashed through him that he had to do something, but he really didn't know what it might be, and went on talking. About the completely naked woolly rhinoceros he had seen in Kraków, and the dinosaur skeletons in the run-down Natural History Museum in Berlin.

'The Natural History Museum in Vienna is completely different again,' he said. 'For example they've got a white shark, and they found the shoe of a sailor of the Austrian Navy in its stomach. They also have the whip scorpion of the Cistercian Father Dominik Bilimek, who accompanied Kaiser Maximilian to Mexico and, after his assassination, brought his scientific collections back to Vienna in very dangerous circumstances. Then there's the chimpanzee Honzo, who looks mutely past you when you look at him. Ernst Zwilling, African explorer and big-game hunter, brought him back from Cameroon, but in the Schönbrunn zoo the ape quickly became so vicious that he could only be kept on his own. Honzo is supposed to have been a passionate smoker and beer-drinker.'

'They gave the chimpanzee alcohol?'

'Yes. But even more famous is the Java rhinoceros that died in 1801 at the age of only fourteen months on the way to Vienna. It was stuffed for the Imperial cabinet of natural curiosities, and it's one of the oldest preparations of its kind. And you know what?'

'What?'

'In that part of the museum they still don't have electric lights, and when I was there in the winter it grew dark in the early afternoon, and I looked at that rhinoceros for a long time, and suddenly sensed something of the strange predominance that death-time has over life-time. You're alone in those vast rooms. It's so silent. And when you decide to make your way to the exit, in room 35, behind glass, a whole herd of zebras thunders silently past you.'

CHAPTER FOUR
Venus Smith

That evening, when he put his foot on the first step of the stairs in the Goethe House, his heart was thumping in his throat, and he noticed his knees trembling with excitement. He became aware that he was convinced, for no reason whatsoever, that he was about to see Liz again.

The Goethe House is just on the other side of the park if you're coming from the Hotel Excelsior. The five-storey building is one of two identical narrow town houses that a pair of brothers had built side by side on Fifth Avenue, where the city ended at the newly laid-out Central Park in those days. Only one of the two buildings still stands today. Inside it is dominated by a broad flight of stairs that seems to wind at ever greater speed through the floors before finally pouring like the train of an evening gown onto the black and white marble of the entrance hall.

There stood Niklas Kalf, trying to calm himself. He wasn't late. He hadn't forgotten his typescript, either. He had showered and put on the suit that he had packed for this evening, even though the numbness in which he had been trapped all day hadn't abandoned him for a single moment. But now he was slowly waking up, feeling excited as people bustled past him. His eye anxiously followed the winding banister up to the first floor, where the event room was, and where, he hoped, Liz would be waiting for him somewhere, to tell him everything was fine again.

Then he discovered that he was being watched. On the topmost step of the stairs, so close to the edge of the red carpet that it looked as if the wheels were jutting out above an abyss, there stood a wheelchair. He wondered how long the woman sitting in it had been watching him through the light blue lenses of her sunglasses, as he slowly climbed the stairs and studied her striking form. She wore a light blue towelling catsuit, beneath the broad trouser legs of which the tips of gold Pumas peeped out, the soles as white and unworn as if she could fly. She herself was black.

He watched the guests jostling past her wheelchair, which she didn't move an inch to the side, but when he had finally reached her and hesitantly placed his foot on the third or fourth last step, she swung back with a practised sweep of her arms and let him pass. Kalf nodded to her and was about to walk past, but her voice stopped him.

'How about we get together after your reading?'

She spoke so quietly that he couldn't help bending down to her, and into her aura of sickly perfume. The smell of vanilla surrounded her like an old-fashioned feather boa. Her eyes, behind the lenses of her sunglasses, remained far away in the vague gloom of an early morning. He was sure of it: it was the voice on the phone. He closed his eyes and nodded. Everything would be OK. She drew a light blue visiting card from the bowling-bag purse in her lap.

Venus Smith
ALDEBARAN PICTURES
3810 West Pico Blvd, Suite 200
Los Angeles, CA 90035
Phone: 310–735–6200 / Fax 310–735–6255

The name in gold: Venus Smith. Once again he tried in vain to catch her eye. Her face was so completely immaculate that he found looking at her disagreeable. He put the card in his pocket.

'See you later, Ms Smith,' he murmured, and felt his way into the room.

He was greeted by Dr Schmidtbauer, the director of the Goethe House. Liz wasn't feeling well, Kalf assiduously explained, the air conditioning on the aeroplane, a summer flu, and drank a glass of wine as the room slowly filled.

Finally he was standing next to Lavinia. 'How are you feeling?'

He shook his head, and she stroked his arm.

'You must stay calm.'

'Yes.'

He took his typescript out of the inside pocket of the suit. The sounds of murmurs and shifting chairs could be heard. The waitresses stared straight ahead. The last members of the audience were sliding in to find a last seat. He moved away.

Niklas Kalf found it hard to concentrate. A number of times, when he heard clicking footsteps approaching on the marble and the door was carefully opened, he lost his place. His mind wasn't on it, and he read haltingly and slowly, standing at the small, rather wobbly podium with its lamp and water glass.

Time and again his thoughts wandered, and he imagined her coming in. His lips read mechanically on as he imagined Liz darting into the room, as silently as a fantasy, and of course he noticed her anyway and looked up, and she smiled at him and waved the way she always did, with a small, embarrassed gesture. She wore the white summer dress that she had bought for this evening, the one with the high waist. Liz seldom wore dresses, but she'd fallen in love with that one. She wasn't very tall, or slim in the conventional sense, although her belly had been flat as ever until recently, but her waist was rather childlike, her whole body was compact, and even her neck was muscular. He loved sucking hard on her neck, as he also loved her soft upper arms, the strength of her hands and the rather expansive line of her thighs. She would sit down in the back row and listen. He knew her belly was starting to bother her, and that sitting would be unpleasant for her after a while. But her expression would be as attentive as ever, and he felt how much he loved her, and his eye actually jerked up from the typescript, in search of her. But there was no one there, and once again he had lost his place.

Everyone was watching him calmly and attentively. He tried to smile and cleared his throat. A lot of elderly people had come, most of them women, as ever, most of them probably German, because only a few were referring to the copies of the English translation that had been handed out at the beginning. He apologized quietly and took a sip of water.

The longer he read, the more he thought of the warning not to say anything out of place. Weeks before, a chapter from the first half of the book had been translated, which seemed particularly suitable for this evening. In it he described how Elsa and Eugen Meerkaz had escaped from a refugee camp near Nîmes in the summer of 1940, and gone into hiding in Marseille for a few months, before crossing southern France and the Pyrenees on foot to reach Spain and finally Lisbon, and leaving Europe forever on two separate ships.

Examining each sentence as he read, he was sure that nothing in this passage could cause offence in any way. However, in the brief moment of silence at the end he had been more worried than usual after a reading. Unable to look up, he waited to see what would happen now. Only when the comforting applause began did his anxiety ease a little, and he thanked the audience with a nod, as his eyes darted once again across the rows of seats. But the only thing that broke the regular arrangement of the chairs was the woman in the wheelchair, who had rolled up at the end of the back row. What if there was no news about Liz?

On the way to the buffet people plucked at big pashminas or crocheted jackets, held handbags under their arms and ran spread fingers through steel-blue perms. He took a glass of wine and talked for a while to two old ladies. The alcohol immediately went to his head, and he realized that he hadn't eaten anything all day. The women were very small, and although he bent down to them, he could hardly make out what they said. They spoke German with a strong accent, and very quickly, as though the important thing was for him to remember everything, the story of their families, the emigration and life here in New York, the lives of their late husbands and their own. He drank and nodded, actually forgot Liz for moments at a time and imagined the apartments to match the made-up faces and crocheted gloves, somewhere on the Upper West Side, on the eleventh floor, rather run-down, with beautiful but slightly rickety furniture, long dark corridors full of photographs and the smile of an old doorman.

Lavinia finally drew him into a circle with Marcus Schmidtbauer, whose wife wanted to know who he was writing for. Kalf shrugged. He had to look for the woman in the wheelchair. If he wanted to know what was happening to Liz, he had to talk to her.

'In Germany women buy the most books.'

Frau Schmidtbauer had big lively eyes and a striking, almost drawling, hissing accent. 'People read less and less.'

Her husband, who was talking to an old lady, put his arm around her shoulder without looking at her. Her eyes rested on Niklas Kalf, who didn't know what to say in reply.

She had been very touched by his description of how Eugen Meerkaz and his wife had fled to freedom, she said quietly. She herself came from Porto. She had always read as a child. And it was still the thing she liked doing best. He nodded.

Schmidtbauer wanted to know if he thought there would be a war in Iraq. Kalf said how impressed he had been by the President, and as Schmidtbauer disagreed, Kalf studied the old lady.

She must once have been a very beautiful woman, with big eyes and an energetic mouth, whose lips were now slightly puckered with age. He noticed how tightly she clung to her husband's forearm, could clearly walk only with difficulty, and wore large, old-fashioned hearing aids behind both ears.

'Lovely reading!' she said with a smile. 'You know, Herr Kalf, what we said all the way through the war? We said German is not only the language spoken by Hitler, but also the language of Goethe! We said that time and again! And: one day those who speak for the German people will once again speak in the language of Goethe.'

'Helen Schueler,' said Schmidtbauer by way of introduction. Kalf must be aware that Goethe House was a Jewish foundation, in which Helen Schueler and her husband Jacob had been considerably involved.

'It all started in the spring of '57,' she said, 'but not here, further downtown on 56th Street. We didn't get this building until later.' For a moment she seemed to think about whether she should go on talking. Her eyes gazed into the void. She wore pale gloves that matched her suit. 'John McCloy was our first chairman.'

'The American military governor?'

'Yes, the high commissioner. But lots of other people helped us in those days, too. Lucius Clay, for example, the general. But the most committed people were the immigrants. Many of them donated German books that meant a lot to them, because they'd saved them from the Nazis.'

Helen Schueler paused. Now her eye swung back to him. How did he like America? She had heard it was his first time across the pond. 'Do they still say that, the pond? *Der grosse Teich?*'

Sadly she only spoke German very rarely now.

He nodded. 'How could you not like being in the capital of the world?'

'I really wanted to ask you something else entirely, Herr Kalf,' she said slowly with a faint American accent, the kind that seems to roll each word around in the mouth. 'What do you actually care about Eugen Meerkaz?'

He had no idea what to reply. And he realized with horror that his silence wouldn't end, until someone behind him asked, 'Tell me, what's she saying, Nick?'

He turned round with surprise and saw Albert Snowe, who was rocking back and forth from the balls of his feet to his heels, as he grinned at Kalf. Helen Schueler repeated her question in English and studied the publisher uncertainly.

'Just wait a while, Helen,' said Snowe, suddenly serious. 'The book isn't finished. Or am I wrong about that, Mr Kalf?'

Baffled, Kalf nodded.

Helen Schueler seemed disappointed. 'It's just,' she said quietly, 'that I know Elsa Meerkaz, his widow.'

He knew that, said Snowe. Everyone who had ever met her was fascinated by her. For him, the two of them, Helen Schueler and Elsa Meerkaz, were the representatives of a connection between the Old and the New World, which would soon, sadly, no longer exist.

'Sorry that I missed the reading.' He turned to Niklas Kalf. 'But I couldn't get away any earlier. It's just a shame that Liz can't be here tonight. It was so nice having dinner with you both.'

At the mention of Liz's name, the disaster of her

disappearance began drilling its way back into his head like the steel point of a migraine. He couldn't manage a reply, just shook his head repeatedly as Snowe and Helen Schueler looked at him with surprise.

'Shall we sit down for a moment?' the publisher asked finally.

'That would be great. I'll just fetch us a glass of wine.'

Kalf was pleased to be able to get out of the circle of people. On the way to the buffet he looked uneasily for the woman in the wheelchair. There was hardly anyone left.

The two old ladies he had been talking to were helping themselves to the last white triangular sandwiches. Two German women journalists whom he knew were leaning against one of the tall rococo mirrors, deep in conversation, holding their cigarettes at arm's length. The double doors to the hall, which was now empty and deserted, stood wide open. As he walked past he heard a strange sound in the silence, coming from the place where the bust of Goethe stood on the mantelpiece, but the hope that Liz might be waiting for him in the darkness of the room was shattered by the rapidly approaching, smacking sound of hard rubber tyres on the parquet floor just as he entered the room.

With a light sweep of her muscular arms, Venus Smith steered her wheelchair just far enough out of the depths to stop on the line that marked the end of the carpet of light that spilled from the illuminated corridor, and on which he had just taken two steps into the hall.

'So, here you are!' was all that occurred to him.

The room was as silent as if it was under water. It was an enticing silence, in which the tension immediately eased. He felt how tired he was, and how alone. Without thinking about it, he took the card out of his breast pocket. Her wheelchair made a half-turn, as unnoticed by her as if the chair was an animal that she was riding. The little front wheels turned as if it was scraping the ground with its hoofs. She nodded at the card.

'I work for Phil Gallagher.'

'Sorry, I don't know him.'

He shook his head. 'Aldebaran Pictures,' he read. 'Los Angeles.'

'Phil Gallagher's a producer. An important one.'

For a moment both her hands slid tenderly over the chrome curves of the hand-rims of the chair, and she patted her steed.

'I'm only interested in one thing: where's Liz?'

'She's safe.'

'What does that mean?'

'It means that she's as well as circumstances permit.'

'What does that mean?' he asked again.

'She hasn't been harmed.'

'And when will she be freed?'

'That depends entirely on you. Give us the material that you have about Eugen Meerkaz, and she'll be back with you the same day.'

What material? 'I'll give you everything I have.'

Niklas Kalf's heart pounded in his throat: he was going to get Liz back!

'We're only concerned about the experiments with Parsons.'

He didn't understand. He knew nothing about this. The anxiety immediately returned. 'What experiments?'

'I think I've expressed myself clearly enough.'

Kalf stared at her and didn't know what to say. He tried to remember the perfume that he had smelt before, when he bent down to her. The sunglasses, he noted, had gone. The whites of her eyes were gleaming, moist and completely clear. He had no idea how long their silence lasted. She just let him go on looking at her, and said nothing, as though it was a particular skill of hers.

But finally the wheelchair performed a half-turn and now, even though her gold Pumas hadn't moved, she too was on the carpet of light. Her lower lip trembled with a smile that she could barely restrain. It was vanilla, he could smell it again now. Without thinking, he sat down next to her on the narrow runner of light, and suddenly it was all there again. The quiet room, in which the white spheres of her eyes gleamed, filled with memories. How Liz and he had arrived here. Dinner with Snowe and the days in the city. How they had made love, and how she had disappeared in the morning. Niklas Kalf sensed that his life would be frozen as it was right now until she came back. He thought: the world doesn't exist. And he knew he really believed it.

Venus Smith studied him as if he was about to say something she had been waiting a long time to hear. Her hands rested impatiently on the chrome wheels. Vanilla, he thought, imagining her skin cool and firm and slightly rough. He had no idea what she wanted from him, and had never heard of those experiments. The silence absorbed him. Nothing to be done. He enjoyed her gaze a moment longer.

'Nice shoes,' he said and ran a hand over the tips of

her Pumas. It was a moment before she saw what he was doing, and only then did her wheelchair jerk backwards a little.

'Sorry,' he murmured quietly.

'Fucking idiot!' she hissed.

Niklas Kalf rose to his feet and brushed imaginary dust from his trousers. He saw her features, close to his face, distorted in uncontrollable fury, then she threw herself back in her wheelchair, so that he was worried that she would tip backwards. But she immediately regained control of herself.

'Niklas?'

Al Snowe's voice pierced the silence and echoed in it. Niklas turned towards the publisher, who was standing by the door to the hall, and immediately turned back to Venus Smith, but the space at the edge of the light was already empty. Again he heard the smacking sound of the tyres on the parquet, and just had time to see the wheelchair sliding spookily back, glimpsed a flash of chrome and then, peer as he might into the darkness, nothing more.

'As soon as you cooperate and hand over all your material,' came a hiss from that direction, 'we'll give you back your girlfriend.'

'Who are you talking to?' Snowe asked.

Kalf stepped into the hall. As far as he knew there was no other exit.

'Come on, I've got the wine.'

He slowly shook off his anxiety. He didn't understand what had just happened. But he sensed that everything that had happened since Liz's disappearance was part of a plan of which he was unaware. There was no point getting involved in something he knew nothing about.

'Come on, Niklas!' repeated Al Snowe, as though beckoning an animal.

Kalf nodded to him. He left the hall one step at a time, and tried to calm his thumping heart.

'I thought I'd left something behind.'

'And had you?'

'No.'

They entered the big drawing room overlooking the street, where it looked as if two smokers had opened one of the tall windows and pulled up chairs, because among the pistachio shells on a little plate there were also cigarette butts. The light night wind carried the sound of raindrops on a nearby awning, already wet through, and the sickly smell of dusty streets in the rain.

For the first time since they'd arrived in New York the air was fresh, and had an aroma that he greedily absorbed. They sat down, and the publisher offered him a glass of wine. His face was open and friendly, and yet there was something about Albert Snowe's heavy, uneasy build that made Kalf suspicious. Finally, he thought, and noticed only now, as they drank and looked down on Fifth Avenue, just how much, on all those hot days, he had yearned for rain. The banners outside the Metropolitan Museum hung slackly from their poles. The light rain surged back and forth like a thin and animated curtain. The street lay almost deserted in the yellow light that dragged its way across the many puddles. Only a few taxis slipped past, with a high-pitched buzz of their tyres as the water sprayed up.

The publisher took great swigs of his wine, repeatedly smoothing his tie over his shirt with his free hand. They talked about emigration, and what it must have been like for Germans in America in those days.

'They're absolutely fascinated by the States.' Snowe looked at him curiously.

'Yes, of course. When I saw Bush speaking at the UN today, not with a time delay or on some unreal night, but under the same sun, I began to understand the power of power.'

Snowe smiled complacently. 'Did you know that the Vice President was the director of the Texan oil company Halliburton? That Condoleezza Rice was on the board of Chevron? I think they've named an oil tanker after her.'

'You get that kind of interconnection everywhere.'

'Of course. But the network that people like Cheney or Rumsfeld belong to is much more extensive. You know Thomas Donnelly and his *Project for the New American Century*? And Richard Perle? Have you read Donald Kagan's essay "Power and Weakness" in *Policy Review*?'

'No.'

'Have you heard the name Zalmay Khalilzad?'

Kalf shook his head.

'He was a special ambassador in Afghanistan, stewarding the transitional government. Now he's travelling in the Middle East.'

'Do you think there's going to be a war?'

'In Iraq? Everything seems to be heading in that direction.'

The publisher fell silent and looked outside. He had

swung one leg over the other, and locked his hands on his knee. 'Do you really believe that this is the centre of Empire?'

'Isn't it?'

'In my view it depends entirely what age we're living in. In the Republic or the Rome of the Caesars. Or the late Empire, when the Caesars were roaming the borders like wolves, getting involved in persistent defensive battles against the barbarians, and being born and crowned in cities like Trier or Byzantium. They no longer knew Rome.'

Niklas Kalf looked out the window and drained his glass. He was surprised that Snowe's voice suddenly became very soft.

'Don't go to the police,' the publisher said quietly.

'But I've got to do something.'

Snowe shook his head. 'You have no idea what you're involved in. Someone I trust completely has assured me that it's best for your wife if you don't go to the police.'

'But I'm being blackmailed. Liz's life is at stake! They want material about Eugen Meerkaz from me.'

'And? Have you got it?'

'No, I haven't. I don't even know what it could be.'

'Then let's wait a while. You stay in New York and wait. I beg you: don't go to the police. I'm sure it would make the situation even worse for Liz.'

Niklas Kalf looked back down on Fifth Avenue at night, and into the even, pleasant rain. There was so much going through his head that he didn't know what to say. I've got to decide, he thought again, without knowing what about, and when he finally left no one remained in the hall or on the staircase, just a sleepy porter by the front door, and he was surprised that Lavinia hadn't said goodbye.

He walked into the park behind the Metropolitan Museum, and down a small hill, then past baseball fields. It was all so quiet and peaceful, and the rain on his skin was so agreeable, that he wasn't afraid. So he didn't take the direct route to his hotel, and instead went in search of the fountain where Imogen Engel's victim had been found, but ended up at the reservoir, still circled by joggers even in the middle of the night, pale, emaciated men, most of them with little bicycle lamps on headbands.

Reflected in the water he saw the palaces that stood around the park just as Snowe had described, and became aware that the panic which had still held him firmly in its grip when he had come to the reading seemed to have disappeared. He knew he had no idea what he could do to help Liz, and he himself didn't understand why he wasn't doing the right thing. But something in the way Venus Smith had looked at him wouldn't let go of him, and he sensed that his meeting with her had only been an initial anticipation of what was to come. The world was busy disappearing. He became aware that he was trembling with loneliness. But at the same time he keenly studied the silhouettes of the surrounding skyscrapers and wondered which one Imogen Engel might have lived in.

CHAPTER FIVE

You're welcome

Day broke behind the window, and the three-legged water tanks above the roofs glistened in the red dawn. The rotor of the air-conditioning system turned slowly with a metallic scrape. Niklas Kalf woke from his troubled sleep, looked around, and the emptiness of the hotel room ticked in his head. On the floor and on the untouched side of the bed there towered the material for his book, which he had scoured time and again for clues since Liz's disappearance. He picked up the remote control and pointed it at the television.

A man, naked to the waist, with a cloth wrapped around his head as an improvised turban, with a pistol and hand grenades in his belt, holds his machine gun close to his body and looks round. He wears a full beard. Under his protection, the Afghan President quickly boards a black off-road vehicle with tinted windows. PENTAGON TELLS TROOPS IN AFGHANISTAN: SHAPE UP AND DRESS RIGHT. The soldier is still in the picture, the camera zooms up to him, his expression flickers as he looks around. A Special Operations officer appears in a little window in the top right-hand corner of the screen. *'On Monday we got the word: some general in Washington ordered no more beards.'*

Kalf's eyes closed again, and he immediately sank into memories of Liz, who filled every free space in his dreams. Powdery snow lay on the tarmac and paving stones, and was whirled in the wake of cars and beneath their shoes into baroque corkscrew flurries as they walked slowly towards the river. He still remembered clearly, it was early evening, there was still quite a lot of traffic, they had to wait before they could cross the street, and they hurried to knot their scarves and put on their gloves. On the other side of the street they stopped on the right, to reach the river near the Iron Bridge, and found themselves beneath the leaky roof of the avenue of plane trees, three rows deep, that pushes its way like a broad, heavy basilica filled with knotty bracework. In the summer the weekly flea market is held under that dense leafy roof, otherwise people play boules on the bright gravel between the trees, but now their joints were frozen in the bitter cold that fell from the sky.

He and Liz leaned against the railing and looked across to the opposite riverbank, to the Commerzbank that loomed over everything, to the narrow turret of the EZB and the two skyscrapers of the Dresdner Bank. Niklas Kalf had lived in Frankfurt for almost twenty years, and when he and Liz asked each other, yet again, when they were finally going to leave and where they would go, as everyone in this city does all the time, he was surprised to discover that he wouldn't find it easy.

They lived in a big but rather dark ground-floor flat in Sachsenhausen. In the summer it took Liz a quarter of an hour by bike to get to her editorial office. She huddled against him, and he took off a glove and ran the back of his hand over her cheek until she smiled. Their frozen breath hung in front of their faces.

No one knows what will remain. Of us or anything else. A drift has gripped us, a drift that will change everything we know. We sense that much of what we love will disappear in that motion. Maybe even that thing which we call love will disappear. Just like a war this motion seizes all the places in the world and takes every life with it, as an earthquake runs through rock. A war like spreading music. And the crucial thing about it all is that we don't know what to do.

'Nico?'

Perhaps, he thought, we are left defenceless by the fact that we were born so long after the last war. Or perhaps by the fact that we're European. Or both.

'Yes?' he said and kissed Liz on the nose.

There wasn't much more of her face to be seen than her bright, laughing eyes and that nose, everything else was hidden beneath her thick curls and her big scarf. She pulled him closer.

'Let's get married,' she said and looked at him seriously.

Niklas Kalf couldn't help grinning.

'Yes!' he said, took off his other glove and gripped both of her hands. The memory made him smile, and he was awake again.

He turned the TV to mute, reached for the phone that lay next to him on the bed, and pressed redial. He didn't know how many times he had dialled Elsa Meerkaz's number already, and he had long ceased to care at what time of day he called. As always, it rang for a long time without anyone answering or an answering machine coming on, and he was about to hang up when a woman's voice spoke. After he had, with surprise, said his name, the heavily accented English voice immediately became that of an old Viennese woman.

'No, Mrs Meerkaz is not here.'

It had been agreed for a long time that he would call from New York and arrange a date for his visit to Los Angeles. He looked once again at the material that he had scattered and distributed all around the room. There were no references to the experiments mentioned by Venus Smith. But some detail in it, a story, a fact, an expression, that he knew at least, was responsible for Liz's abduction. But he didn't know what it was, and if there was anyone who could tell him what they wanted of him, it was she: Elsa Meerkaz. He didn't understand why she wouldn't speak to him on the phone, and wondered once again whether he wouldn't be better off simply going to see her in LA. But he still couldn't make his mind up to leave New York. It was here that Liz had disappeared. And here he wanted to wait for her.

'No, I can't say when she'll be back.'

Niklas Kalf stared at the screen. A soldier against the background of several Apache fighter helicopters, their black, angular contours almost wiped out by the haze. The soldier is wearing a dirty baseball cap, and a pair of sunglasses covers the top half of his face. The bottom half is covered by a beard, which reaches almost to the lenses of his shades. Several ammunition belts stretched over a torn white muscle shirt, both hands clutching his machine gun. He wears white, very soiled golfing gloves.

His face blank but uneasy, he looks around the bright, dusty plain.

'She's gone, yes.'

Kalf assumed he was talking to the last secretary of Eugen Meerkaz, who had looked after his widow since his death. What reason could she have for hiding from him? He could find no answer to this question.

'I'm sorry,' said that soft old voice, full of charm and regret.

He picked up the remote control and turned the sound back up. 'In this culture, men respect men who have the ability to grow facial hair, and the longer the better.'

Always the same mistake, he thought. Perhaps they'll bring back a new Mithras cult. He turned off the television, even though the silence was hard to bear. Loneliness welled up in him like cold water in a flooding basement. At first he had been convinced that someone would call him, but nothing happened. Finally he tried to get through to Venus Smith, but the people at Aldebaran Pictures told him she wasn't in town at the moment. She'd call him back.

When she did call back two days later and asked him what he had for her, the routine of his waiting immediately collapsed, and he understood that there was nothing he could do to help his wife, even though she seemed closer right now than she had since her disappearance. Kalf almost thought he could hear her breath rather than her kidnapper's. His heart thumped crazily.

'Nothing?' asked Venus Smith, and when he didn't reply she hung up.

He had lunch one day with Lavinia Sims on the quays

at Fulton Fish Market. Then they walked over Brooklyn Bridge, and she showed him her parents' home, where she lived with her mother. Her father was dead, her family had lived in the city for over a hundred years, and he somehow thought he knew that already. She wanted him to talk to her about Liz as they sat on the steps of the narrow brownstone house, and Niklas Kalf told her how they had met at university. She was an editor in the local section of a Frankfurt newspaper, writing mostly about art. She cycled to work. She liked swimming. Kalf stopped and looked down at the steps, and managed to hold back his tears.

On another occasion they met Albert Snowe near his office at Lincoln Square. Lavinia fetched three big lattes from Starbucks, and they spent half an hour sitting on one of the green, gently curving park benches. Snowe fed the pigeons with his double chocolate brownie, and Niklas Kalf asked him what he should do now.

'Nothing,' said Snowe without looking at him. 'Just wait.'

He couldn't do that any more. He couldn't bear the idea that someone might be doing something to Liz.

'What are the kidnappers after? Have a good think. Don't you know, after all?'

Niklas Kalf tried to stay calm. The question had kept him awake for days.

'There's nothing. The only exciting thing in Eugen Meerkaz's life was his escape from the Nazis. I don't know anything about the experiments that woman Venus Smith talked about. There's no secret.'

Snowe stuffed the rest of his brownie into his mouth, leaned back on the bench and studied him. Kalf watched the people coming out of the subway and quickly crossing the little park. At the edge there was a playground and a dog run. When he held out his hand to say goodbye, Snowe begged him once again not to go to the police. It would put Liz in danger.

'What's he really like?' he asked Lavinia as they walked down to the subway.

'What do you mean?'

He shrugged. 'Is he to be trusted?'

'In what way?'

'No idea.'

Kalf thought about what he really wanted to know. The subway train thundered up, driving a gust of hot air into the station.

Lavinia grinned. And into the noise she shouted, 'No. Absolutely not.'

At that moment he knew that he could no longer listen and wait for Snowe. He wouldn't be able to bear the present situation for much longer. And when he was back in the hotel, lying on the bed and looking out the window, watching the summer day fading, he recalled once again his dinner with Snowe, and how he had talked about his work as a biographer. That a stranger's life could be concentrated on a single moment. Yes, the publisher had replied, a strange life was probably about secrets. Perhaps, thought Kalf, I didn't take it seriously enough, the idea that there might really be a secret in the life of Eugen Meerkaz.

He sat down on the floor and began once again to look through all the documents, the letters and essays, the photographs and postcards, the copies of testimonies, IDs, encyclopaedia articles and laboratory books, all the newspaper articles and obituaries and all his own notes, and as he did so he looked everywhere for the iceberg tip of a hidden secret rather than simply sorting out the bits he didn't understand, as he had been doing up till now.

A secret, he improvised, must be something capable of reassessing everything already known. Something that worked like a key where no one had seen a door. A magic word. Niklas Kalf took another look at all the pages of formulae and incomprehensible calculations, and as though in slow motion he finally pulled, by the corner of the envelope, a letter from the stack of papers. It was, he knew at first sight, a letter of condolence after Meerkaz's death. Two lines that had never struck him as particularly important, but now he read them again. *Dearest Elsa*, it said. *My deepest sympathy at Eugen's sudden death. What happened strikes me dumb. Don't worry! Yours, Hans*. He remembered the phrase about being struck dumb. But what about the bit that came after?

Kalf said it out loud to himself: *Don't worry! Don't worry!* Didn't it sound conspiratorial? And who was this Hans? The paper wasn't headed, and there was no sender's address on the envelope. Kalf inspected it, and deciphered the postmark. Marfa, TX. Marfa, Texas, he repeated to himself. Elsa Meerkaz had never mentioned the place in her conversations. Or a man called Hans. That's not really a secret, he thought. But it was, he knew only too well, his sole clue, and if there was a secret, it was plainly something that Eugen Meerkaz's widow was hiding from him.

As long as he had nothing against her in his hand, it was pointless to go to LA. He knew she wouldn't help him, even if he didn't yet understand why. Better to head off to Texas first. Where else was he supposed to start his search?

Niklas Kalf began preparing his escape as carefully and inconspicuously as possible. He called Liz's office and told them something about complications with the pregnancy that meant they had to stay in the USA longer than planned. No, Liz didn't want to speak to anyone right now. He said the same thing to her mother. No, nothing serious. She'll call. He phoned a few friends, and the story that he and Liz wanted to spend some time travelling through the country fell more easily from his lips with each conversation. A plan that they had both had for a while, but hadn't told anyone about. A sabbatical that could be nicely combined with his research for the new book. They'd be back home before the child was born.

He spun out the story more and more as he talked, and at the same time he repeatedly found himself wondering what a person would normally do in his situation. He thought that anyone else would have informed the authorities, gone home, hoped for news. He was startled by how far he had already removed himself from that normality. But why? All he knew was this: his friends' voices came from a different life, and he could feel the current that had seized him, had dragged him far from everything he knew. Out into the country outside the window. It was about Liz. And at the same time it wasn't about Liz. What was it about?

Niklas Kalf had the credit limit raised on his Visa card, and both their savings transferred to his Giro account. He FedExed the key to their flat to a friend who promised to take care of the post and the plants. Then he was ready: he stood for the last time in the hotel room where he had spent almost three weeks.

Still lying on the chair by the bed was the shiny DKNY raincoat that Liz had bought in a shop in TriBeCa. He went into the bathroom to look through her stuff, all of which was useless now. He couldn't use any of it, and he wouldn't take any of it with him. He had asked Lavinia to check out for him the following day and look after his luggage. He hoped that meant his escape wouldn't be noticed at first. He stuffed the Meerkaz material right down to the bottom of his bag, then added a few pieces of clothing and last of all the little pocket-sized *Traveler's Atlas* that Liz had given him.

The dark green leather was embossed on the front with the image of a compass card, the gilt edging gleamed like a mirror, and the pages were made of stiff, smooth paper. Liz had discovered the little book in a stationery shop in Chelsea, somewhere on 23rd Street. It contained everything you need to know as an American, maps of all the federal states, the national parks and the highways, a map of the world and plans of all the major American cities, the time zones and the weather in the capital cities of the world for every month of the year, calculation tables for inches and yards, miles and feet, pints and quarts, grains and pounds, all the American embassies from Albania to Zimbabwe and the toll-free numbers of the airlines, parcel services, credit-card companies and hotel chains. He sat back down on the bed and flicked through it. Liz had said: *So that you can find me wherever I am!* Her smile, which he remembered right at that moment, was as familiar to him as his own face. He had never been with the same woman for so long. But when he looked at Liz, it still always felt as if he liked everything about her, just as he had done right at the start. *So that you can find me wherever I am.* I'll do that, he thought. But he had to get a move on. Marfa was the name of the place in the postmark on the letter, and it wasn't listed in the index of the atlas. But El Paso was, right on the border with Mexico. Niklas Kalf swung his bag over his shoulder.

And just as he was about to pull the hotel-room door shut, the phone rang. Venus Smith, he thought, and froze. They weren't letting him out of their sight. They were very close by. The phone went on ringing. He couldn't move, and wondered again whether he was doing the right thing, and he felt as if he was leaving Liz in the lurch. But he knew that if he picked up the receiver now, he himself would become a prisoner, and he couldn't do that if he wanted to help her. Finally the ringing stopped, and he pulled the door shut behind him.

Two hours later, at Newark International Airport, Niklas Kalf swapped his ticket to Los Angeles for one for the last flight via Houston to El Paso, and booked a hire car there. He was pretty sure that no one had followed him from the hotel: first he had taken quite a long walk through the park, and only then had he taken a taxi. He paid for the ticket and the car in cash, even though Avis had the number of his Visa card stored, and he didn't spend any more time than necessary in the public area of the airport.

When the plane flew west between Washington DC and Pittsburgh, over Pennsylvania and Maryland towards the Blue Ridge Mountains, he closed his eyes.

Lavinia's goodbye three days before in Central Park came back to him.

It had been Sunday, precisely ten days after Liz's disappearance, and football was being played on the Grand Leaf. Little boys and their fathers in sports gear walked past the bench where they sat, and countless people were walking their dogs, a lot of golden retrievers, their owners elderly, with grey-streaked hair, a king-size white poodle on the lead of a very tall Asian woman whose eyes were expressionless behind the pink-tinted lenses of her sunglasses, pairs of pugs, and beagles and lots of lapdogs that were startled by the grey squirrels, on long dark red leather leashes. Dog-walkers with seven or eight dogs trotting in front of them in a wide phalanx. Young couples conversing loudly, walking very quickly and not even looking at their buggies, and older couples, themselves grey as squirrels, thin and bent and incredibly urban. Spanish families and Asian, Indian joggers, of course, and young women reading books as they walked and wearing big headphones, remote from everything around them.

Niklas Kalf read on the screen: Charleston, Raleigh, Charlotte.

Lavinia gave him a sidelong glance as he stared across at the skyscrapers that soared above the trees, and tried to remember which one of them Imogen Engel had lived in. That first evening in New York now seemed unattainably far off.

'What are you going to do now?'

He thought about what he could say. He hadn't stopped feeling suspicious about Snowe, and his liking for Lavinia did nothing to change the fact that he was on his guard against him. They were sitting close to one another, side by side, and he noticed the thin film of sweat on her top lip. She was wearing her hair in a ponytail, and he looked for a long time at her face with all the freckles that had become so familiar to him. She allowed him to look at her, as if they really were old friends.

'I want to get away.'

'What does that mean?'

'That I have to get away, is what it means.' He nodded in affirmation.

'But that's impossible. What's happening about Liz?'

He said he didn't know what was happening about Liz. That was why he had to get away.

'But where to?'

'I don't know yet.'

He could see that Lavinia had noticed he was lying to her. Something in her eyes recoiled.

Nashville and Atlanta were on the left, and to the right lay Cincinnati. The whole breadth of the country. Kalf tried to imagine Texas. The plane passed West Virginia; Lake Huron and Chicago were far to the north.

'Niklas?'

He had become very used to Lavinia saying his name. It sounded close and friendly. He regretted it very much, but it seemed best to trust nobody.

'No idea! I don't know yet. But I'll call you. I want to know if anything happens here.'

On the horizon to the left the Mississippi and St Louis. Nothing would happen to Liz as long as they wanted something from him.

'You'll do that, yeah?' Lavinia laid her hand on his forearm. 'Please, really, do!'

At some point, on their third or fourth evening in New York, he and Liz had gone for a drink in the Oak Bar, and when they got back quite late from the Plaza Hotel there was hardly any traffic left on Fifth Avenue, but it had still smelt very strongly of the horses that waited for tourists by their carriages in the daytime.

A step towards the kerbstone, out of the warm light, and suddenly a beggarwoman was standing in front of them, a big-eyed black woman. She held her right elbow exhaustedly in her left hand in such a way that her right hand, holding a few coins, pointed at Kalf like a cantilever. He couldn't understand what she was saying, but unlike in Germany, where he had always found it easy to avoid homeless people, he couldn't do that here. He felt that her eyes were directed at him alone. As though he was being held to account. And he knew it wasn't about the fact that he didn't feel like giving this woman the same amount as he had just left as a tip in the bar. It was more as if, as they looked each other in the eyes, they were actually responsible for one another. Like all human beings. But also in a way that he had never experienced before. Here, where there is nothing to catch a human being.

No one is caught and barely anyone remembers that he is falling. Niklas Kalf shielded his eyes with his hand. Outside the plane window there was gleaming bright, completely monotonous blue. So it didn't matter what she said. None of the stories of lost tickets or money for food came into it. It was all a pretext, and she knew it. He gave her ten dollars, and Liz watched without saying a word. The beggarwoman disappeared across the street and through a little swarm of yellow taxis into the park.

Tennessee. They were past Memphis. It was always, at the same time, a donation to the dead. The plane turned south, towards Houston and the Gulf of Mexico.

In the in-flight magazine Brad Pitt was advertising a blue perfume, the girl next to Niklas Kalf played with her Game-Boy, the young Mexican with the acne scars read a motocross magazine. Kalf settled into the lonely sound of a woman in the row behind him, who couldn't stop talking.

He had given Lavinia a goodbye hug and got into the taxi without looking round. That only occurred to him again when he was sitting at the gate in Houston, waiting for his connecting flight to El Paso, and it grew dark, but not cooler, and the distance from New York was apparent not only in the sound of the announcements, but in all the movements of the people. He saw men actually wearing wide-brimmed hats and narrow-hipped tight jeans with belt buckles. Mexican families laid siege to the waiting areas. When the little turboprop plane took off for El Paso, it stretched up into the black night like a scrawny cat.

The night was completely clear, and they flew low over the flat land. All the urban conglomerations looked the same from up here. In the neighbourhood of the big highways that gleamed white the residential areas lay, the houses long since darkened, only their driveways lit, surrounded and watched by mindless blackness. The face of a landscape that he didn't yet know. He remembered that figure that he had suddenly thought he had seen on the screen above the seats in his half-sleep on the flight from Frankfurt. Europe as the head of a sleeping boy, his neck stretched towards America, which was his body. It's really very simple, thought Niklas Kalf: I've got involved in a story I know practically nothing about. He stared steadily out of the little window. Liz was somewhere. Every road drew a different Chinese character in the blackness with its warm yellow light. Shortly before midnight he landed in El Paso, collected his car from Avis and took a room in the nearest motel.

The window didn't open, the night porter told him wearily, for security reasons, and it occurred to Kalf once again that El Paso was on the border with Mexico. The air conditioning had cooled the room down to the point that it didn't smell of anything. The sheets felt clammy, and he slept badly, still just below the water surface of his dream, with Liz always nearby.

'Your profession?' asked the immigration officer, and he replied in his dream, 'I'm a writer.'

The officer nodded and looked up from Kalf's passport, which he was holding with both hands. 'Are you here for professional reasons?'

He thought of Trotsky. Are you or have you ever been a member of a Communist Party? According to the anecdote, Trotsky had smiled as he said he hadn't.

'No. Just for a holiday.'

'The officer stamped his visa. 'Enjoy your stay!'

Kalf took the passport and nodded to him. 'Thank you.'

'You're welcome.'

When he woke up early the next morning, he still had that sentence in his ear: *You're welcome.* Shortly after seven he went to the car park. It was still damp in the dawn light, and the cars on the six-lane highway glittered with chrome and paint. He was glad to have escaped the night, threw his bag into the boot of the red Oldsmobile Alero which, with its bulging wheel-cases and a spoiler on the tailgate, looked like a cheap Japanese sports car, and set off. It only took a moment to get used to the automatic gears. The young woman behind the counter of the Holiday Inn had pointed to the left when he asked which way was east, so he drove under the expressway at the next crossing and then onto the highway.

On the lanes in the other direction, the commuter traffic was queued up to enter El Paso, and in the back window there rose the foothills of the city, wretched-looking grey houses, climbing an equally grey collection of mountains. A shame, he thought, I haven't seen the Rio Grande, then the road bent, and the city had disappeared. Undulating gently, the highway led to the comparatively glamorous Interstate 10, heading, with its motel chains and burger stalls, the huge masts with their neon signs and the billboards, into open country. The tarmac was flanked on both sides by dull, crumbled stone in every shade of red and yellow, as though crammed together by enormous bulldozers, and only sketchily covered by a loose web of some kind of plant whose greyish-green leaves, even from a distance, looked fat and waxy.

After three hours Kalf stopped in Van Horn and went into Burger & Shake, where he ate what was on the breakfast menu: tortillas and coffee. A gloomy old place without air conditioning. The owner didn't like Mexico.

'Third World,' he said.

He leaned against the icebox, his hair gelled back, and his wife behind the counter played up her age.

'Frankfurt? My brother was there in the army.'

Cicadas in a stinking wooden hutch with a wire fence, and little fishes in inflated freezer bags with a puddle of water in them. Can you go fishing here? They both shook their heads. Kalf was sweating so much that he hurried to get back out into the dry heat. After he'd filled up the car, he switched from Interstate 10 to Highway 90. To Marfa, he read, it was another seventy miles.

Highway 90 is single-lane and runs dead straight and parallel to the railway line, next to low wooden electricity poles, on which porcelain insulators gleamed. No vapour trails marked the huge sky, not a car to the horizon. The channel-searcher on the radio dashed tirelessly through the frequencies without finding a signal.

Once Kalf stopped the car and got out. The wind immediately carried every sound away. Then it was silent. As an experiment he switched on his Nokia and watched for a while as the icon of the transmission mast scattered pixel dots over the little display that was supposed to represent radio waves. Even after five minutes his mobile couldn't find a network, and he switched it off again. Roads like these, he understood, connected places little older than he was himself. The settlements along them could grow and be abandoned again; in the end it wasn't worth keeping them going. All that survived was the distance.

The prairie behind the barbed-wire fence was as empty as the sky. Sometimes an iron gate marked the driveway to a farm, although no buildings or paths had been seen, sometimes a farm road led from the highway, a gravel track that he watched till it disappeared among the grey undergrowth. At some point he passed through Valentine, an almost deserted former train stop, eroded in exactly the way that places here decay. Empty houses, through whose half-blind windows you can see the mountains behind, nailed-up doors, sagging roofs, mountains of rubbish surrounding the place like dunes, with car parts of every age and provenance. He couldn't help thinking of that time near the cathedral in Barcelona when he suddenly found himself standing by a wall with strangely alien arches and buttresses, huge, pale blocks whose foundation lay far below street level, and immediately knew: Rome.

The remains of an empire that crumbled two thousand years ago are everywhere, like the bones, on a beach, of a fish long rotted away. They are our world's open skeleton, sunk deep into the cities like a piece of black-rusted barbed wire into a tree. He tried to imagine what it might have been like back then: you settled into what happened to be left behind, desert all around you, the lights out and all the inscriptions forever on standby. But thirty feet above a cemetery and an oil press, at some point they built a chapel and in it, suddenly: figures and faces. As if mirrors had abruptly been called into existence. No more running inscriptions. Instead, gestures and glances everywhere. What remains in the void, after the end of order. You look at each other.

And only three hundred years to Florence. And another three hundred, thought Niklas Kalf, to the familiar furnishings of our world. The thin, blindly seeping trail of time.

He slowed down slightly. All of a sudden levelled dust spread nervously along the tarmac strip of Highway 90, to the left the white star of Texaco, behind it Dairy Queen and Dollar General, to the right Pueblo Market and the Thunderbird Motel with its fifties neon sign that seemed to be throwing itself across the road. But the road was already beginning to sweep towards distant mountains that stood out darkly against the horizon. Kalf looked through the town, the last stop the Exxon sign on the high steel mast at the crossing, where Highway 90 meets Highway 67. Sixty miles to Presidio, the border town with Mexico at the Rio Grande and said to be the hottest place in the United States. Niklas Kalf stopped at the gas station and got out of the car. And he wasn't sure if he was really here to uncover a secret that might not even exist, or perhaps just to hide.

CHAPTER SIX

Marfa Ignatyevna

'Has anyone actually told you how this place got its peculiar name?'

Niklas Kalf shook his head and stared out into the hazy afternoon. In the newspapers you could follow how the troops were being brought to the crisis region. After the President's speech it seemed to him that the whole country was preparing for war. A NATION CHALLENGED, the *New York Times* had called a special supplement on 12 September. He couldn't get out of his head images from a little town in Iowa, in America's heartland, where children in blue, red and white T-shirts had formed the American flag in a harvested field for a flying camera. *It's not another world, it's not another place. Iowa is the same as New York. Iowa is the same as Texas. America is America.* There was no reason to be afraid. Here, in the heart of Empire, there was no threat of danger. An empty cattle transporter crashed past.

'Do you know?' Marvin asked again.

They were sitting at the bar in Joe's, drinking beer. Niklas Kalf had met Marvin in the bookshop where he worked, and when he discovered him here in the bar, he had sat down next to him.

'No idea.'

Marvin was somewhere in his mid-forties, weedy and with a somewhat receding chin emphasized rather than concealed by his three-day beard, and he had a stammer. His speech repeatedly got stuck on individual words, like a car on a sand dune, but in the end he always managed to get over it. So Marvin told the story of Marfa, which isn't really a story, but just a scene, a moment. Back in the summer of 1883, when the first train of the Galveston, Harrisburg & San Antonio Railway stopped here to take on water. It's here, as you head westward, that the track crosses the Chihuahua trail, an old trade route that has led north from the Gulf of Mexico since ancient times, and which the gold prospectors also travelled on their way to California.

The railwaymen had considered what name the new station should be given. Marfa, the engineer's wife had said, and then returned to her book.

'And why Marfa?' asked Kalf.

Marvin nodded. That was what her husband wanted to know, too. What sort of name was that? It's the name of a character in the novel I'm reading, she replied. And that was how it stayed.

'Is that all?'

'That's all.'

A water station in the prairie. The stations in the prospectors' maps are nothing more than the rhythm with which the trains will breathe. But the steel tyres still roll in slow motion metre for metre behind the workers, unbearable the heat and the bright light and the shouting and hammering that creep through all the cracks of the Pullman car. A glance outside, a word on a page of the new book, the husband's uncomprehending expression, his skin white under the rim of his dust goggles, white as a dog's fur. Her smile when the man finally shuts the door behind him: alone at last!

'And what was the name of the novel?'

'No idea. I think it was by a Russian.'

They had another few beers. Joe's is the only bar in Marfa, a traditional adobe building made of air-dried mud. There's a neon Miller's sign in the window, and a long bar made of dark wood, a television hangs from the ceiling, and there's a pool table near the toilets. Kalf asked Marvin if he knew of any Germans who might once have lived here, and whether the name Hans meant anything to him. Marvin shook his head. No, he didn't know him, but the Germans had been here in the war. His parents had told him. Kalf nodded. He knew that already.

There had been a prisoner-of-war camp in Marfa during the Second World War, but everyone told him there was nothing left of it. Now the little town was defined by the art scene, since Donald Judd had moved here in the seventies and bought up the grounds of the former military base.

Countless stars in the sky as he walked back to the hotel. As he flew into Houston, it was the first time he had seen such a desert city lying in the landscape, a thin cocoon of lights in the night fading away into the distance. Places without a beginning and without any discernible shape, the kind that don't exist in Europe.

Trans-Pecos is the name given to this part of Texas between the Pecos and the Rio Grande, nothing worth staying for, a border region and even today one of the most thinly populated stretches of land in the United

States. Everyone passed through here, Spanish and French conquerors, Indians on their war trail, and soldiers of the incipient nation, white settlers heading west, and Mexican farmers coming from the south. Another two years after the engineer's wife in her railway train had given Marfa a name, the adventurer Lucas Brite noted here in his diary that there wasn't a single sign of human presence for miles around.

On his first night in Marfa, Niklas Kalf was woken by the shrieks of the trains, sounding as if they were pushing time in front of them. He stared at the ceiling of his room and knew that the whole vast sky above the night-black prairie was the echo chamber for those shrieks. Up to six yellow Union Pacific diesel trains pull behind them through the country the mile-long chains of wagons, laden two storeys high with containers. They are the agents of distance. When you watch them, space seems to unfold before their slowness. They often sit for an hour or longer on the open track, waiting for a signal or whatever, and in the night their rattling is unceasing, as if the endless chains of wagons divided not only the town, but the whole country as far as the horizon and on from ocean to ocean.

Half sleeping, he reached for his cellphone, and set it to search for a network again, and as the wagons clattered through Marfa he looked in the dark at the transmission mast on the glowing blue display, its flashing pixels disappearing into the void. More than anything at that moment he wished he could finally speak to Liz again, and hear her say that she was well. That nothing had happened to her.

As he kept falling asleep for moments at a time, her

voice settled as gently over the rattle of the wheels as it had done when she had told him she was pregnant. His hand on her belly. The way she laughed the first time the child moved beneath it. The way she laughed that night when she fell pregnant. It was always her laughter that he remembered first, since her disappearance. The way she brushed her curls back behind her ear and the way she seemed to look through him when she was listening to something with special concentration. The way her lips pursed when she was asleep. The softness of her hand. Her stubbornness, and the way she wouldn't let anyone change her mind. Her head in his armpit and the way her hair tickled his nose. And the fact that she never forgot anything.

Niklas Kalf blinked into the blue of the mute mobile phone on the pillow next to him, and felt how firmly loneliness had him in its grip, that paralysing, deadening emptiness around him, which he hadn't been able to shed by fleeing New York. He kept nodding off, and Liz's laughter drew him painfully into a dream, then the rattling of the train finally grew quieter, the silence darted back into the room in its wake and carried Liz away with it. He woke up, turned off the mobile, and the blue light disappeared. He stared at the ceiling and cried.

The very next morning he set off to the public library in search of literature about the prisoner-of-war camp, about which, it was plain, hardly anyone in the town knew anything more than the fact that it had once existed. More pickups than usual were parked outside the post office, a dog yapped on the bed of one, an empty horse transporter stood next to it, women chatted, ranchers collected their mail from the narrow PO boxes. The sky was cloudless and high and almost dark blue, the air fresh and very dry. It got pretty hot in the sun, at about midday a thermometer in the hotel often showed more than 80 degrees Fahrenheit. The public library was in a side street, by something like a little park whose grass had turned yellow long ago.

For a place with just two thousand inhabitants the selection, particularly of American classics, was very generous, although it wasn't Steinbeck, Arthur Miller and Michener who drew most of the custom, but the Internet terminals and the DVD shelf. An elderly lady with a brooch on her blouse shook her head when he asked her about the German prisoners of war in Marfa. The name Hans meant nothing to her, either, and she studied him sceptically as if he was intent on causing trouble in the town. He quickly changed the subject and asked about the name Marfa, and her expression cleared immediately. Without a word she took out a copy of *The Brothers Karamazov* by Fyodor Mikhailovich Dostoevsky, a battered paperback nine hundred and forty pages long, which opened up all by itself at the place where Marfa Ignatyevna first appears.

Niklas Kalf was surprised. He hadn't expected to find this town in Dostoevsky. '*I understand what duty means, Grigory Vassilyevitch, but why it's our duty to stay here I never shall understand.*' A witty woman, the engineer's wife, he thought, who probably hadn't been too fond of Texas. Grigory Vassilyevitch replied to Marfa Ignatyevna that it didn't matter what she understood. *And so it was. They did not go away.*

He decided to borrow the book, go back to the hotel and spend the day reading. And just as he had filled in the requisite form, a dainty Mexican-looking woman was suddenly standing next to him. She handed a voluminous DVD case over the counter, looked at his German address and asked with a smile where he came from, and what he was doing in Marfa. She was very small, and looked curiously up at him. Her face seemed made of warm wax, and her lips were the matt red of a candle. Kalf couldn't help staring at her. She wore her heavy black hair parted in the middle and in a bun at the back. Her eyelids were as heavy as her hair. She was taking out the first series of *Sex and the City*, which he didn't know, but when he saw Sarah Jessica Parker on the purple cover he remembered seeing her face in New York on all the buses. The librarian scanned the DVDs in and they went out together. He answered her question by asking for her name.

'April,' she said with a laugh, wishing him a good time in Marfa. Kalf watched after her until she had disappeared around the corner, before he pushed open the heavy chrome swing door of the hotel.

The Paisano had once been the best hotel between San Antonio and El Paso. Built for an oil boom that never came, it had its heyday in the mid fifties, when the film crew stayed there during the filming of *Giant*, with James Dean and Liz Taylor. Now it was almost always quiet in the big hall, with its decorative tiles in opulent colours. From one wall a massive bison's head and, next to it, the head of a longhorn bull, sometimes seemed to gaze at him attentively. The reception desk was unoccupied, as ever. In the long corridor on the first floor the two Mexican chambermaids came towards him and gave him a friendly greeting. Almost all the rooms were open. The drone of a vacuum cleaner reached him. He stepped out onto the little balcony. The fountain in the central patio was dry.

He picked up *The Brothers Karamazov* and lay down on the bed. The novel, published in 1957 by Signet Books in New York, flapped open again like an old seashell. It was a strange feeling reading this story in English, and he noticed how closely his memory clung to a German Dostoevsky, who had never existed any more than this English one had. He read as though behind glass: Marfa Ignatyevna had a child, a six-fingered boy who, his father said, was not worth baptizing.

'*"Why not?" asked the priest with good-humoured surprise.*

'*"Because it's a dragon," muttered Grigory.*

'*"A dragon? What dragon?"*

'*Grigory did not speak for some time. "It's a confusion of nature," he muttered vaguely, but firmly, and obviously unwilling to say more.*'

The child actually dies of thrush. On the night of its burial, mad Lizaveta gives birth to a child, which is taken from her and given to Marfa. The boy, christened Pavel, becomes a cook. Kalf read all day without thinking of anything else. Only when it began to grow dark under the awning on the little balcony did he get hungry and went down to have dinner in Jet's Grill, the hotel restaurant.

Among the changing guests who studied the menu for the first time each evening, while he struggled to keep from recommending the T-bone steak with mashed potatoes and advising against the fish, which was fat and bony, Niklas Kalf began to feel strange after only a few days. No one stayed more than one night. He gazed with amazement at the gay couple in their late forties. The Asian family with two children, travelling in a white Pontiac Trans Sport. The fair-haired biker and the three retired couples who occupied the tables this evening, all with white trainers and two of the men with moustaches. He had decided at the start of his stay on a type of beer and a dessert that he ordered every time, and each of the waitresses had stopped next to him for a moment to ask him his name and where he came from. No one wanted to know when he was setting off again. The answer would have been the same smiling shrug with which he answered the question about what he was doing in Marfa.

Niklas Kalf knew that it was time to admit the failure of his plan. Time and again he tried in vain to contact Elsa Meerkaz. He had considered, in spite of the suspicion that he felt for the publisher, asking Albert Snowe what to do. He had stared at Venus Smith's card and repeatedly tried to imagine what he could offer her. Every day he planned to set off for LA.

But that same paralysis that had seized him the moment of Liz's disappearance kept deadening his despair. He only felt the loneliness at night, in his dreams. At every opportunity he had asked about a German, without finding a trace. Instead he started observing people going about their everyday business, trying to memorize how they walked and nodded to one another and how they got into their cars. He studied their smiles and how they talked to each other, and he always had a sense that there was no alternative to the way they did it. Everything here was in its place. Everything, it seemed to him, was called by its proper name in English, and the prices in dollars gave everything its actual value. The police sirens and the car horns had the right sound, all the lights their proper colours.

Arriving at the centre of the world, Kalf understood, meant that all the promises of the television world of his childhood longing were now redeemed, and he understood how terrible it had been as a child to find nothing of the world of the television series in his own world. Everything always in the wrong colours. Everything had to be dubbed, even, later on, concepts like 'war' or 'family' or 'kiss'. Except that when there was no precise correspondence the running translation in his head came to a standstill. How did you head west in Europe? You never saw dolphins.

Kalf reflected whether this might be why his generation, amidst all these second-rate copies, had been so determined to see the world as aesthetic. To understand the difference that divided one's own life forever from the images from the heart of Empire. What does someone think about himself when he always sees a strange face in the mirror? Niklas Kalf couldn't help smiling: the only German he had found here was himself.

He watched the sheriff with his deputies, breakfasting on eggs, bacon and pancakes in Mike's Place, a diner with purple-tiled tables. Morning after morning the sheriff joked with the ageing blonde in the kitchen, who wore a purple T-shirt with the names of the Marfa Shorthorns 2001, the high school football team, on the back. He saw how he tipped his hat as he left, watched after him and slowly drank his coffee. In the supermarket he tried to memorize the names of the breakfast cereals, Lucky

Charms and Magic Stars and Cheerios and Cocoa Buffs and Cocoa Crunch and Honey Bunches and Cookie Crisp and Trix and Kix and Fruity Shapes and Waffle Crisp and Alpha Bits and Shredded Wheat and Raisin Bran and Capt'n Crunch and Frosted Mini-Wheats and Frosted Flakes and Crisp 'n' Fruit and Apple Phils.

One evening he saw the re-elected German Chancellor on television, and switched channels with surprise. A funeral procession with singers and dancers in African costume moved from the harbour in New York to Ground Zero, black coaches full of coffins bearing the remains of four hundred slaves, four hundred of twenty thousand corpses from a slave cemetery that had been discovered during building work. He reached for the remote control on the bedsheet, switched the television off and heard laughing voices in the corridor. The sign INTIMACY PLEASE on the door rattled in the wake of the people passing.

He tried repeatedly to imagine the wife of that engineer, bored as she waited all day for her husband supervising the excavation of the tunnel. As she sat behind the half-lowered curtains of her Galveston, Harrisburg & San Antonio Railway Pullman car, peering out into the heat of the endless Texan plain, in which her eye could find no purchase.

At some point it occurred to him that she herself must have been Russian. *The Brothers Karamazov*, as the afterword to his battered copy from the public library in Marfa revealed, had not been published until 1880, just three years before she had passed through here. So he tried to imagine pages in Cyrillic, and the way the woman held the book. As he did so he saw nothing more than her pale face in the shadow of the curtains that shielded her against the light.

But in his imagination no book would fit on the little table under the window. It was only when he imagined a stack of Russian newspapers next to her, on the rather worn carpet with its dark red and brown pattern, that his mind's eye recreated the way she read. Now he saw her spending the whole day reaching down next to her seat, picking up one copy after another and opening the gossamer-thin, soft paper at the same place every time, where the serialized novel appeared under the title *Bratya Karamazovy*. She never set foot on the piece of land to which she gave her name. The last trace that remained of her was a pack of old paper rotting away in the wreck of her Pullman, or in some barn along the railroad track, or in an attic in San Francisco.

Strange, he thought, that we don't know what will stay and what will not. The days passed like that. In his dream she looked wearily out over the plain. And slowly the iron wheels rolled on, always balancing on a tiny ridge of metal in the rigid prance of frozen speed.

CHAPTER SEVEN

Storm

For a long time the army was Marfa's livelihood. A good dozen military posts along the Mexican border were kept supplied with soldiers, horses and material from there. Double-deckers that flew along the border were stationed here. After the First World War the tents slowly made way for solid buildings, Camp Marfa became Fort D.A. Russell, and in 1935 the 77th Field Artillery Battalion was stationed there with up to a thousand soldiers. All that remains of the officers' mess is the outside walls. A road curves gently up a slope that is still called Officers Hill, ending in a T-shaped cul-de-sac in front of the commander's former villa.

Niklas Kalf got out of his car and looked out over the fort and the town, and further eastward to the far-off, shadowy mountains on the horizon. His eyes followed the roads that ran in all directions out of the town, he felt the faint breeze on the top of the hill and the sun on his skin. He saw the fort vanishing into the prairie. The German camp must have been somewhere over there. He had been in Marfa for two weeks now, without finding a trace of that secret that he had hoped was hidden inside Eugen Meerkaz's life. The impulse to travel to Los Angeles and tackle Elsa Meerkaz was strong. But he had no proof that she had anything to do with Liz's disappearance. In the end he didn't know anything. And he had nothing he could use to haggle for Liz with anyone at all. So he simply waited, called Avis and extended the rental on his hire car. Stay still, he thought, looking out for a long time over the prairie to the mountains. Then he decided to drive down to the fort and see if he could perhaps find something more at first hand.

Today the grounds belong to the Chinati Foundation, which is administered by Donald Judd's estate. Until his death in 1994 the artist worked here, gradually rebuilding the whole area. When Kalf stepped out of the car in the dusty car park by the front entrance, he noticed that the wind had stopped. Guided tours, he read, daily at ten. Solid shoes. Sun protection. No unaccompanied visitors. There was no one to be seen, the car park was empty. He climbed over the chain and walked all the way around the barracks.

Those few steps were enough to drench his shirt with sweat in the oppressively sticky heat. Fine grey haze condensed in the calm, on the blue glass of the sky. There was not a sound to be heard. Kerbstones carefully marked, like chalk lines in a children's game, the edges of streets in the stony dust, turn-offs going nowhere, parking bays and empty crossings. Even before he felt it, he saw the wind billow up again as a fine, feathery spiral of sand, rolling, rising and slowly spreading. Then he felt it on his skin, very light at first, but as surprisingly cool as if it was much later in the day. Clouds dropped from the glassy sky, dark clouds that quickly swelled and pushed their way in front of the sun.

Donald Judd had had two factory halls extended with

big windows, and topped with corrugated-iron barrel vaults from former aeroplane hangars, which creaked and clanked loudly in the cool wind that was quickly turning cold now.

He ignored the first flash of lightning. It came down somewhere near the mountains, but when the thunder rolled the wind hit him like the mild shock of a very small explosion. He was still scouring the sky for the streak of light that had flashed at the edge of his field of vision when he felt the first drops on his skin, and then the rain broke. The drops landed densely in the red dust, leaving little craters that united within minutes to form puddles and streams, while the car park, when he looked around, had already turned into a body of water perforated by the rain. Although his shirt was now sticking coldly and wetly to his skin, he hesitated for a moment about running back to the car, and then ran over to the nearest hangar, almost slipping in the wet dust. The water sprayed under his trousers and up his ankles and dripped into his trainers.

Of course the door on the narrow side of the hangar was locked. But the big embrasures of the windows on the side facing away from the wind provided some shelter. Niklas Kalf pressed himself against the wall and wiped the water out of his face. The dark, wet plain stood there like a menacingly high, cold wall, and he felt just as alone as he had on the morning of Liz's disappearance. He repeatedly wiped the rain out of his face. I don't belong here, he thought, and had no idea why he should have remembered now, of all times, how Liz and he had stood in the apartment of a German journalist on the twenty-seventh floor looking down at the ribbon of light on First Avenue. It was night, and the river glistened blackly between the buildings. Behind it, the radiantly illuminated Queensboro Bridge and, quite far to the south, surrounded by all the brilliance of the city at night, the silver helmet of the Chrysler Building.

'That's the most beautiful building in the world,' Liz had said, so quietly that he alone could hear it. He had laid his face in her fragrant curls and closed his eyes.

Behind the sky's eyelids lightning twitched down like exploding veins. Curtains of rain drifted, lit for a fragment of a second, across the night-black prairie, and garish afterimages also twitched through the hangar. For moments, as they did so, Judd's artworks appeared out of the darkness, a hundred aluminium cubes standing in both halls. He peered into the dark room and observed how in the gloom the flashes gleamed in the matt-finished material after a perceptible interval, light and somehow smooth, as if eyes were opening sleepily, briefly.

And for a moment the storm seemed like a punishment for doing nothing to find Liz, but instead, as he admitted to himself for the first time, beginning to feel strangely at home in this place. He was losing himself in a world that wasn't his, its strangeness wouldn't let go of him, it worked tirelessly away at his senses, and he knew there was nothing that he could do about his hunger for observation. And the more time passed, the further Liz moved away from him. But he enjoyed the rain running into his shirt, which stuck cold and wet to his back. And the thunder rolled in fresh waves across the endlessly wide plain, and so over him, too.

CHAPTER EIGHT

Then the world disappears

Knocking. First quiet, then louder. Someone was calling. It took him a while to understand: the knocking was coming from the door to his room. Then he also understood what the voice was calling.

'Mr Kalf.' It was the chambermaid. 'Telephone. A call from New York.'

There were no phones in the rooms, the one for guests was on the counter in the lobby. He nodded. It was shortly after six.

'Mr Kalf! Quickly!'

'I'm coming!' he called, annoyed that his nods were being ignored. He quickly slipped into his shirt and trousers. Liz, he thought.

When he opened the door, the chambermaid had disappeared. There wasn't anyone in the hall, either. The receiver lay next to the phone, an old-fashioned black instrument on the brightly glazed tiles of the front desk. He hesitated for a moment and closed his eyes as he imagined Liz's voice flowing into his ear. The receiver was lighter than its appearance suggested, and yet he felt the opening up of that spectral space of creaking depth into which, with old analogue telephones, the voice dropped like a plumb line, to sound across an immeasurable echoing distance, in which the seas surged above submarine cables as thick as your arm.

'Liz?' he asked into that old, familiar space.

'Nick? It's me, Lavinia.'

'Lavinia,' he repeated.

Not Liz. And the space he had expected didn't open up. Instead Lavinia spoke right next to his ear, her voice embroidered onto a dull void leading nowhere.

'A digital connection,' he said, disappointed.

'Niklas!'

'We're talking over the Internet.'

Liz was still missing. Only when the realm of ghosts opens up, he thought, will I have her back.

'How are you, Nick?'

At some point in the night, when he no longer knew how he would endure the loneliness, he had phoned her, thus revealing where he was. 'Lavinia! Do you know what time it is?'

'Sorry if I woke you, but I've had an email with photographs that you've got to see.'

'Photographs?' Kalf didn't understand.

In the silence of her hesitation the electronic connection broke the thread of her breath. 'Yes: pictures of Liz.'

Bait. That's a bait, he thought. 'Of Liz?'

His heart thumped with joy, but in the same instant the tone of her answer took his breath away. 'I can't describe them.'

Her voice broke in the silence after that sentence.

'Can you receive email?' she asked at last, and again it was a long time before he understood what she had said.

'No. I can't access my account from here.'

Now he noticed that he was barefoot, the floor was suddenly terribly cold, and he hopped from one foot to the other. Next to the front desk on a little table stood two Thermos flasks, as always, one with ordinary coffee and one with decaffeinated. Plastic cups and little bowls of sugar, sweetener and creamer in bright paper sachets next to them. White napkins and white plastic stirring paddles. I mustn't be discovered, he thought.

'Niklas?'

'Yes.'

'Why don't you set up a Hotmail address? Do you know how to do that?'

'Yes, of course.'

'niklas.kalf@hotmail.com?'

Again he nodded, completely pointlessly. 'What kind of photographs are they, Lavinia? And who sent them?'

'I don't know, Niklas.'

Soft and golden, the morning sun entered the hall and hurled itself in a wide orbit across the brightly coloured tiles. On the wall the bison's glass eyes glittered as though a fire burned in them. The bull's eyes stayed dull and black.

'Snowe wants to know where you are.'

'Snowe,' he murmured.

'Can I give him the number?'

'No, absolutely not. What's the deal with these photographs?'

'Take a look at them.'

The space of her voice was as dull and black as the bull's eyes, Kalf thought. 'What date is it today?'

'Eleventh of October. Why?'

THOMAS HETTCHE

He gave a start. He had been in Marfa for over two weeks, and nothing of all those days seemed to have remained, not even a sense of passing time.

'Oh, just.'

'You take care, yeah?'

Kalf hung up.

Marfa Book Company is two hundred yards down the main street from the hotel. Marvin nodded to him as always, but paid him no attention, just pushing the stool to the place where the computer's flat screen and keyboard stood, next to big jars of chocolate-chip cookies and ginger snaps, so that guests could surf the Net. The account was quickly set up. Then Kalf waited for the pictures.

The bookshop always opened at 9.30. Apart from Internet access there was black tea and croissants, and apart from the tourists, most of them retired couples with big white camper vans parked outside the front door, the same guests came every morning. The lawyer with his office on the corner picked up a large frozen latte, the young artists from the Chinati Foundation exhibition space dropped by for an espresso, and a woman with her two children talked loudly to Marvin every morning, as he made her a double cappuccino to go in a big cardboard cup.

It didn't take long for Lavinia's email to come. The text consisted of only two sentences: They were still waiting for the material. It was high time to cooperate. Niklas Kalf nervously dragged the browser frame smaller as the analogue modem slowly built up the first picture. His hands were wet with sweat, and an eager anxiety inside him waited impatiently for what he was about to see.

First of all he recognized only the outline of a figure, then he made out Liz's face, but it was a few more seconds before the expression in her eyes appeared. She was sitting on a chair or a stool, her head resting against the wall behind her. Striped pastel-coloured wallpaper, in the top edge of the picture the corner of a shelf. Liz was looking face on into the camera, and Niklas Kalf immersed himself in her gaze, which reached no further than the white fire of the flash in her pupils. The picture must have been taken at night, or else there was no natural light in the room. Liz was wearing an oversized white T-shirt that he didn't recognize. He studied her expressionless mouth. One hand rested in the other, in her lap. He saw with surprise how her belly arched. He reflected that she was already in her fifth month. That's my child, he thought, and he was ashamed of his surprise, all the more so because he really had nearly forgotten it. Liz is tired, he thought.

The digital picture was very low-resolution, the skin was surreally reddened, blue shadows under the lids, which he'd never seen like that. He opened the second picture, and the frame settled over the first one. It was clearly a detail. Kalf recognized Liz's hands in her lap. He impatiently opened the third photograph. Liz was sitting on the stool again, but this time the camera's reaction time had been too slow for the movement, and everything was blurred. At first he thought Liz was just vigorously shaking her head, and he imagined the accompanying energetic *No!* that her open mouth seemed to be uttering, but then he understood that the pale shadow on the upper edge of the picture was a fist.

A fist that must have just caught her face. Her mouth was the open mouth of a scream. The flash-animated icons in the Hotmail advertising banners revolved mutely. He clicked hesitantly again on the other two pictures, to take comfort from them. As if he could rewind what had happened to Liz. And again he wondered about the apparently unnecessary detail. But then he noticed the reddening of the left hand and understood that they had wanted to draw his eye to something that he might have overlooked in the other picture. That it wasn't her fear. And that Liz wasn't, as he had thought at first, simply holding her hand wearily in her lap. Her hand was swollen. Breathing deeply and as slowly as possible, he tried to calm the cramp that gripped him. Liz, he could now clearly see, was holding her left hand in her right as though in a bowl: her hand must have hurt, it was injured, perhaps broken. Once again he clicked back to the first picture and now he understood: her head hadn't slipped against the wallpaper because she was tired. Liz was clearly concentrating on bearing the pain.

Kalf looked into her eyes until everything human vanished from them and all that remained was a random gaze, the dull stare of an animal, the gawp of fish in supermarket aquariums. Nothing but indifferent, unshared pain mutely gazing at him.

'You seem to like it here.' A voice tore him from his thoughts.

Caught by surprise, he hurried to close the browser window. Through the pain it took a moment before he recognized the Mexican girl he had met in the library, who was now standing next to him at the counter.

'Yeah, that's right,' he replied thickly, and cleared his throat. He was finding it hard to conceal his anxiety. 'I might even stay a while longer.'

April, he remembered, that was her name.

'Great!' April nodded with a broad smile. She was a teacher, she said, and she always had Fridays off. The last time they'd met had been a Friday, too, had he noticed?

No, that hadn't occurred to him, said Kalf, thinking all the time of the pastel-coloured wallpaper, the wall and the shelf. The hand and the scream. He knew he would have burst into tears if he had tried to speak at that moment. So he moved away, nodded to Marvin and turned to leave.

'Sunday?' she asked quietly.

When he turned to look at her in bafflement he saw that she was studying him carefully as if she could really read his face.

He nodded.

The sky, when they emerged together, hung stiff and blue above the street and didn't stir. Again he watched after her as she walked down the street after they'd said goodbye. Everything in this landscape is defined by distance. It leaves nothing as it is, but pulls objects so far apart that gaps form between everything, in which silence opens out. There are no birds in this landscape, no cicadas and no trees in which the wind can rustle. Not even the dry grass whispers, everything is waxy and hard, every sound its own island in this silence. The fear in Liz's eyes ticked away in it.

Kalf walked to his car and drove a little way out of the town. To the south of the railroad and the highway, towards the border, lies the headquarters of the Border Patrol with its big transport fleet of off-roaders and buses for the removal of illegal immigrants, and five miles outside Marfa there's a checkpoint with roadblocks. Somewhere before you get to it is the bleached, towering Stardust motel sign with its broken bulbs and the five-point Texan star at the top. A white airship belonging to an Air Force research station stands unchanging in the air, attached to a steel cable. Highway 67 leads directly south, beyond the rim of the basin in which Marfa lies, and into the desert.

Again and again along the road abandoned houses, rusted cars and farm equipment appear. No radio reception on UKW, only long-wave country music from a station calling itself Force of the Last Frontier. Nasal membranes torn and bleeding from the dry air. Twenty miles north of Presidio on the right a rock formation in red sandstone called Lincoln's Head, quite clearly showing a prostrate face in the profile of the landscape. Just before Presidio, Lajita International Airport, a dusty track next to the road. A little later the massif suddenly appears like an enormous wall that the Rio Grande has eaten into the soft stone.

The highway leads wide and undeviating through the town and straight to the border river. At the roadside there are barred gas stations, breakdown recovery services and liquor stores. In a diner, Niklas Kalf ordered beef enchiladas and iced water that came in a pink half-litre cup made of chipped hard plastic. The silhouettes of the Mexican men, who, with their massive heads and stocky torsos, seem to balance, narrow-hipped, above their tight jeans, with silver buckles as big as hands on their belts, and white cowboy hats. After a glance across the Rio Grande, which runs shallow and muddy far below the town, he turned and drove back.

He stopped at the point just before Marfa, on the top of a little hill, where a rotting billboard the size of a house stands. The water tank gleamed silver as a fish above the town. The lights were scattered sparsely against the distant mountains. He heard the far-off sound of one of the many wind wheels that stand everywhere in the fields, pumping up water for the cattle, the metallic grind of a wing. It always made him think of the creaking of a door screen, and a rusty spring pulling it shut with a clatter. APRIL, it said on the card that she had given him, no surname. Another business card, he thought, and rubbed the firm paper between thumb and index finger.

APRIL

BODY MIND CENTERING

1001 Waco Street

Marfa, TX 79843

Phone: 435 719 4862

He listened to the wind and waited for it to subside, because as he summoned the images repeatedly before his inner eye, the feeling of oppression constricted his throat more and more. Only when the rigidity of the photographs dissolved into memories of Liz did he feel better for a moment. How he had first told her about Meerkaz, one evening in their local bar. The heat in New York and how they had kissed. He didn't hear the car, and didn't see it in the wing mirror as it drew up. What tore him from his thoughts was a deep, rather drawling voice.

'Are you an American citizen?'

A uniformed man bent down into the open side window, his right hand resting on the knob of his holstered gun.

Kalf looked round, startled, and was surprised to see the high radiator grille of a black off-road vehicle filling the lower half of his rear-view mirror. Above it, on the windscreen of the car behind him, were the words Border Patrol. His eye jerked over to the side window, and he was staring into his own eyes in the mirrored sunglasses.

'No, sir.'

The sudden desire to tell everything. *Officer*, said his voice in his head, *meine Frau wurde gekidnappt. Bitte helfe Sie mir.**** He bit his lip. He no longer knew if he had been right in his decision to leave New York. He felt guilty and cowardly.

'Your passport!'

The border official took the passport and walked back to his car. Niklas Kalf watched him going through his documents in the rear-view mirror. Another car appeared on the horizon, an old green Chevy that was slowly getting bigger. The sound of the engine was thin at first, stretched high above the earth, but sinking lower and lower the closer the car got, until it was clenched like a fist inside the vehicle. Behind the steering wheel an old farmer with a dirty white hat and eyes narrowed in the midday glare. When the car had sped past the sound of the engine spread out again, as wide as a roaring train.

The policeman briefly flashed his headlights into Kalf's rear-view mirror and, when he looked round, beckoned him over.

'You're Dutch?'

The window was lowered and the car was so high up that Kalf could see the official flicking through it, but couldn't see the passport itself.

'No, sir, I'm German.'

'Here it is: Dutch.'

The border guard pointed to a page. At first Kalf couldn't understand what he meant, but then it occurred to him.

'That's *deutsch*,' he explained. 'It's the German word for German.'

The border guard had taken off his sunglasses. An ageless, Indian face with a broad nose and a clear-cut mouth, the corners pointing downwards. The black pupils gleaming the same colour as his gelled-back hair. He looked indifferently at Niklas Kalf. Not uncomprehendingly, but without recognition, and Kalf was startled when he realized that the man in front of him associated nothing with either term.

He had never before uttered the word *deutsch* without seeing an echo in the face of the person he was speaking to. Ever since, interrailing in his youth, he had first crossed the German border heading westward, his origins had constituted an inescapable identity, however fluent his French might have been. But here all connections to Europe had been severed long ago. He had to keep himself from speaking the name of Adolf Hitler to check whether the border guard might prick up his ears, and the name was already on his lips when he caught his reflection in the GMC's big exterior mirror and gave a start.

No idea how long he'd been wearing this shirt. The skin of his face had turned much darker and dull in an unfamiliar way, as though worn away by the sand. Pale strips across his temples marked the arms of his sunglasses. His hair, on the other hand, seemed to have got even lighter, and longer than he had worn it for years. Behind him in the rear-view mirror the sun hung over the wide plain. I'm no longer young, he thought suddenly. His whole life in Germany seemed infinitely remote from him. With scorching envy he recognized that he too could have been born here, in the centre of the world. He had to struggle to remain calm, the desolation jolted him so, and the thought of the photographs of Liz made him shiver again. He had never really been sure how one was supposed to act, had only ever registered what was going on around him. He wiped from his forehead the fine sand that the wind here always carries. Never had the world seemed so real to him as it did now. And never a situation seemed so hopeless as the one in which he found himself. I'm forty, Kalf thought, when the border guard asked what he was doing here.

He was on holiday. In Marfa.

'Marfa? What's going on over there? The art thing?'

Niklas Kalf nodded. *The art thing,* he repeated in his mind, and the border guard gave him his passport back.

'Enjoy your trip, sir.'

Kalf thanked him. And when he tried to look himself in the eyes again, the picture blurred in the quiver of the exterior mirror. He stepped aside, and the Border Patrol car drove off.

Back in the hotel he stopped hesitantly by the telephone whose receiver, heart thumping, he had pressed to his ear that morning. There was no one in the lobby, although nearby, from the restaurant, the few guests could still be heard. The picture of her scream. Her injured hand. That paper on the wall of a room whose whereabouts he didn't know. Nothing now was as it had been yesterday. Clearly they had assumed that Lavinia was in communication with him, which was why they had sent her the pictures. Their calculation had proved correct, and now they had established contact with him. He pulled out the piece of paper from which he had so often read Elsa Meerkaz's phone number, and his heart pounded as it always did when he called. Even though he had never managed to reach her.

'Ja?'

He gave a start. Actually hearing her voice for the first time since he had been in America took his breath away. Why, it shot through his head, was she answering the phone in German? An agonizingly long moment seemed to pass before he was able to answer her.

'Mrs Meerkaz,' he said very slowly, 'this is Niklas Kalf.'

'Mr Kalf, how lovely of you to call!'

He had to close his eyes to stay calm. He called to mind the only picture that existed of Elsa Meerkaz in recent years. A fat woman on the beach in a long black robe, as ageless as a Greek shipowner's widow. Even a few years ago she was said to have strolled down the steep hill from her villa in Pacific Palisades to the sea to swim each morning. By now she was over ninety, but her voice still had that Austrian lilt which, as her husband once wrote in a letter, had not only been preserved in exile, but had intensified with age.

Kalf wondered how to start, but before he could say anything she asked him about the reading in the Goethe House. Trembling inwardly with excitement, he passed on Albert Snowe's greetings.

'A most charming man.'

'Yes, that's true. He urgently advised me against leaving New York.'

'I don't understand.'

Once again, as when he had spoken to Lavinia that morning, the echo chamber of the digitally connected conversation. He knew this was the moment he had been awaiting all along. Now his wife's fate would be decided. The cotton-wool silence left him breathless, and he couldn't control himself any longer.

'What's going on?' he yelled, aware that his voice was breaking. 'Why couldn't I contact you? We made an appointment. Have you any idea what's going on?'

At the same moment he became afraid that she might hang up. But she just said she didn't know what he meant. She was sorry if he'd called her for nothing.

Niklas Kalf fought to stay calm.

'My wife has been kidnapped,' he said in as relaxed a tone as possible. 'And I can't give the kidnappers what they are demanding of me.'

'How dreadful,' she said. 'I'm really very sorry, Mr Kalf.'

'Yes,' he said after a long pause, the black nothingness of which took his breath away once again.

'I wish there was some way I could help you.'

'I very much hope you can, Mrs Meerkaz.'

'I don't understand.'

The coldness in her voice made him furious. He was sure she was lying. And again his voice rose: 'You're keeping something from me! My wife's life is at stake! Speak!'

'What? I don't know what you mean. I'm sorry about what's happened to you, but I find your suspicions quite unseemly.'

'Mrs Meerkaz,' he began again, 'please listen to me. The kidnappers plainly believe I'm in possession of certain material about your husband. Material so explosive that they're threatening to kill Liz over it. It's about some experiments. The name Parsons has been mentioned.'

'Yes,' she said.

Niklas Kalf breathed deeply. Could it be that she'd finally allowed herself to help him after all?

'Do you know what they might be?'

For a moment he hoped again.

She had really no idea what he meant. Her husband and she had had nothing to hide from each other as long as they lived, that was what happened when you fled from Hitler. As he knew, they had gone to California immediately after their arrival in the United States, because Eugen Meerkaz had known Theodore von Kármán, the Hungarian physicist, at the California Institute of Technology, and he had offered him a job. Everyone knew what her husband had gone on to achieve in his research. It was all documented in countless articles and research reports, there was no secret there. She really didn't know what he was imagining.

'I'm not imagining anything, Mrs Meerkaz. I have received photographs today, in which it's apparent that my wife is being mistreated.'

She didn't reply.

'We had an appointment, Mrs Meerkaz. Let's talk about the whole thing when we go through your husband's documents at your house. Something's bound to turn up then.'

'I can't imagine that.'

'Mrs Meerkaz, if I set off today, I can be in LA within two days.'

'Mr Kalf, I don't think it's a good idea for you to come here. Please let's postpone our appointment for a while.'

'No,' he cried, 'you can't wriggle out of it like that!' Nothing mattered now, anyway. 'You've landed me in this. It's your fault that my wife has been kidnapped! I insist that we meet!'

'No, Mr Kalf.'

'You've got to help me!'

'I can't do that,' she replied calmly. 'And I don't know what you're thinking of, either. Please stay where you are. That's the best thing. For your wife and for you.'

Her voice had hardened. Then her silence engulfed the space. Kalf knew: it was a threat. There was nothing left for him to say. So he said nothing. Closed his eyes and listened to time passing.

'So where are you?' she asked quietly after a while.

Her breath in the receiver started and stopped again.

For a moment Niklas Kalf considered whether he should reply to her, but instead he hung up.

Almost all the streets in Marfa lead nowhere. Repeatedly, as he drove through the town, he had finally ended up driving down a piece of unsurfaced roadway to an embankment or one of the dry riverbeds, and had had to turn the car with a glance at the mute, indifferent prairie. Now, that night, when Liz's face and her gaze and the way her hand seemed to hold the pain appeared before his eyes when his consciousness tried to slip even slightly towards sleep, he stared into the dark and imagined the people here in Marfa now, in the middle of the night, getting into their cars and driving just two or three blocks, turning off the ignition and letting the wheels roll to where the asphalt ends.

Only at that edge, Niklas Kalf thought to himself, finally breathing his way calmly into sleep, do the cars stop, and the drivers turn off the headlights. Then at last it's all over. Then the world disappears.

CHAPTER NINE

That's not bad for the devil!

Waco Street lies beyond the highway that cuts through the town from east to west. Marvin had told him that in the old days mostly Mexicans had lived south of the highway and the railroad tracks, while the whites had tended to live around the courthouse. Marfa consists largely of one-storey houses, few have more than four rooms and they always stand precisely in the middle of a plot of land, flanked by a garage and a drive and surrounded by a knee-high fence. While in the north of the town trees or bushes are often planted on the patch of lawn in front of the houses, which help to block the view of the usually large lattice windows of the sitting rooms, the plots south of the highway mostly look as if they've been swept clean. Green plants seem to grow only in the shade of the houses, otherwise the ground is pale and dusty. Brightly painted metal fences, little American and Texan flags in empty flowerpots, cement grottoes with Mary in a light blue cloak, Disney's Bambi and the Seven Dwarfs in faded plastic in the sand. Small white Japanese cars are often parked outside, dark holes eaten into them by rust.

Galveston, Austin and Plateau Street, Ridge and Hoover Street. It was only when he got out of the car in front of 1001 Waco Street that he noticed to his surprise that he had driven through the town quite as naturally as if he lived here. Persephone? He was sure she'd said Persephone.

'No!' she replied with a laugh, and her red lips revealed very white teeth. She brushed the heavy hair out of her face and blinked into the bright sunlight. 'It's Penelope!'

And April? He pulled the card out of his trouser pocket and she laughed again.

At some point her husband had started calling her that. And it had stayed that way for her company. 'He died two years ago,' she said after a moment's hesitation, and the laughter vanished from her face.

He'd completely forgotten how small she was. Quickly, as if she wanted to avoid the blazing light of that Sunday afternoon coming in, she shut the door behind him. A curtain in front of the big sitting-room window filtered intense blue light, thin, white beams beside it. He said he was sorry about her husband.

'A turkey is a funny bird,
His head goes wobble, wobble.
And he knows just one word,
Gobble, gobble, gobble!'

A little boy in a high chair at a counter leading to the kitchen, with an empty plate in front of him, beat out the rhythm for himself with a spoon.

'That's Dave,' said April. 'He's just turned four and thinks it's Thanksgiving today.'

The boy had black curls and big, laughing eyes.

'Hi, Dave!'

Instead of answering, the little boy started up his song

again. 'A turkey is a funny bird,' he crowed, but this time he crossed his thumbs and spread his fingers out into fluttering wings, 'his head goes wobble, wobble.' He wobbled his head until Niklas Kalf laughed. 'And he knows just one word,' the little boy continued as loudly as he could and, cheering and exultant, he lifted himself up in his high chair and stretched both index fingers over his head. 'Gobble, gobble, gobble!'

As he did so, he laughed so loudly that he shook, and Kalf couldn't help laughing too, as he looked into his beaming eyes. At first he didn't notice that the endless laughter had mutated into a low, jerking cough which, strangely, didn't seem to extend as far as the child's laughing mouth and laughing eyes. Only after a few minutes did the coughing become so violent that Niklas Kalf understood what was happening, and his own laughter caught in his throat.

His heart leapt with pity when he saw Dave's face going into spasm, and the mask into which the laughter had long since frozen, so hard was he coughing, simply fell apart. Kalf was sure that the child must be familiar with this cough, indeed that he must have been long used to it, and he must also have learned bravely to ignore the barking tremors. But it was terrible now to see him subject to this coughing fit, unable to be the things he yearned with all a small child's strength to be. Kalf would never forget that moment when the boy's radiant expression started flickering in the storm of coughs that suddenly raged unchecked through his little body, desperately tried to defend itself and finally went out. Just as many circus artistes can roll their eyeballs back into their skulls, the child's gaze turned inwards, focusing entirely on the cough, which had manage to capture his undivided attention, the spasm produced by the irritation, the monotonous twitching of the strained windpipe and the pain that Kalf imagined he could feel himself.

That's not bad for the devil! Kalf thought furiously and sadly as he saw that the coughing simply wouldn't stop. *That's not bad for the devil.* He'd recently read that sentence in Dostoevsky. Ivan says it at some point to the devil, a rather ramshackle figure with a big, soft hat who is suddenly sitting by his sickbed. Not bad at all, thought Kalf, looking quizzically at April, who was now holding her son's head. As she cushioned the groaning and shaking and the gurgle of phlegm, she didn't take her silent gaze off him. The spasm gradually subsided.

'Cystic fibrosis,' she said as if by way of apology, and stroked Dave's back as the internal storm withdrew.

'Gobble, gobble, gobble!' murmured Dave quietly and opened his eyes. And although he felt terribly sorry for him, Kalf couldn't help smiling at the child's mischievous grin as, now quite calm again, he snuggled into his mother's arm.

After a moment she kissed him on the forehead as if nothing had happened. 'Hurry up! We have to go!'

As the little boy jumped up, April explained that they were about to go to the cemetery. Did he want to come along?

'Come on, it's not so bad!'

She smiled as if she was all too familiar with the reaction to her son's illness, and stroked his arm. The awkwardness melted away and he managed to smile at her. He became aware how close he felt to them both, even though he barely knew them. As if they had been waiting for him. Of course he would come.

They took the old Datsun that stood in the driveway. Dave climbed in the back. April, as he still thought of her, said nothing until she turned on the indicator just before the edge of town and said he'd see in a minute: the racial divide still existed in the cemetery. And as she slowly drove along the wide, untarred path between the rows of graves, he understood what she meant. The graveyard was clearly divided into two sections. Here there were trees and old graves surrounded by cast-iron railings, while beyond a fence the gravestones vanished into the prairie. But in contrast to the white people's cemetery, plastic flowers in all colours gleamed there, and tinsel and Christmas baubles, pictures of the saints and flags.

How did the living manage to live together, he wanted to know. April grinned and let the car bump through the potholes. It worked well enough, as long as you accepted that the Mexicans generally got the bad jobs. But that was changing slowly, and by now there were even some affluent Mexican ranchers in the surroundings of Marfa. April stopped at the edge of a puddle from a hissing sprinkler, and they got out.

The jet jerked tirelessly in a circle and covered a piece of lawn that held, as though sunk in the soft green, the regular rows of the soldiers' graves. Next to many of the narrow slabs that bore nothing but a name and dates of birth and death, little American flags had been stuck into the grass, their sole decoration. Outside the area encompassed by the jet of water, the cemetery was stony and dusty as it was everywhere else, and barely a pale bunch of grass grew in it. Identical grey concrete borders surrounded the graves, stone slabs the shape of king-size beds, unadorned and undecorated. The sun glittered coldly in the rain of drops from the lawn sprinkler. April was now holding a thin bunch of flowers in her hand. Dave had already run the short way to his father's grave, and was waiting for her there.

MARCUS LENOX it said on the stone, with two dates beneath it:

* 12.3.1968 and † 8.10.2000. The American eagle in gold, lightning in both claws.

'Marc was with the Border Patrol.'

April had seen his quizzical expression.

He nodded.

'Get us some fresh water, will you, Dave?' she said, took the withered flowers out of the vase that had stood next to the gravestone and gave them to her son.

The boy ran off and they watched him go. Marcus Lenox had been only a little younger than himself. Kalf couldn't help thinking how quickly the belief had begun to erode that everything would stay as it had been since his youth. Now he often felt the pull of that desolation with which the horizon began to close in. And at that moment he very clearly imagined he sensed the empty space that the dead man had left behind.

'He doesn't say much, does he?'

'No, not really.'

She bent down and plucked out a few stalks that were growing over the slab. 'I always think it has something to do with his father's death.'

'Yes.' He didn't know what to say.

'It must be hard with a child who's so ill.'

She stood back up. 'My parents live in Terlingua. That's near the Rio Grande. About an hour to the south. If I want, my mother comes and helps me.'

'That's good.'

'And next year they may be setting up a kindergarten here.'

She blinked past him into the sun. Then she threw the stalks away. Lightly and just a few inches from the grave. 'The phlegm chokes him. Isn't that what you wanted to know?'

Kalf said nothing.

'It's horrible: his body itself produces what's going to kill him, at some point. But the dry climate here does him good.' She smiled when she saw his questioning expression. 'You're right: otherwise I probably wouldn't be here.'

Dave came back, carefully balancing the narrow plastic vase, filled to the brim with water.

April put in the flowers.

'And what's this Body Mind Centering on your card?' he said, changing the subject.

'I heard about the BMC pretty soon after I found out what was wrong with Dave. Then I took him to see someone who offered this treatment, and when I noticed it was helping I took some courses myself.'

She brushed her hair out of her face. 'And now I'm the one helping others.'

Dave was standing next to Niklas Kalf and had taken his hand. April smiled when she saw.

'Come on, guys, let's go!'

Dave would shortly have his afternoon nap, but first

he'd have to inhale, April explained as they drove home, and as soon as they were back Dave ran to the corner of the sitting room where the two sofas met. Without looking, he pulled out a transparent plastic hose with a similar mouthpiece and sat down on the couch below the big sitting-room window, through which blue light still fell, filtered by a thick curtain. A kind of compressor started humming and Dave pressed the mouthpiece of the inhaler firmly to his nose and mouth.

Kalf sat down next to him. White steam spilled out from the edges of the mask and lingered in the blue light. Dave leaned into him and rested his free arm on his knee. A damp, aseptic smell rose to Kalf's nose. He tried to calm his breathing to inhale in as little as possible of the antibiotics and cortisone that were being released into the air. April sat down on the other sofa. The front page of a *New York Times* on the floor showed a picture of Imre Kertész. NOBEL FOR HUNGARIAN WRITER WHO SURVIVED DEATH CAMPS. Kalf bent carefully down and picked up the paper with his fingertips. New York, Friday, October 11, 2002. CONGRESS AUTHORIZES BUSH TO USE FORCE AGAINST IRAQ.

Dave cuddled up against him as the machine fumigated his pulmonary alveoli, and Kalf admired him for his calm and composure. He laid his hand on his back and beneath the thin shirt he felt too clearly the hard muscles trained by endless coughing. Dave started making strange signs, nimble figures with his free hand that looked like signing for deaf people, but also those headless puppets that children invent, the legs the index and middle finger and above them the hand, the body. Something like that danced on his knee for a moment, then Dave looked at him, his face distorted by the mask, and he understood that the boy wanted to know if he understood him. Kalf nodded, and again the fingers drummed on his trousers, and again he nodded, understanding nothing that the child was trying to say to him. Instead he understood why Dave didn't speak. How, thought Kalf, was he to trust a language that doesn't work under that mask, and is therefore of no use to him when he needs it most urgently? He was amazed at how fast the child's hands were.

Perhaps, it suddenly occurred to him, Liz had been dead for ages. Just as dead as Marcus Lenox. Such things happened. It wasn't impossible. Not even unimaginable. He repeated her name to himself, but the magic of the sound was ebbing increasingly away. Or was he just convincing himself of that? Wasn't he the one distancing himself from her? The one beginning to turn her disappearance into her death, as something easier to live with?

'You look exhausted,' April said quietly.

He shook his head.

'You don't want to talk about it?'

'I can't.'

'You can't.'

'No, I can't.'

Nodding, she sucked air through her teeth. Then the compressor grew quieter and stopped, Dave threw the breathing mask on the floor and immediately started leaping about on the sofa. The mask on the floor still streamed thin white steam that settled on the carpet like sleet on a calm day.

'That's enough,' said April at some point. 'Afternoon nap!'

The child threw his arms around Kalf's neck and laughed at him, and he hugged the hard body once again, then carefully pulled the little hands away from his neck and set the boy on the floor. He ran out and threw the door to his room shut with a loud crash, and all of a sudden it was very quiet.

Kalf thought of the rapid evenings here, that seemed to rush every day from all sides across the prairie to the town; the sky, withering in time lapse, capitulating day after day, with all its shades of red, to the black night. And he thought again of that letter with the Marfa postmark. That, he said to himself, is why I'm here.

'Do you know anyone called Hans?'

'Hans,' repeated April, shaking her head. 'No, never heard of him.'

'A German. I know that he lived here in the fifties, or perhaps still does.'

'A German, you say?'

'Yes.'

'Frank's father was a German, I think.'

'Frank?'

'Frank Holdt, an artist.'

'Could you introduce me?' Niklas Kalf's heart was pounding. He had never been so close to his secret, if indeed it was a secret.

'Sure. But right now he's in Hawaii with his partner. They wanted to be back for Open House, the annual Chinati Foundation party.'

That wasn't for a month. It meant he would have to

go on waiting. But he realized how relieved he was by the hope that he might have found just a clue to that letter which he had taken from the pile of documents in New York, and which he had brought here. He felt as if he and April had known each other for a long time. Her immaculate skin still reminded him of wax, and he imagined her velvety smoothness. He felt that he didn't want to go.

But what do I want, then, he wondered. To stay, thought Niklas Kalf, and said into the silence, 'You must tell me what BMC actually is.'

April nodded and smiled. He watched as she laid one hand on the other and seemed to reflect for a moment.

'BMC,' she said then, 'makes it possible to communicate with all the cells of your own body, the organelles, the mitochondria, and the DNA and finally with the molecules themselves.'

'What do you mean by that? What does *communicate* mean?'

April rubbed her hands around each other as if preparing for an athletic exercise, not especially carefully, but thoroughly, and Kalf noticed that her fingers weren't particularly delicate, and that her hands looked as if they'd been shaped by gardening, brown and with short fingernails. 'You go on a journey into your own body. And you follow your body fluids. Lymph, blood.'

He shook his head. 'I don't get it.'

April nodded, stood up without a word, fetched a chair from the dining table and sat down so close in front of him that he had to part his legs. Tied her long hair back in a single movement in such a way that it no longer fell into her face. Laid her arms on her knees and held the palms of her hands vertically in front of him.

'Lay your head in here.'

She smiled and looked at him. Her eyelids were so heavy. He hesitated for a moment and looked at the open shells of her hands.

'OK,' he said, hitched his shoulders and did as she asked. Laid his head into her dry, warm hands and closed his eyes. He cautiously relaxed the muscles in his neck. He slowly breathed out and in, smelling the rather powdery, fresh scent of hand cream.

'Rock your head slowly and softly from side to side,' she murmured.

He did so, and her hands held him gently.

'Organs,' she continued quietly, 'are soft parts in the container of your body. Your brain's an organ, too. When you move the container, you can influence the organs. The slightest movements of the head cause alterations in the brain structures.'

And it really was as if he could feel his own brain, feel it move in the slow roll of his head. But above all he felt a weight, which he hadn't noticed at all before, being lifted from behind his eyes.

Her hands went on rocking his skull gently.

'Lie down on the floor, please.'

For a moment he wondered why he was doing what she asked him to. But then he slipped silently from the couch, lay down on his back and closed his eyes again. Immediately he felt her carefully laying four fingers of one hand under the corner of his left jaw, and beginning to stroke his neck, first up, then back down again.

'It's possible,' she said, 'to accompany the flow of lymph inwards, through the lacy vessels of the skin surface to the larger collection points, the cisterna chyli, the ductus thoracicus, all the way to the point where the lymphatic fluid flows back into the bloodstream at the vena subclavia above the heart.'

Her other hand settled with very light pressure on his ribcage, and seemed to be looking for something there. 'Don't be alarmed,' she murmured, reaching carefully under his shirt. Her hand slipped over his belly to a particular spot to the left below his nipple, and waited as if listening for a hidden signal.

'I was wrong,' she said thoughtfully. 'It isn't your brain. It's your heart.'

She started running her hand gently over his ribs, and slowly the movements of her hand became wider and firmer, and he actually felt as if she were, with his ribs, pressing his lungs against the place where his heart must be. Again and again, against that numb, deeply buried point that you don't feel and know nothing about, except that it's the lever of the only movement that never stops. Niklas Kalf felt the desire finally to talk to someone about everything growing more intense than ever before. I don't want to miss Liz any more, he thought, and he so longed to tell April everything that he was already moistening his lips with his tongue to begin his confession when he heard her quiet voice.

'The heart has a particular connection with the eyes. When the dynamic flow between heart and eyes is disturbed, the patient often experiences that as a disintegration of the inner and outer world.'

Inner and outer world, he repeated to himself, and

then she suddenly stopped. He noticed with surprise how hard his heart was beating now, all the way up to his throat, and he tried to breathe calmly as he opened his eyes. Saw with some bemusement April walking over to the kitchen units and pouring a glass of water. His heartbeat slowly eased, and he sat up. He drank the cold water in little gulps.

'Better?'

'Yes.'

'Yes?'

'Yes!'

She grinned. 'Good,' she said.

Shortly afterwards they said goodbye. They stood for a moment in the mild, reddish afternoon light that lay over the Marfa plateau on the edge of the Chihuahua desert, and he felt calmer than he had in a long time. Everything around him was in some way familiar to him, so that there was no room for homesickness.

'And Dave?' he asked.

'You mean how long he'll live? They don't know. Two years or ten. With good medical care perhaps even twenty. No idea.'

She blinked into the soft light. BMC, she explained quietly, hadn't just helped Dave, it had helped her a lot, too. 'I see the body as being like sand. It's difficult to study the wind, but if you watch the way sand patterns form and disappear and re-emerge, then you follow the patterns of the wind or, in this case, the mind.'

He nodded to her before turning round and walking to his car, and he didn't stop thinking about what she had said until he walked into the bar and Marvin tapped his index finger to his forehead. The neon sign wasn't yet switched on, the bar was still empty. Just Marvin, as if he were always here, at the bar.

'Hey, stranger, still here?' he asked, apparently unable, for a long moment, to get over the obstacle that the *still here* placed in the way of his utterance.

Kalf nodded with a grin and waited until he got his beer. Only then did he ask, 'You remember that woman I talked to recently in the bookshop?'

'Sure, April. Why?'

'I've just come from hers.'

'Ah!'

'No, not what you think.'

'No?'

'No,' he said again, although he didn't really know what there was between them. 'Do you know Dave, her son?'

'Yes. Sad business. Last winter we held a collection for him.'

'Money for medicine?'

'No, for a trip.'

Marvin paused as if he had to take a run-up before he could go on talking. He carefully wiped the beer from his thin grey beard and took a deep breath.

'April went round telling everybody there was this therapy that was good for Dave, swimming with dolphins and stuff.' He hissed the last word in an agonizingly long trembling s and an elongated f, until he was able to go on talking. 'Somewhere around Corpus Christi. We paid for the journey.'

'Who's we?'

'Just about everybody.'

Marvin picked up his glass and emptied it. Kalf hurried

to copy him. He nodded to the barkeeper, a bald, bent-backed man in a white shirt, who poured two fresh glasses from the tap. Kylie Minogue sang 'Can't Get You Out Of My Head', and the two men turned around to look at the screen.

'I've found the book that Marfa appears in,' said Kalf.

'Really? What's it called?'

'*The Brothers Karamazov*. By Dostoevsky.'

Marvin nodded. 'And who's Marfa?'

'A maid.'

'No shit? A cleaning lady?'

'Yes,' he said. 'And the devil's in it, too.'

'Bullshit!'

'No, he is. He said: *Nihil humanum a me alienum puto*. That means: Nothing human is alien to me.'

'That's not bad for the devil!'

He stared at Marvin in astonishment. Had the feeling he was suddenly in a time-lapse film, the kind they'd shown in biology class. All around him the trembling shoots of a rapidly growing plant bent towards one another, turning into an impenetrable tangle of green stems and buds and leaves full of sticky soft sap. 'Say that again!'

Again the word *bad* caused Marvin a lot of trouble, his lips twitched damply, but he got there. 'That's not bad for the devil!' And with a grin he raised his new glass to him. 'To the devil!'

In Marfa, distance extends even into the barren front gardens. You can feel it even in the abandonment of the children's toys. Niklas Kalf now remembered seeing in passing, very close to April's house, which was already being sealed against the night, a climbing frame of iron poles which looked as forlorn as if it was already in no-man's-land. Next to it stood Dave's abandoned pedal car, whose painted headlights seemed to gaze down across the street to the distant Chinati mountains, its steering wheel slightly smashed in, as if the car had stopped while travelling at great speed. Something had changed irrevocably, and he wondered whether it might have had something to do with the way April had held his head in her hands.

What was Marfa Ignatyevna's question again? *Why it's our duty to stay here?* Anyone who went away, he understood that evening for the first time, would never learn the answer.

CHAPTER TEN

I don't know

Just as Lavinia's voice stuck close to his ear like a thin film covering the furry black space, Niklas Kalf suddenly remembered standing at the gate behind the glass facade at Frankfurt airport before departure, and watching the compressor blade of one of the two engines of the Boeing 747 slowly turning, the motion gradually coming to a stop.

It was midday, very hot outside, and in the sharp shadow that the wings cast on the airfield, tankers and cargo transporters had shunted busily around the under-carriage, like pilot fish, always close to the immaculate silvery body of the plane, whose hatches were still wide open. A hulking, ungainly animal, unfit to live on land, its breathing slow and tired. Two hundred thousand litres of kerosene being pumped into its tanks, while refrigerated containers of food were hoisted to the hatches. Kalf's eyes had darted across the massive white nose to the windows of the cockpit, and for a moment he had actually thought he could see the flash of a pilot's glasses behind the reflective windscreen, but then every-thing was once again opaque and motionless behind the glass which, he could clearly see, had been worn by hail and sand and ultraviolet radiation.

'Niklas?'

'Yes.'

'Liz's father phoned the Goethe House, and they gave him my number. He wants to know how you are and how he can reach you.'

Kalf thought for a moment. Germany had disappeared so far behind the horizon that he had long ago stopped considering the possibility that anyone over there might miss him.

'And what did you tell him?'

'That everything's fine, and you're travelling in areas where there's no mobile network.'

'Good.'

'I promised I'd call him again as soon as I'd made contact with Liz. What should I tell him?'

'Tell him we'll call. That his daughter is well.'

'Nick?'

'Yes?'

'And I've got a message for you from Al Snowe.'

'How does he know where I am?'

'He doesn't. He said you might call me, and if you did I was most emphatically to offer you his help again. You can approach him whenever you like.'

Kalf closed his eyes. Her voice reminded him of that dinner with Snowe, and the way the publisher chewed ice cubes and talked about that underage murderess. How he had driven downtown with Liz in the taxi, through the sultry summer heat on her first day in New York.

'I understand.'

He didn't understand a thing. He'd spent the last little while in bed reading Dostoevsky. The sky was overcast, and it was raining often now and getting cooler by the day. 'Do you know *The Brothers Karamazov*? I borrowed the novel from the public library here. And you know what? It's actually all about why you shouldn't leave the place where you are.'

Lavinia laughed as if he'd made a joke, and Kalf changed the subject.

'I'd like to know the name of the restaurant we all went to. I forgot it straight away.'

'L'Acajou. It's on 19th Street.'

'Are you sure?'

'Yes. Snowe often goes there with his European authors.'

'Do you remember how strange it was that he spent the whole evening talking about that girl, the murderer?'

'Imogen Engel, yes.'

'As if he was trying to tell me something, give me a clue, something like that.'

'I don't think so, Nick. You're brooding too much. He was just really interested in the business about that girl Imogen at the time.'

'But why? The murder was years ago.'

'Well, because she'd been let out about a week before. Didn't he say that at the time?'

'No, he didn't.'

'Oh!'

How could he ever forget? Imogen Engel was at large. But what did that mean?

After a pause, just long enough for her bafflement to be apparent, she asked, 'What are you actually doing in Texas the whole time? And how are you, Niklas?'

He shrugged. 'I don't know.'

Niklas Kalf stood next to the telephone and started feeling very cold in his summer clothes. At night the temperature dropped close to freezing, it was windy, and the hotel thermometer, even during the day, even when it wasn't even raining, barely showed more than fifty degrees Fahrenheit.

Kalf now often spent half the afternoon in his car on the edge of town, letting the windscreen wipers shovel the rain aside. Liz was now in her twenty-third week. He tried to imagine the child moving in her belly. Huge cloud formations, vertiginous cliffs with dark, often night-black cores, drifted over the plain, many-veined lightning flashes twitched through them like a twinkling light wandering across milky glass, and plunged from them like swift, pointed roots trying to bore their way into the ground. The dry arroyos that criss-crossed the landscape turned within hours into raging streams, while banks of rain hung like wet sails from the cloud-ships as they glided slowly away. He felt inaction paralysing him more and more. The days simply passed. Toads emerged from the earth. And the air that had seemed for so long, in that dry landscape, to be made of glass, suddenly smelt so spicy and heavy that he almost felt ill.

We are the first, he reflected, who are not drawn to this place. All the immigrants have sought their fortune here, in the heart of Empire. But that pull is past, thought Kalf, and saw the wind sweeping the empty prairie, either away from a new storm front or into the area of falling air pressure left by a rain-drained cloud formation. He often thought of that boy he had suddenly thought he could see on the monitors on the flight to New York, that lascivious sleeper over the continents, and how he had set off from the boy's forehead, from the edge of the Empire to the middle of it, here, into this void where he waited, not knowing what for.

'I don't know,' he said again to Lavinia Sims. 'I'm waiting. They'll have to break cover sooner or later, I guess.'

He didn't believe what he was saying. He knew very well that nothing would happen while he did nothing. But he also sensed that there was nothing he could do about his inaction. Lavinia didn't say anything. In the end she said he could call her at any time, and then they hung up.

The weak light of the gloomy day glimmered in the glass eyes of the bison's head. Time passed almost invisibly now that there were no guests in the hotel. He had forgotten the last time he had seen a stranger, and the staff weren't much in evidence since there was nothing to do. Only the two ancient heaters turned stiffly from left to right and back again, snorting their warm air into the lobby. The doors lining the long hotel corridors stood open, and Kalf looked into the empty rooms, which seemed to be in twilight all day. Again and again he studied the Marfa postmark on that letter that had lured him here, and thought about what April had said about the separation of the inner and outer worlds. He had never understood whether his mania for observation was a form of flight, or whether his permanent indifference towards himself was the very thing that allowed him to have a precise perception of the outside world. Like a huntsman undistracted by a shaking hand.

But now he was lacerating himself for his inability to act. The only thing that got him up in the morning was the prospect of the newspapers and the computer in the bookshop, and day after day he persuaded himself yet again to make the short journey on foot in spite of the rain. He followed for days, in the *New York Times*, the hunt for the sniper who was executing people at random during those weeks. Pictures of perfectly lit gas stations at night, car parks with the victims' cars, finally a photograph of the perpetrator, laughing arm in arm with his son. John Allen Muhammad, 41, and John Lee Malvo, 17. *A photograph taken by Mr Muhammad's former sister-in-law*. He read in *Spiegel Online* about a man in a little town near Lucca who had said goodbye to his family in the late 1950s and declared that he was emigrating to America. Now his corpse had been found in a walled-up niche in the cellar. Beside the man's skeleton, a rifle, a bricklayer's trowel with bits of mortar and a bottle with a letter of farewell. Sometimes in those weeks he no longer knew if he really was waiting for news of Liz. And he felt as if he'd been caught red-handed when he checked his Hotmail and actually had mail.

Nervous and surprised, he clicked the news window shut. The mail was from Lavinia Sims: it contained only a short greeting and a forwarded email with a picture file attached. The sender was a combination of numbers at GMX. Liz! he thought, feeling like a traitor, because all of a sudden all that past and lost time shrank into a recognizable period, and he wondered how she was. And the child. Wanted nothing now but to feel her gaze at last, even if it was the deep-frozen gaze of a photograph.

His heart pounded as he opened the GIF. It showed nothing but an unmade-up, smiling mouth, the lips slightly parted. He was sure it was Liz. He eagerly studied the photograph. Her lips were chapped, the corners of the mouth torn, reddened like the skin above the upper lip, and to the left, near the point of the smile, there was a spot right in the finely arched wrinkle. That was all. He was relieved not to be shown any fresh injury, and yet fear constricted his throat. He didn't see what he wasn't supposed to see. He felt as if these close-ups were actually cutting her into pieces. He stared helplessly until he couldn't bear it any more. He quickly clicked the picture shut. *Spiegel Online* reported that what was probably the oldest animal in the world lived on the seabed in Antarctica. He turned to Marvin.

'A giant sponge,' he explained, feeling the anxiety ease as he spoke. 'Two metres tall and ten thousand years old.'

The animal had already been discovered twenty years ago on the seabed in Antarctica, and repeatedly measured since then. But hardly any growth had been established. The size of the animal could only be attributed to its great age.

'I don't understand. How do they know how old the thing is?'

'By investigating the sponge's oxygen consumption. The less an animal needs, the lower its metabolism and growth.'

Niklas Kalf turned on his bar stool to face the window and watched as a car with an empty horsebox slipped through the rain. He shivered, although it was very warm in here. He didn't understand what that photograph showed.

Was it a threat? And if it was, what was he supposed to do? Liz's breath on his cheek when she whispered with him in bed. Her lips so close to his skin that he felt the vibration of the letters when she formed them. He ordered another tea.

'Bad news?'

He shook his head. As Marvin turned round to the coffee machine to let hot water into the cup, he closed his eyes for a moment and imagined how he would write to her. *Dearest! I don't know where you are or how you are. I'm very worried. What should I do?*

'I've read,' said Marvin, pushing the cup over the counter, 'that in the White Mountains there's a forest of bristlecone pines that are supposed to be over four thousand years old.'

Kalf wondered whether he should click on the reply button while Marvin told him they now planned to clone the trees. Scientists at the University of California in Davis were already collecting cones, branches and needles.

'Not in Fort Davis, you understand?'

'Yes, of course!' Kalf felt the passing of the moment when he should have acted. His heart was in his mouth.

'In Davis, not in Fort Davis. But that's why I remembered it, I guess. Because it sounds so similar: Davis and Fort Davis. You ever been to Fort Davis?'

Kalf shook his head. Marvin lived on a ranch. His father had died at an early age, and when his mother died he had sold the largest part of land a few years ago. At some point he'd apparently been married, too. It had actually stopped raining. I'm going to stay here forever, Kalf thought. He felt cold.

'I need something warm to wear.'

'Go to Alpine.' Marvin put the empty teacup in the sink and wiped the counter with a damp cloth.

'Yes,' said Kalf, but it was a few days before he took up Marvin's suggestion and headed east along Highway 90.

At first the road runs parallel to the railway in a dead straight line, then it climbs slightly to the Paisano Pass, no more than a bump on the edge of the plain, and still the highest point on the railway line between New Orleans and Portland. A memorial next to the road recalls: THE SPANISH EXPLORER JUAN DOMINGUEZ DE MENDOZA CAMPED HERE ON 3RD JANUARY 1684. Alpine lies in a dip, fraying away, as though dumbfounded by vastness that offers no purchase or boundary.

Kalf immediately discovered the shop that Marvin had mentioned to him. Hats and cowboy boots, but also saucepans and rifles, stood in the shop window, draped with Texan flags. A peroxide-blonde woman, whose thin lips contrasted painfully with her powder-white skin, silently spread out what he asked for on the glass sales counter. Shirts, two pairs of Dockers, stout, high-sided, rough-soled leather shoes, a warm down jacket with a hood. He kept on the things he'd tried on in a little cubicle behind the counter. At last he was warm again.

He bought picture postcards in a souvenir shop, and on the way back, as it was early in the day, he stopped in a muddy car park scattered with puddles, under a red neon sign saying Kitty's. None of the men at the bar paid any attention to the girl stripping in the back area of the bar, on a little dance floor that was rather dark and also cluttered with stacks of cardboard boxes. She was Mexican, and she didn't have a particularly good figure.

Niklas Kalf had called Liz's parents a few times when he knew no one would be at home, and left messages on the answering machine. How well they were, and that they seldom had the chance to phone. Now he spread the postcards out on the bar and wrote to them and to some of his and Liz's friends, to say how great the country was and how much they were enjoying getting away from it all. The mountains and the prairie. The lonesome roads. The big sky. He signed in his own name and in Liz's with two different-coloured pens that he borrowed from the barkeeper. Then he drained his beer. When he left the strip joint, he had made a decision that surprised even him.

He drove back to the town and found a car dealer's forecourt. He looked around under the red, white and blue glittering garlands, seeing mostly American models, as new, a lot of SUVs and pickups, and also two old BMWs. A young salesman held out his hand in greeting and guessed after his second answer that he was German. In that case he had something for him. He led Kalf to the rear of the compound.

'You're kidding!'

The salesman was standing by the very same light blue model of a VW Beetle that Kalf's father had once owned. He hesitated for a moment, but then he couldn't help grinning and sat down in the driver's seat. When he touched the thin steering wheel the smell of the plastic seat in the summer came back to him, the way his bare legs had stuck to them, and at the same time he registered what was different: the automatic gear system, the speedometer in miles. Kalf wondered whether there had been headrests in those days, turned the thin, kidney-shaped ignition key and listened to the familiar sound of the engine. A white New Mexico State University sticker below the ventilation slits on the bonnet. Four hundred dollars, said the salesman. Niklas Kalf took his hire car back to Avis in Alpine.

On the way back he opened the quarter window a little and turned the heating high, while the automatic transmission switched unhurriedly, with long pauses, to fourth gear and the car accelerated to just below the permitted seventy-five miles an hour. He had to get a move on, because today was the Chinati Foundation's annual party, at which he hoped to meet the son of a German, whom April had told him about. Even by morning the town had been full of strangers, young men in jackets stood outside the Foundation's town office, and on the door of the Foundation itself he had seen a poster for a reading. He read the names Marilyn Chin and Sigrid Nunez and today's date. It was already almost mid-November, which meant that Liz had now been missing for two months. At about half past seven he parked the Beetle in a long row of cars outside the former main gate of Fort Russell.

It was so cold that his breath formed clouds in front of his face for the first time that year. The sky was low, full of clouds arranged dramatically in echelons to the horizon, and the groups of visitors seemed as strangely introverted as godforsaken skaters in the gloom of a Dutch landscape.

A young man who looked like an art student was distributing the programme. 'Boris Groys will give a lecture on Kabakov's years in Moscow.' After that there was to be a 'sound performance'. 'New York-based artist Stephen Vitiello, sharing a programme with musician/ composer Tetsu Inoue, will perform on Friday and Saturday evening at six p.m.' He had missed both already, and soon dinner in the Arena would begin, 'one of the Chinati Foundation's most impressive and characteristic spaces, architecturally adapted by Donald Judd. The dinner will begin at eight p.m., with music by Mariachi Aguila, and will be followed by a traditional bonfire after dark.'

The various groups of visitors met up outside the hall, and as soon as Kalf got there he found April. After his visit to her on Sunday they had arranged to meet once more in the bookshop, but not again, although Kalf didn't understand why. But now he could think about possibly meeting, at long last, the son of that Hans who had known Eugen Meerkaz. April had put up her hair and wore her dark-red-lipsticked mouth as if it were a trick that she had mastered. He saw her talking to a couple with their backs to him, and hurried over to them.

'Here's Niklas!' she cried, and even before she had greeted Niklas Kalf she grabbed him by the upper arm and drew him into her circle. 'And these are Asia and Frank. I told you about them. Asia works for the Foundation.'

'Hello,' said Kalf to Frank.

Frank nodded and shook his hand. His face had rather big pores and a very soft mouth from which his smiles quickly trickled away.

'So you're the stranger in town that everyone's talking about,' he said with a grin.

Niklas Kalf nodded.

'Hi!' said Asia.

Her vertebrae were clearly visible, and the pulsing veins under her thin, pale skin. She was very young and had the transparent blue eyes of a husky. 'Nice to meet you!'

'I haven't seen any of the art yet,' Kalf apologized. 'And I'm sure it's too late now.'

'It's never too late.' She looked at him curiously.

'She has the keys,' explained April. 'But what about dinner?'

'I'm not hungry anyway.'

'But it'll be dark soon,' said April.

Frank took a pack of Marlboro from the breast pocket of his blue pullover and lit a cigarette. 'But it's still light enough.'

Asia nodded and gave Kalf an enquiring look. By now they were standing in the middle of a big crowd of guests, all waiting for the doors to be opened.

'Fine,' he said, 'then let's go.'

Asia took a drag on Frank's cigarette. And as they set off against the flow of visitors, she asked Kalf what he wanted to see.

'What is there?'

He struggled to keep up with her.

'The most important thing's the prints by Kasimir Malevich and other artists of the Russian avant-garde. We're also showing illustrated books by Ilya Kabakov, whose big installation *School No 6* is part of the collection.'

'And apart from that?'

'Dan Flavin's *Marfa Project*. It's very important for us. A monumental work with brightly coloured neon tubes, taking up six buildings. The *New York Times* called it "the last great art of the 20th century".'

'And Judd?'

'What about Judd?'

Niklas Kalf told her about his attempt to visit the two hangars, and being caught in the storm. Again the view of the plain opened up, the two great halls standing on its rim. As he felt the night getting closer and closer, he suddenly understood how essential a part of those gleaming metal cubes it was that one should go towards them, and he remembered once more his own journey from El Paso to Marfa.

'We've had a thousand guests in the last year.'

'Not bad!'

'Yes, when Judd died in 1994, the Foundation faced a choice of either dissolving itself or making some money. But since the opening of the big Flavin installation in 2000 more and more visitors have been coming. More than ten thousand over the past year.'

They were standing by the narrow door at the front end of the first hangar, and Asia took out a key.

'What answer do you think Donald Judd would have given to Marfa Ignatyevna's question?'

Asia looked at him curiously, her hand on the door handle. 'What question's that?'

Kalf told her the story of Dostoevsky and the railway engineer's wife.

She nodded with a smile. 'I know that one. But what was Marfa's question?'

' "Why it's our duty to stay here?" '

'I don't understand.'

'Why did Judd choose this particular place, in the middle of the desert?'

'It has a lot to do with the landscape,' she said quietly after a moment's hesitation, looking back over her shoulder as though to check the prairie that ended at the weathered brick wall from which the wind had long since licked the mortar.

Then at last she opened the door, and they slipped from the open expanse into the interior space. When the door clicked shut, he was surprised by the suddenly expectant, breathless silence.

A concrete roof with two rows of columns in a square grid divides the space into the three naves of a basilica. The faint, thin winter light still entering the big windows along the whole of the long sides seemed to accumulate in the aluminium cubes that stand in three rows on the smooth concrete floor. They glowed. In the two lateral naves they stand close to the window, almost outside in the sand and brushwood of the prairie. Hesitantly, Kalf entered the space one step at a time.

'There's no electric light.'

Asia had stopped by the door, leaving the space to Kalf. 'Judd had the plugs removed.'

He nodded. His eyes eagerly felt their way along the surfaces of the waist-high cubes, trying to discover the differences, because although they all consist of the same polished aluminium and clearly have the same outer dimensions, none of them is the same as any other. He walked slowly between them.

None of them, he thought, is complete. And yet it would be wrong to claim that there's anything lacking from them. It was more as if the *One Hundred Aluminum Pieces* were examples of a species, just as he was. Eyeless and faceless as they are, and mute and motionless, their diversity of form alone suggests individuality. Donald Judd, who merely seems to be playing out a conceptual sequence in constantly new variations of reflections and shadowing effects, in fact succeeds in doing something quite different. Niklas Kalf looked out into the Texan prairie and saw how the dry grass gleamed. No less than life, he thought. An almost dead, almost inanimate life. In forms as similar and hard as the cacti and the grass, motionless and endlessly preoccupied with itself, like all the autistic, lonesome life here.

'As if they're alive,' he said, without looking at Asia.

' "Masculine art", according to the *New York Times*.'

The thin soles of her Converse All-Stars squeaked with every step, but he had no time to look round to her or answer her. Instead he kept on slowly following the middle row of cubes. This art was in love with strength, that much was true. Like everything that holds out beneath this sky, he'd understood that much over the last few weeks. He stopped in the middle aisle of the hall and felt within him the echo of the expanse that he had experienced here, and the merciless clarity of the sky. He remembered the monotony of waiting, and how it had gradually eaten away at him. He barely knew who he was now.

Asia had reached the end of the hall some time ago and leaned in the embrasure of one of the industrial lattice windows, where a last scrap of red sun still came in, and looked out. Only when he was standing right next to her did she turn towards him.

'Finished?'

He shook his head with a smile. 'I don't know. For today, perhaps.'

The skin of her face was stretched firmly over the bones and the mouth an incision cut into it, almost colourless and as though worn away by sun or wind. The eyes so pale blue that already he couldn't see the pupils in the twilight.

'How old are you, Niklas?' she asked, and he felt as if he'd been caught out. 'It's OK if I call you Niklas?'

'Of course.' He nodded. 'I'm forty, why?'

She laughed.

'Why are you laughing? Too old?'

She shook her head. 'I don't know. Frank's exactly the same age.'

Neither of them said anything for a moment. Then he said, 'You've got a strange name.'

'Asia?' she asked, as if she had to think which one he could mean.

'Yes.'

'My father was in Vietnam.'

'That doesn't strike me as much of a reason.'

'I don't know,' she said again. Then, after a pause, 'Do you want to see the second hall?'

'Not today.'

'Shall we go, then?'

Again he nodded.

Silently they hurried now to cross the almost dark hall, back to the entrance. He caught himself trying not to look at the boxes as he did so, the way you don't look people in the face when they pass you in the street. And then, when she was already holding the key in her hand, he suddenly noticed a sentence on the front wall of the hangar. *DEN KOPF BENUTZEN IST BESSER ALS IHN VER-LIEREN,***** he read – and stopped with surprise.

The letters shimmered red in the gloom of the space, which had already yellowed the whitewashed walls to ivory long ago. Surprised not to have to translate what he was reading, it was a moment before he understood that the sentence was written in German, and it felt like the rocking of the ground beneath your feet when you've been aboard ship for a long time and you first stand back on land.

He slowly walked closer to the wall and read the sentence out loud: '*Den Kopf benutzen ist besser als ihn verlieren.*'

Asia, already at the door, turned round to him and nodded.

'So how did that get here?' he wanted to know.

'POWs,' she said, each of her steps a squeak on the smooth concrete floor. 'Prisoners of war. There was a camp for German prisoners of war here during the war.'

'I know. But I thought there was nothing left of it.'

She shrugged. 'You should ask Frank. His father was one of them.'

'Really?'

He tried to conceal his excitement and took another good look at the lettering. He was in the immediate presence of a clue that seemed to refer directly to Eugen Meerkaz. If he had, until now, merely hoped he would come upon the trail of that letter here in Marfa, all of a sudden he was almost sure of it. One last time his eyes roamed through the space, now completely filled with night. Only in Judd's creation did a last remnant of light still hum, stored in the hundred different cubes, as silent as nature itself. And like nature, he thought, waiting, hesitating, perhaps even observing.

'Were they in here?' He noticed that he was whispering.

'No,' she said quietly. 'But let's go. Otherwise there will be no dinner left at all.'

When they were outside and Asia was locking up, the sky was very clear and, apart from a bright, watery strip on the horizon, a very even, deep black in which the stars were just rising. And although Asia stood very close to him, her smile was barely visible.

'Come to us for Thanksgiving. There's turkey and all the works.'

That wasn't for two weeks. 'Can't I meet Frank beforehand?'

Asia looked at him with surprise.

'No, sorry. We're travelling again. Frank has an exhibition in Houston. Come at Thanksgiving. Then you can ask Frank about his family and the camp.'

'What about on the phone? I've got to talk to him!'

Asia shook her head reluctantly.

He tried to smile. So once again he had to wait. The thought was unbearable.

CHAPTER ELEVEN

It's better to use your head than lose it

April looked at him across the white tablecloth. Dave, kneeling on the chair next to her, was pushing a Matchbox car back and forth and bubbling an engine noise with his lips. She brushed back her heavy hair with a swift motion.

'In September 1620, a group of pilgrims sailed to America on a ship called the *Mayflower*,' she began. A smile darted across her red lips when she noticed Kalf's expression. 'After sixty-six days they reached America. They were hungry and sad, the first winter was long and cold, and many died.'

Almost two weeks had passed since their meeting at the Chinati Foundation, and when she had collected him today with Dave, it had almost seemed as if he was part of the family. Time had long ago melted away into a glittering, gleaming mass. All he remembered was receiving another picture of Liz at some point. He couldn't remember how long he had sat there with his index finger on the mouse button before he dared to open it. However stupidly his eyes wandered all over the colourful browser window, Liz was nowhere to be seen. The picture showed a plank bed with rucked-up sheets, crumpled pillows and a wool blanket, thrown back as if she'd just got up and gone out. Relief trickled through him, but then his eyes began to look for what wasn't there. The sheet was dirty, and the dark patches could be blood. What did her absence mean? Was it a threat? Or was she gone because she was dead? He noticed April staring at him.

'In the spring an Indian came to them, his name was Squanto. And he showed them how to plant maize and other vegetables, and the harvest in October was so good that the Pilgrim Fathers had food in abundance for the winter: grain and fruit, vegetables and salted meat.'

Dave sent his right hand running over the table on forefinger and middle finger. April nodded. 'The pilgrims and the Indians had the first Thanksgiving party. It lasted three days and there were more than ninety Indians along with the pilgrims.'

Frank, sitting at the head of the table, took a swig from the bottle of Michelob in front of him. His house was one of the old army houses on Officers Hill. From the dining table one could see through a big window into the garden, with a tree and a large brick grill. Kalf imagined the officers' families inviting each other to barbecues on Sundays, he saw the men's white casual shirts and the women's slender dresses. He took a swig of beer, and April went into the kitchen to help Asia. Dave trotted after her, the swing door squeaked a little, then the two panels quivered quietly together. Kalf couldn't wait to ask Frank about his father at long last, and when he did, he had trouble speaking German.

'Asia said your father was a prisoner of war.'

'That's right, he came here in 1943.'

'It might be a strange question, but was your father's name Hans, by any chance?'

Frank was amazed. 'Yes, that's right. Hans Holdt.'

Niklas Kalf gulped with excitement. It flashed across his mind that he shouldn't immediately reveal his concerns, and that the best thing was to stay calm and not to press his questions too much. He knew these situations from his research, but never before had he been so anxious about driving away a story that was now so palpably within reach. As though a quiet sound was all it would take for it to disappear. A breath of wind that would blow everything away.

'I had no idea there were many German prisoners of war in the United States.'

'About half a million altogether. Rommel's army in particular came to the States. My father had been in Africa since 1942.'

Frank set the empty beer bottle back on the table. He drawled, as if chewing every word, and with a heavy accent. Did Kalf want to see his works?

Kalf nodded. He knew they had time. After the weeks of waiting there was no reason to hurry. Frank led him through the kitchen, where April and Asia were busy fetching the plates from the cupboards. Dave was playing on the floor, and there was a smell of potatoes and spicy meat. They weren't to stay away for too long, they would be eating soon, April called after them as they walked outside.

Frank used the former garage as a studio. A neon light flickered for a moment, then shone brightly. In the middle of the room was a plywood trestle table with some objects lying on it, more or less the size of a human head; at first Kalf could tell neither what they were made of nor what they represented. Next to an office chair stood an old glass-topped sofa table with a few tools on it, various pliers and awls, twine and a little saw. On the floor, a pile of things that Kalf couldn't identify, but which clearly formed the source material for the half-dozen or so filigree objects on the trestle table. When he bent over them, he recognized the skin of a flattened squirrel, some little bones and the delicate skull of a mouse, paper everlastingly bleached by the sun, the plastic straw from a fast-food restaurant that looked as if someone had bitten it in half. Around all these human products or animal remains, the fine but stable gossamer of plants, whose white branches, chiselled like bronchi, seemed to hold and connect it all.

'Do you find all these things in the desert?'

He turned towards Frank, who had stopped at the door and hesitated with his answer as though he didn't know what to say.

'No,' he said then, 'I actually don't.'

'But?'

'I assemble it.'

'But you do get the material from the desert?'

'Yes, that's true.'

Niklas Kalf waited.

'Asia finds it,' he said finally, as though betraying a secret.

'She collects it all?'

'Yes. She collects it for me.'

'Then you work together?'

'Yes. You could say that.'

Frank lit a cigarette. 'But we live apart.'

Kalf watched the way he drew on the cigarette. Registered how nervous his eyes were, small and watery.

Frank's exactly the same age as me, he thought, and suddenly it was as if he recognized a lot of himself in Frank's way of working. There was something familiar in the precision of the objects. The way the deadness in them was almost brought back to life by the skill of the montage was something he recognized. We know what we can do, he thought, and we sense that the power will eventually subside.

'Can I touch that?'

Frank nodded, and Kalf carefully picked up one of the objects and turned it slowly back and forth between his fingers. Something between totem and animal. How good it was after so long to have someone who was like oneself. When they came back into the house the turkey was on the sitting-room table, served with corn cobs and potatoes, and April was clutching a carving knife and a meat fork.

'It's your turn, Frank.'

Frank nodded and carved the food, while Dave sang his song again:

'*A turkey is a funny bird,*
His head goes wobble, wobble.
And he knows just one word,
Gobble, gobble, gobble!'

Everyone laughed and clapped, then they raised their glasses and Dave, quivering with excitement, clinked a big glass of Coca-Cola against their beer glasses.

Over dinner they talked about how war with Iraq was becoming increasingly likely. It wasn't easy being an American right now, said April, cutting the boy's meat into pieces. Niklas Kalf nodded and told them about the impression that Bush's speech to the UN had made on him. What did people in Germany think about America? Fundamentally, he said, there was still a feeling of profound gratitude to the United States, but the intellectuals were traditionally pacifist. Sadly that was no longer the case here, April replied. Many people, even in the universities, now applauded the new role of the United States as the sole world power.

'Sometimes I think,' said Kalf, 'that we Europeans don't understand what's happening because we live in a completely different world.'

She shook her head violently. 'We're against the war, too. A war against Iraq isn't the way forward in the fight against terror.'

'Who's we?'

The art scene in Marfa, which had grown substantially over the past few years. The Foundation had about ten employees, and then there was the guest-artist programme. Then there were always a few writers living on grants from the Lannon Foundation in Marfa. And about two dozen artists had gradually moved here, and over the last few years a few lawyers and businesspeople from Houston. There were a few gallery owners, and a photographer from New York lived here now as well.

'Everything's changing,' Frank winked at Kalf, 'the whole infrastructure of the place. You can even see it in the layout of the streets. Marfa was mostly a supply centre for the cattle breeders. There used to be nothing but pickups and men in cowboy boots. Now the emigration has stopped, Marfa has a population of over two thousand again, houses that were empty for decades are being sold, new shops are opening.'

'They're all here because of Judd,' Asia said tonelessly,

careful not to meet anyone's eye. Kalf looked at Frank's young girlfriend, who hardly ever said anything, and looked a little twitchy and nervous.

At some point Dave asked if he could watch TV, and when April said yes he hurried into the sitting room, which was only separated from the dining area by an open arch. Shortly after came the typical concert of a cartoon, with all the various blows and crashes and the whistle of the falling bombs, the squeak of the car tyres, the groaning and screaming.

'Turn it down, Dave!'

'And what happened to your father?' asked Kalf. 'Did he stay here after the war?'

Frank set down his cutlery. 'He met my mother when he was still in the camp. That was why he stayed at first. But later he went to California.'

Kalf nodded.

'He was ill. Epilepsy. And when he heard about a new kind of treatment they'd developed in Los Angeles, he went there.'

Frank hesitated for a moment before explaining. 'Something in the patient's brain was divided to restrict the discharge of the epileptic attack.'

'And then?'

'My father came back to join us in Marfa at first. But only for a while. Then he went to LA for good.'

'And was he cured?'

'The attacks weren't as severe. But the operation had one particular result that I thought was very funny when I was a child. Whenever I put something in his left hand he didn't know what it was called, and when I then put it in the right hand, he suddenly did. I could play that game with him for hours, and laughed myself sick every time he touched an apple with his fingers and shook his head in despair.'

'Alien hand syndrome,' Asia explained quietly.

'That's really strange!'

'Yes,' said Frank.

'No, that's not what I mean.' Kalf cleared his throat. 'I'm writing a book about a German immigrant in Los Angeles, Eugen Meerkaz, and when I was doing my research I found a letter from a certain Hans, with a Marfa postmark.'

He laid the crumpled letter on the table.

Frank hesitated for a moment before picking up the envelope and taking out the letter. He cast his eye over the few lines in it. Yes, he confirmed then, that was his father's handwriting. Niklas Kalf was so excited that he didn't know what to say. He repeatedly nodded to Frank Holdt, who silently put the letter back into the envelope.

'I think you should move house.' April finally broke the silence that lay over the table, in which everyone listened to the coughing of the boy that settled distinctly over the carpet of sound from the cartoon. 'As it looks like you have good reason to stay in Marfa a while longer.'

'Yes.' Kalf was suddenly very serious. 'I'll probably stay here for a while.'

Frank got to his feet and fetched some beer. April went into the sitting room to check on Dave. Kalf and Asia said nothing and didn't look at each other until Frank came back out of the kitchen.

At some point in the night, when the boy had already

been asleep for a long time, they all went outside and along the road until they could look down the hill and across the wide, night-black land. Kalf felt chilly, and was holding a bottle of beer, the glass of which was getting colder and colder. The sky was clear and wide and full of stars, and he envied the three of them for belonging here. Music drifted across from one of the other former officers' houses, a thin, fluttering seam through the total silence, and Asia and Frank kissed and hugged as April and he stared wordlessly into the night. He would never have thought that he could feel so much at home in a foreign country. For a moment he thought he could see a white light in the blackness where he suspected the horizon must be, several lights, in fact, moving back and forth, but he wasn't sure. Eventually it grew too cold for all of them, and they went back and sat down around the table, on which empty plates and bowls remained. Frank went into the kitchen one last time to fetch some beer, and when he stood in the doorway with the four bottles in his hand, he grinned at Kalf.

'I think I've got something for you.'

And the following week Niklas Kalf did move out of the Hotel Paisano and a few blocks along to Neville Street. It was lined with narrow strips of green, and behind them head-high but mostly gappy wood fences, over which one could see the roofs of one-storey houses and trees whose leaves seemed to have turned yellow long ago. Wooden electric poles stood a short distance apart, their slack cables crossing the street.

The house belonged to an artist friend, they told him, who had lived for a long time in Marfa, but had recently moved to Dallas. He wouldn't be back before next spring, said Frank, and opened the door.

'So?'

Frank grinned and slumped on the wide sofa as Kalf looked around. The musty smell of a room that had been unaired for too long. The big window was curtained, and the sitting room was bathed in gloomy, glowing, reddish light. Between sofa and door a low table whose dark imitation wood looked artificial even in the dim light. Two little chairs and an open fireplace. The door to the bathroom was ajar. He pushed it open. The dripping of a leaky tap in the washbasin, toilet, the shower behind a pink plastic curtain, above it a small vertically sliding window. The cool smell of old damp.

'And you're really writing about someone who knew my father?' asked Frank, as Kalf inspected the kitchen.

'Yes,' he called, and opened the fridge. Steak sauce and Mexican beer. He fetched two bottles and went back into the sitting room.

'Does the phone work?'

Frank picked up the receiver and nodded.

'Tell me about the man you're writing about.'

Kalf gave Frank a bottle of beer and sat down on one of the little chairs. The fireplace gave off a sour smell of cold ashes, which covered the floor of the fireplace like a soft, baggy black-and-white bed. They drank.

'His name was Eugen Meerkaz and he was a Jew, born in Berlin in 1903. But his family came from southern Germany. In the same year that Hitler came to power, he met Elsa Landmann, a Viennese girl who had come to Berlin to study. She's eight years younger than Meerkaz. They fall in love, but the situation quickly gets difficult.'

'Is she Jewish as well?'

'Yes,' said Kalf. 'In 1935 the author Bruno Frank, an acquaintance of Elsa's father, invites them both to Sanary, a fishing village on the French Riviera.'

'Great!'

'But that meant exile. Aldous Huxley lived there, René Schickele, and then Thomas and Heinrich Mann, Ludwig Marcuse, Alma Mahler and Franz Werfel. Brecht and Arnold Zweig came by. Elsa and Eugen married there.'

'And how long did they stay there?'

'After the war broke out, early in 1940, all the Jewish exiles in France were put in camps. Eugen Meerkaz near Nîmes, Elsa in the big camp at Gurs in the foothills of the Pyrenees.'

'Were those German camps?'

'No, but there was the constant threat that the prisoners would be handed over to the Germans. Elsa escaped that summer.'

'She escaped?'

'Yes. And she looked for her husband. She wandered through southern France, which was suddenly full of refugees after Hitler's coup, and, disguised as a black-market trader, finally made contact with him. Then they both managed to flee.'

Frank nodded and got up to fetch them another beer.

'Happy ending,' he said as he dropped down onto the sofa again. 'But how did this man Eugen Meerkaz meet my father? How did the Jewish immigrant meet German soldier Hans Holdt of the 334th Infantry Division?'

'Eugen Meerkaz knew other immigrant scientists who were all working in California. That was why he went there.'

'And he got a job.'

'Yes. At Caltech, the California Institute of Technology in Pasadena.'

Frank looked at him in astonishment. 'That's where my father had his operation.'

'Exactly. And that's where the two of them could have met.'

Something, thought Kalf, was beginning to fit. And he asked Frank Holdt to show him the former prisoner-of-war camp. Tomorrow.

'But I don't want you getting too excited. You can hardly see anything.'

'I don't care,' said Kalf, but when they drove along the old camp road the next day and Frank seemed finally to stop where the road disappeared into the wide prairie, he was surprised to see that nothing at all remained of what must once have been there. Only when they got out did he discover to his amazement that beneath the dry scrub and between the red, stony sand the kerbstones of the road went on running. He noticed crossings and junctions, a whole road system that seemed to have sunk into the dust beneath the knee-high scrub like a decayed body, leaving nothing but the pale bones. The wind creaked loudly in the corrugated-iron roofs over the *One Hundred Aluminum Pieces.*

Bald, woody, trunkless growths, their branches growing concentrically straight out of the ground, not dense but dark and dry. Next to them, in the dips in the stony ground, almost entirely white tufts of grass like the remains of hair on the dry, sick skin of a mangy animal. A species of cactus whose lancet-sharp, wax-hard leaves stuck out in all directions. Silent, beige-coloured birds with big black beaks on the ground in the shade of the bushes.

'As the American soldiers were being sent to the front, the German prisoners of war came here,' Frank announced. 'At times there were up to two hundred. Gradually female civilians replaced the crews of guards.'

'And your mother was one of those civilians?'

'Yes.'

They followed one of the sunken roads into the bushes and felt their way slowly up the slope towards Officers Hill. Soon the remnants of the roads seeped away in the sand, and they walked along a narrow concrete strip, already largely overgrown on both sides, that might once have been a path between the prisoners' barracks. On either side, ankle-high foundation walls kept appearing now, enclosed elongated rectangles, in which one could still make out the steel pins that had once held wooden constructions.

'What kind of German soldiers were they?'

Frank shrugged. 'Young, well educated, not yet exhausted. It was the start of the war, and many of the soldiers in Rommel's Afrika Korps were probably still convinced that they would win it. Convinced Nazis.'

In the ruins it was possible to make out concrete rostrums and gutters, and in his mind Kalf completed the laundry rooms and toilets. He peered up to Officers Hill. The houses looked infinitely remote, but at night the lights must have seemed very close. He tried to imagine the everyday life of the prisoners, and the world in which people could have imagined waging war against the United States. When this had been a foreign, distant land, and not the model of everyone's dreams. And he imagined how it might have been to climb out of a wagon in Marfa after travelling for weeks, suddenly in the middle of a boundless continent, the sparkling horizon revolving around you at night.

'The prisoners of war left Marfa in November 1945. And at the end of 1946 Fort Russell was closed completely. The government sold the land. Civilians moved into the officers' houses, the rest fell into disuse. Until Donald Judd bought it all.'

The wind was cold across the plain.

'The terrible thing about this landscape is,' Frank Holdt said quietly, and the wind tore his words from his lips, 'that nothing here means anything. Even Auschwitz wouldn't have meant anything here.'

Surprised, Kalf turned round to look at him.

'And I'll tell you something,' Frank went on. 'That's exactly what you like about this landscape.'

'Rubbish,' said Kalf, horrified.

'Of course.' Frank looked at him mockingly. 'You're always raving about how this landscape doesn't have a face. That nothing here looks at you. That's exactly the same thing.'

'Nonsense,' he said, but he felt dizzy. The wind across the grass. The hard light, melting the contours of things. It always seemed as if something was missing. Could it be the eyes of the dead?

'The camp,' Kalf began quietly, but didn't know how to go on.

Frank nodded. 'Two hundred men, removed.'

'Removed?'

'From history. A blessing, if you like.' He smiled. 'Isn't it strange that the direct road to Mexico from which the illegals are coming into the country today is the very same road that the prisoners gazed down back then? Mexico is only sixty miles away. They watched after the cars until they slowly disappeared. Freedom.'

'Using your head is better than losing it,' Kalf tried to joke.

'Using your head is better than losing it,' Frank replied with a nod.

After he'd brought him back, Niklas Kalf sat for a while in the dark on the sofa, picked up the receiver and heard the dialling tone. Finally he went into the bedroom and opened the door to the garden.

A fence of white painted boards that had been nailed alternately on either side of the post, producing a transverse structure. The garden was as narrow as the house was wide, and the grass was yellowing in that rectangle. There was a tree at the end of it. A rope hung from a branch, with a car tyre as a swing. A camping chair lay toppled next to a stack of firewood by the brick grill, its red anodized metal smeared with wet ash. Behind the trunk of the tree, near the fence in the corner of the garden, he discovered a grey concrete birdbath full of brackish water, and dipped his finger into it.

CHAPTER TWELVE

Mystery lights

Niklas Kalf had fallen asleep on the sofa in the sitting room in the afternoon, and woke heavily from a strange dream. Old newspapers on the worn carpet. A rabbi hires a hit man for his wife. The Christmas tree outside the Rockefeller Center in New York. US marines training in the Persian Gulf. The war another thing you went on playing with the way you don't stop scratching the scab on a cut because the pain tickles. He pushed the red curtain aside and looked out at the street, seeing nothing but his Beetle, which still stood where he had parked it. No idea when that was. He let the curtain fall again, and the merciful red filter settled on everything once more.

The newspapers smooth on the soles of his feet as he shuffled over them into the kitchen. He took a bagel from the bag next to the sink and the carton of milk out of the fridge, and filled the plastic cup that bore the words MARFA SHORTHORNS.

He remembered every detail of the dream. Another flight. The plane landing hesitantly on the shimmering runway at Fiumicino. Very new, deep black asphalt, looking liquid in the heat steaming above the hot river. When the cabin door opens and he comes down the aluminium steps blinking in the white light, the needle-sharp heat penetrates his clothes, which are suddenly unbearably heavy. And even before the taxi has left the autostrada and entered Rome via the Porta Portese, the sand, always carried across the sea in August by African winds, is already rubbing between his teeth. On the borders of the old empire the temples and theatres are still sinking into it, at night especially the refreshing wind slowly grinds the travertine into desert. Rome's decline has only just begun.

Niklas Kalf took a drink of milk and stared at the tap from which a drop hung, quivering and growing until it broke away and burst with a little drumbeat in the basin. An appointment, but he doesn't know with whom. He has a headache, and again a thin film of sweat on his skin. He drinks latte macchiato, peeling with pointed fingers madeleines, *fatto con latte*, from their little waxed papers, in which they have risen like fat flowers.

Then he is sitting in a taxi. The engine sounds irritated when the car leaves San Giovanni in Laterano behind and accelerates for the first time when they reach the Via Appia. Abandoned industrial land with house-high billboards, sandstone crevasses with bricked-up caves and tiny plots with grapes and shrubs. Head-high reeds where the ground is boggy, overshadowed by the concrete posts of bridges that were never finished. He recognizes the Alban Hills on the horizon, and he winds his window down at the same time as the driver does. Radio voices scatter. The road starts winding, forest approaches the asphalt, in its shade the air is cool and smells of pine and slate. The narrow facades of old villas, their washed-out chalk-red retreating into the shadows as the car approaches. A dark blue limousine is parked alone in the forest. A high-fenced tennis court.

Niklas Kalf closed his eyes. He didn't know where the sudden, deep sadness came from, and ran his hand over his face. In the dream he is standing on the terrace of a restaurant, on the edge of a steep slope, looking down into a crater. He recognizes the Lago Albano and now knows at last where he is: Castel Gandolfo, the Pope's summer residence, he came here once with Liz. Boats in the dark blue. It's hot, not a cloud in the sky. He takes off his sunglasses and cleans them on his shirt.

A waitress comes and asks what he wants. I'm waiting for someone, he says. She nods and leaves.

Tables with white tablecloths along the parapet. No guests apart from him. He unpacks his notes, photocopies and books, Dictaphone, pens and notepad, and knows now who he's waiting for. He tests the batteries of the Dictaphone, records the silence, winds it back, listens to it and discovers a bird that he hadn't heard before. His breath is on the tape. He listens to it again. He runs through his questions once more and takes off his jacket.

The sun has long passed behind the ridge of hills when a car approaches, a BMW whose engine dies at the last moment. An old white 7-series, broad and squat. A woman – at first he notices little more than her big sunglasses – is sitting at the wheel. In the sudden silence she can be heard engaging a gear, and the engine and exhaust immediately begin to cool with a bright and perfectly even ticking sound. Niklas Kalf only sees Eugen Meerkaz when he gets out. At that moment a sudden gust stirs up sand, red, very fine sand of a kind that he hadn't noticed here before, which now drifts across the ground in small, chiselled whirls. Then the woman gets out, too, and as soon as she has left the car she pulls her short beige knitted jacket over her chest as though she were feeling the cold, and immediately he knows: it's Liz.

Meerkaz is wearing a white T-shirt and sandals. He clutches a brown envelope in one hand; there is a beige jacket on his other shoulder. He walks very slowly. He turns and says something to Liz. She takes off the sunglasses. Niklas Kalf's heart is in his mouth. He jumps to his feet and wants to go to her, but he knows he mustn't let anything show at first. So he just waits next to the table, his fingertips on its rim as though to calm himself. It is as if the sky has inconspicuously changed its blue. Something menacing creeps into his dream.

Meerkaz has liver spots on his almost bald head, and the skin under his chin lies in those folds on either side of the larynx that lizards have. Bowing slightly, Kalf shakes his hand, which is soft and rather small. Suddenly the waitress is back, too.

This is Liz, says Meerkaz, my daughter. Kalf has to control himself to keep from crying out, while Meerkaz opens both hands in a tired gesture across the table on which he has spread out his material. Everyone sits down. Liz, who seems not to know him, immediately starts to order, and he notices with surprise that she is speaking Spanish.

Meerkaz stares out over the parapet, and only when Kalf follows his gaze does he see to his horror what has meanwhile happened behind his back. The pines have disappeared, and the sea. Instead, his gaze descends over red, sandy stone into a deserted canyon, with nothing but low grey bushes and individual cacti growing in it. Infinitely sad that Europe is no longer there, he carefully tidies up the photocopies and books, the notepad and the photographs and packs everything back in his bag. Meerkaz watches him as he does so.

'Would you like to see it?'

As if he had been waiting for that all along, Meerkaz asks again, when the table is finally cleared, 'Would you like to see it?'

He's right, thinks Kalf, that's exactly why I'm here. Nothing else is of any importance. 'Yes, of course,' he says.

But first the waitress reappears, bringing cutlery and napkins, a little plastic breadbasket and big glasses of beer.

As soon as she has gone Meerkaz shoves everything aside, opens the envelope that he had on his knees all the time, and takes out a stack of typed paper. Kalf carefully pulls the papers across to him, sets the title page face down beside the pile and looks at the first page of the text. It has been typed with a mechanical typewriter, the 'o' is almost always filled, and the 's' clearly jammed and has sometimes slipped upwards. Kalf feels with the palm of his hand the depressions that the letters have made in the paper. Meerkaz has stuck in changes on gossamer-thin tracing paper, covering individual words and sometimes whole paragraphs. The pages are paginated by hand, and the chapters have also been given handwritten titles. The text often flutters to the edge of the paper.

THOMAS HETTCHE

Meerkaz points to the manuscript with a dismissive gesture of his pale, liver-spotted hand and tells him, 'You can keep it.'

His gesture is so violent that a glass falls over and beer sloshes over the tablecloth. Kalf quickly pulls the manuscript away and hurries to fetch napkins from the next table. Liz too has jumped to her feet.

'Keep it!' she hisses at him, her eyes, wide with fear, right in front of his face.

Niklas washed down a mouthful of the dry bagel with the milk. The pictures from the dream disappeared very slowly. Liz, he thought, only ever her name: Liz. He put the Marfa Shorthorns cup in the sink, poured some water into it and stopped by the sitting-room table. Her sentence from the dream still echoed: *Keep it!* Was it possible that he already had what he was looking for, that he had had it for ages? He studied the things on the table that Frank had brought, letters, photographs, newspaper cuttings, and remembered their conversation once again.

Frank had repeatedly mentioned that he had never understood why his father had stayed in LA after the end of the treatment. He had only ever appeared in Marfa on short visits. He seemed to be earning very good money now.

'But he never said exactly what he was doing. All top secret, he said.'

Even the letters remained vague in that respect. In them, Hans Holdt wrote about experiments that were being performed on him, about screens and electronic brains to which he was connected. He talked repeatedly about his wartime experiences. The desert played an important part, and the terrible feeling of loneliness that must have overwhelmed him as a young soldier in a foreign land. *Many of my comrades, dear Frank,* he wrote once in a letter to his son, *found their way back to the faith of their childhood. That may surprise you, particularly after everything that was said afterwards about German soldiers. But you should know that the warrior, not only in battle and in the fear of death, but also in the tedium of marching and waiting for the enemy, is in some special way aware of the experience of the divine. That has always been so. Even the Roman soldier learned faith in the war and returned to the Tiber with Mithras.*

'I don't understand!' Niklas Kalf lowered the page.

Frank silently handed him another letter, in which Hans Holdt described his encounters with the natives. Above all some of the auxiliary troops who had been busy in the company kitchen seemed to have fascinated him. He wrote that the Berbers, as he called them, had withdrawn to the edge of the camp at night, to the open desert to pray. *Some of us,* he wrote, *had the privilege of having access to these rituals, because they knew how to gain the respect of our allies.*

'I don't understand,' Kalf repeated.

'Neither do I,' agreed Frank Holdt thickly. 'Tell me again what Caltech really is.'

Kalf nodded. 'The California Institute of Technology was founded after the First World War by Ellery Hale, the astrophysicist, who also built the Mount Wilson Observatory.'

'The one the Hale–Bopp comet's called after?'

'Exactly. Hale had the vision of a research association in California, to which his observatory, the Huntington

Library and Caltech were to belong. If you like: the start
of the scientific-military-industrial complex in the USA.
Hale brought the physicist Robert A. Millikan from the
University of Chicago to Los Angeles, and he actually
managed to establish research facilities and private companies. The Jet Propulsion Laboratory, for example.
Hughes Aircraft, the Air Force Space Technology Laboratory, Douglas Aircraft Company in Long Beach,
Aerojet General, TRW, and the Rand Institute.'

'Wow!'

'Yeah, impressive, isn't it? While the geologists of the
Institute solved problems for the Southern Californian oil
industry, and other scientists started experiments with
rockets, aeronautical engineers, in the world's first wind
canal right next to the Caltech clubhouse, started work
on fuselage models for the Douglas DC3.'

'The *Rosinenbomber*, the plane that dropped supplies
to the Germans after the war?'

'Exactly.'

'Millikan sounds like a pretty clever guy.'

'Maybe, maybe not. He increasingly became the ideo-
logue for a particularly Southern Californian vision of
science. For him, California was "as England was two
centuries ago, the westernmost outpost of Nordic civilization". He wanted Aryan hegemony through science
and entrepreneurship.'

'What crap!'

'Yes. But it somehow suited California, which must
have been pretty esoteric in those days. Some people
compared Millikan and Einstein to Nostradamus. All
three were Masters of the Age.'

'Why Einstein?'

'Einstein taught at Caltech, as a lot of immigrants did. Von Kármán, Oppenheimer, Pauling, Noyes.'

'And what about Eugen Meerkaz? What did he have to do with it?'

'Meerkaz worked for von Kármán at the Jet Propulsion Laboratory.'

'Then this man Parsons that my father sometimes writes about, was he a colleague of his?'

'John Parsons? Yes. A pioneer in the field of rockets, co-founder of the Jet Propulsion Laboratory. He developed propulsion systems for liquid-fuel rockets. Parsons died in June 1952 in an explosion at his villa. And you know what?'

Frank shook his head.

'Meerkaz was there.'

'In the explosion?'

'Yes, they were both blown sky-high. No one knows what really happened.'

Niklas Kalf still quite clearly remembered saying that to Frank. Perhaps because he couldn't forget Frank's face at that moment, his rather soft mouth, from which a small, uncertain smile seemed to trickle, as if he was about to say something. Instead he had lit himself another cigarette and laid the lighter on top of the Marlboro pack.

What if someone knew what had happened in that mysterious explosion in John Parsons's laboratory, in which Eugen Meerkaz had lost his life? Kalf was still standing by the table piled with the documents of a past life. After Frank had smoked his cigarette, he offered him the documents to keep, and since then Kalf had studied them countless times. He couldn't rid himself of the idea that he might finally be getting close to the secret whose existence he hadn't even believed in.

There were only a few pictures of Hans Holdt. None from the camp. One on which the year 1947 had been written in pencil. A tall, gaunt man with dark eyes. A lot of pictures of Frank's mother, a very young girl whose face one immediately forgot. A few letters from the time of his treatment in Los Angeles. In one of them he mentioned Eugen Meerkaz, but there was no suggestion that he knew anything about his scientific work.

Niklas Kalf fetched a beer from the kitchen and wondered if he might have overlooked something, but he couldn't think of anything. He flicked through the notes he had made in Marfa, beginnings of letters to Liz, all breaking off after half a page. Individual sentences. *The wind that never stops. Darling . . .* A list of names that he simply jotted down to try to make sense of what had happened.

Al Snowe's name was listed there after the first dash. Kalf didn't really know what he wanted of him, and his interest in the book about Eugen Meerkaz seemed unbelievable. Below him came Lavinia Sims, who had helped him so much in New York. Kalf couldn't understand why they had sent her the pictures of Liz. Could it be possible that she knew Venus Smith, the woman in the wheelchair? She was next on the list. At least he thought he knew what to make of her. But what did Phil Gallagher want, the man she worked for? Was he behind the kidnapping? Kalf had found no clue on the Internet that Gallagher did anything but produce fairly successful films, not one of which he knew. But what would a

Hollywood producer want with his wife? What interest did he have in Eugen Meerkaz? And how was Imogen Engel involved? He wasn't sure if her name even belonged on the list. And last of all: Frank Holdt and Asia. Below them Hans Holdt, anti-tank personnel, 334th Infantry Division. April. The last name that Niklas Kalf had written down was Elsa Meerkaz. It was around her, he knew, that everything revolved.

And as he thought about the widow of Eugen Meerkaz, and involuntarily put Hans Holdt's letter in its correct temporal sequence, he suddenly had an idea that electrified him: the last of the letters that Holdt wrote from LA to his wife and son in the summer of 1952 dated from Monday June 16th. But now Kalf knew that that explosion, the one that had killed Eugen Meerkaz, had occurred on the 17th of June. Wasn't it very strange that Hans Holdt had been in Los Angeles just one day before that disaster, and in Marfa four days later? Because the postmark of that letter, the one that had brought him here in the first place, was dated 20th June.

That's one thing, thought Kalf, that she's got to explain to me. And without thinking he picked up the phone and dialled Elsa Meerkaz's number, which he had long known by heart for ages. Meanwhile night had fallen, and it was dark outside the red curtain. But his attention was focused entirely on the voice of Elsa Meerkaz and sure enough, when he mentioned Hans Holdt, she fell silent for a moment at first, and then sounded very uncertain as she asked if he was still in Marfa.

As he said yes, he knew that he had made a mistake. Now she knew where he was.

'Ask Pinky,' she said after a long pause, as if she had

been thinking about what needed to be done under these changed circumstances. 'But please don't come here.'

'Who's Pinky?'

'You don't know Pinky?'

Her voice sounded as if she meant in that case it was really his fault if he didn't find out what he wanted to know. But Kalf just waited. He had the certain feeling that he was now on the right track.

'Palm Springs,' Elsa Meerkaz said at last.

Nothing else. But that was the first time that she had given him any information. That's the clue, he thought, and couldn't help grinning. And he was about to say something in reply when he heard someone knocking. He hurried to end the phone call and went to the door. Hadn't known the bell didn't work.

'Hi!' said Asia. She came a step closer. Her pale, gleaming blue eyes looked at him expectantly. The night was high and cold behind her. 'Come with me, I want to show you something!'

He looked at her in disbelief. 'At this time of night?'

But when she shifted impatiently from one foot to the other, he asked her to wait just a moment and fetched his jacket. He had to hurry to catch up with her. She was wearing a checked windbreaker with a white lambskin collar, the sleeves of which reached over her hands, and walked silently down the middle of the quiet street. Above the deserted crossing the traffic lights swayed from their wires in the cold wind, blinking their relentless yellow fire.

'Were you born here?' he asked breathlessly, and she turned towards him with a smile.

'Yes.'

Her grandfather had been coach to the Marfa Short-horns for over ten years. When he died in 1985 she had been five. But she still remembered him very clearly. 'There's a plaque to him at the high school!'

'And your father?'

'He works on a ranch.'

'But he was in Vietnam, you told me.'

'Yes.'

'Hence Asia.'

'Hence Asia.'

'And your mother?'

'Lives with her second husband somewhere on the East Coast. Any more questions?'

Asia looked at him seriously. She had stopped by a green Dodge.

'Where are we going?'

'I bet you haven't seen Marfa's Mystery Lights yet,' she said. 'I love them!'

Asia turned and drove, after they had left the town behind them, straight through the night for about a quarter of an hour. Niklas Kalf had read about those supposedly inexplicable light phenomena in the prairie, heralded on big billboards as one of the town's special attractions. Something for the esoterics. Finally she stopped in a car park right by the highway, full of cars. Behind a low building a terrace opened up onto a night-black prairie. It took him a few moments to get used to the silence and the darkness. First Asia's face appeared in it, and gradually the outlines of what must have been two dozen visitors, their pale faces trained mutely into the darkness, like telescopes.

'And now?' he whispered in her ear.

She shook off his voice like an annoying insect. He stood quietly next to her, and was looking at the frozen breath in front of her mouth, a ghostly shimmering, lightless aura that opened up and subsided again like a geyser, when a murmuring sound started up around them. Some people took a few steps forward, others pointed into the blackness and whispered to their companions, and Niklas Kalf saw the shimmering aura in front of Asia's lips disappear. She was holding her breath. For a moment she stood completely rigid, then, without looking round, she gripped his hand, and now he too peered into the dark prairie. But as his eyes hadn't got accustomed to the blackness, at first only a few bright dots danced on his retina, ghostly contours and mirages, until eventually he too saw the lights on the horizon. Lights that looked like motorcycle headlights, that quivered their way very slowly down a hill, disappeared, reappeared, now two, then five again.

On a brass plate fixed to the front of the Marfa's Mystery Lights Viewing Area, you can read that a cowboy who camped here first reported the phenomenon in 1833. He thought they were Apache fires. The Apaches themselves thought the lights were stars dropping to the earth.

Kalf found it hard to concentrate on the slowly dancing lights in the homogeneous black of the prairie. Time and again, he couldn't help thinking that today he had come a little closer to the secret of Eugen Meerkaz, a mystery that involved his death. He thought of Hans Holdt, brought here with hundreds of soldiers, a whole army transported here from the North African desert, and those words about the bull of Mithras and the soldiers' religion. He stared into the glittering starry sky that enchanted the darkness over their heads. After a while he whispered to Asia that President Bush had announced the right of the United States to take preventive action.

What made him think of that right now, Asia hissed back.

'Bush is infringing the Prime Directive of the Federation.'

She giggled quietly and let go of his hand. '*Star Trek?*'

He nodded. The Prime Directive prohibited any intervention in the internal affairs of other civilizations. Asia had to struggle to keep from snorting.

They both now looked up into the sky, which was so transparent that above the sickle of the moon you could see the whole of its dark body. The necklace of the Pleiades glittered clearly. He looked round to Asia and noticed that she was looking at him. She opened her lips, above which her breath still did its ghostly dance, but not to say something. Their fingers glided into one another. He put a palm to her cheek, and she rested her head against it. Her breath stroked his closed eyes like a calming touch. He was very frightened by the thought of how far Liz was from him. He heard the whispering sea of grass. There was no one here but ghosts. Kalf thought of the Indians' spirit paths. The abandoned farms. Of that sleeping boy who lay across the world.

They didn't notice the shimmering lights on the horizon disappearing, or the spectators gradually returning to their cars. Slowly all the oversized vans and campers rolled from the car park to the highway and rocked away into the night, as Asia and Niklas Kalf kissed each other.

CHAPTER THIRTEEN

Who's who?

An old man, bony and very tall, who looked a bit like William Burroughs except that he wasn't wearing a suit but a blue checked flannel shirt under a dark, worn leather jacket. But actually, thought Niklas Kalf, he doesn't look like Burroughs in the slightest, but like someone else, he couldn't think who.

They were both standing by their vehicles, filling them up. The old man had closed the top button of his shirt, and the long, thin tips of the collar revealed that it wasn't a new shirt, but a kind that had long since fallen out of fashion. He wore his Stetson, which had once been white, pushed far back to the nape of his neck. His pronounced jaws worked under his dark, leathery skin, his bright, possibly blue eyes narrowed as though the light hurt him, as the petrol pumped with a loud hum into the tank of his old pickup and he stared disinterestedly at Kalf. Then there was a click, a shudder ran through the petrol pump and the hum stopped. The old man shook off the last drops, hung the nozzle back up and shuffled past Niklas Kalf to the till. He wore jeans and eggshell-coloured snakeskin cowboy boots. When he came back, Kalf was still filling his car. It was as if the tank wouldn't fill up. He suspiciously eyed the dial on the pump. The old man stopped next to him, and tapped the brow of his hat.

'Not Burroughs, you jerk-off! Henry Fonda. I remind you of Henry Fonda. In *Once Upon a Time in the West.*'

It was true. Niklas Kalf nodded in surprise.

A grin spread across Fonda's face, across the two massive sides of his jaw, beneath which his Adam's apple bobbed.

'Heard anything from your wife?' he asked with that tooth-baring grin.

'Excuse me?'

'Have you had any news about your wife?'

'What do you mean? What do you know about Liz?'

'Nothing, not a thing.' Fonda shook his head, and his grin vanished. 'Don't get too excited. I don't know anything about Liz.'

Niklas Kalf stared at him, unable to say anything. For a moment he registered that the petrol was still pouring into the tank. And as Henry Fonda looked him in the eyes, the grin spread across his face again like a light being turned up.

'But I know a few things about Asia.'

Kalf stopped leaning against the pump and stood up straight. A terrible fury pounded within him, and he knew that only if he lashed out, if he brought his fist over and over again into the old man's face, only then would that fury ease, and he clenched his right hand into a fist and prepared to strike. But in the middle of the movement the feeling was extinguished. As if it had been blown out.

'Come on, let's drive for a bit,' said Henry Fonda comfortingly, and nodded across to his truck. Kalf was surprised to feel himself being taken gently by the arm.

'Just relax,' the old man said, smiling calmly. 'Just relax, it's OK.'

And Henry Fonda led him away from the humming pump, held the passenger door open to him and let him in.

'Here we go!' he said cheerfully, swung himself into the driver's seat, started the engine, which sprang into life with an unusually deep growl, and set off.

'No, it isn't Henry Fonda,' said Niklas Kalf, completely astonished by what was happening.

The old man laughed. 'Correct! And who is it now? Come on, say it!'

He struggled to think who he was being reminded of now. He was still tall and gaunt, but suddenly the old man seemed a little younger than a moment before, and his eyes were no longer narrowed, neither were they blue, but mocking like his mouth. The film title came to him first: *Colors*.

'Robert Duvall,' he said with relief.

'Yeah! You got it, son!'

Robert Duvall struck the steering wheel with the palm of his hand as he left Marfa, heading north. Kalf realized to his amazement that he couldn't cope with the question of whether the man in whose vehicle he was now travelling just looked like Robert Duvall, or really was. He had a sense that the change had swept across the old man's face like a wind wrinkling the still surface of a lake. One image disappears with a soft ripple, another appears. That was all.

'What's it like being a German in the United States, son?' Robert Duvall asked into the silence, knocked a cigarette from a soft pack of Marlboro and clamped it between his lips.

'How do you know I'm German?'

The old man laughed that Robert Duvall laugh, in which the cheeks settle in countless wrinkles and the eyes get small and menacing. The smoke curled unhurriedly in front of his face, as if the cigarette was smoking itself.

'Did you know that 80 per cent of all the takings at the world's cinema tills flow to the United States?'

'I did, it's been in all the papers. You remember the film in which you played one of De Niro's brothers, a priest?'

'A priest, you say?'

Duvall seemed to think for a moment, then shook his head. 'No, sorry, I don't remember that film.'

'The church is somewhere in the desert. De Niro is a gangster who comes to you to confess.'

'Yes, the confession. The twilight of truth. That's so European!' Duvall looked at him with a grin, just glancing occasionally back at the road, which was empty and ran straight to the horizon. 'That life is a dream and one is only a butterfly dreaming one is a man. That's the moment of the birth of modern Europe out of the melancholy of the baroque. Few things have excited you so much as the supposition that you can't really tell what's real and what's imagined.'

Kalf looked out into the desert. The old man was right. He thought of all the time that had passed here in Marfa, and he thought again of Dostoevsky and the fact that anything can happen when you don't know what's a dream and what's real.

Duvall nodded, apparently very pleased. 'You got it, son!'

Then he braked and stopped, apparently on the open road. Slowly, as if walking caused him pain, he got out and opened a gate. Dropped his cigarette end and stamped it out before climbing back into the driver's seat.

'It's like this, son: you guys are still thinking about that strange twilight of the dream that you were still persuading yourselves to see as reality, but already you sense the certainty of reality returning. That special weight that gives you the certain feeling that you aren't dreaming.'

He drove on a few yards and stopped again. The engine bubbled in neutral. 'Hang on, I'll be right back.'

He closed the gate. Ahead of them a thin, barely discernible tyre track ran through grey, dry scrub up a hill, before disappearing behind a spur halfway up. The pickup rumbled through the deep crevasses that the torrents of the autumn storms must have dug into the slope, and which you never saw in the solid grey of the prairie until your front wheel was already see-sawing into them. Kalf wondered whether it was the old man's ranch, and at the same time couldn't help smiling at such a naive thought. Ownership, he knew, was something that didn't suit this person who had given of himself so readily.

Finally they reached the point behind which the path disappeared, and he looked back towards the road. They were astonishingly high up above the prairie, and on the horizon he saw Marfa's silver water tower on its tripod. A plateau opened up behind the top of the hill, bounded on one side by the back of the hill they had just climbed, and on the other by a steep rocky cliff. A field sheltered from the wind, fenced in with a gate.

'Get out, son, we're there.'

As soon as they got out of the car, Niklas Kalf heard a heart-rending mooing sound behind one of the rocks that lay scattered in the scrub of the field. Then he saw a little calf hobbling rapidly towards them at the gate, without stopping its long-drawn-out, helpless sounds even for a moment. It was still very young, with black and white patches, and it hobbled, but only when it reached them did Kalf realize that the animal wasn't injured, but had five legs. The left hindquarter seemed to be double, and the unnatural, slightly shorter leg had grown crookedly out of the other one. Robert Duvall held his hand out flat between the old weathered wooden beams. The calf immediately sucked his fingers as though they were teats, taking them right into his mouth. With a laugh the man allowed his hand to be licked, as if it was a particularly good joke.

'Is that supposed to mean something?'

Duvall clearly couldn't stop laughing, so amused was he by the situation.

'What's that supposed to mean?' Kalf asked again and said nothing until Duvall finally stopped laughing at his own joke, pulled out his hand and wiped it on the light blue flannel of his shirt.

The calf mooed again, and when it stretched out its tongue Kalf was startled to see how incredibly long it was. It dribbled over its muzzle, again and again, sticking the tip of its tongue alternately into one damp nostril, then the other. As he watched, repelled, Duvall tramped over to the truck, hoisted a bale of hay from the bed and dragged it over. He opened the gate, for which he had to push aside the still mooing and slavering calf, carried in the bale and cut open the twine with a knife that he suddenly held in his hand and had just as suddenly put away. As he left the field again, pushing his hat to the back of his neck, he now reminded Kalf of Ted Turner.

'You're nuts!' The old man shook his head with horror and brushed the dust off his jeans with his hat.

'I've heard you're very interested in Rome?'

They leaned against the gate and watched the calf eating.

'What's that supposed to mean?'

'Well, I remember damned clearly the times when the caravans were heading for Europe and the fleets for her harbours. That's all in the past. Today, Venice and London have long been deserted. Somewhere running through the middle of you people there runs an invisible Limes, that line that separates the expanse of the barbarian land from the Pax Americana. You've got to understand that we're paying for your paradise! The United States, as my friend Kagan puts it, are patrolling outside your walls.'

He had hung the hat over a fencepost. His eyes, now large again and very bright, shone at Kalf, and all of a sudden there was something feline about him, his head was rounder, his cheekbones more pronounced than they had been a moment before. He took his pack of cigarettes out of his breast pocket and tapped out a Marlboro. Lit it, cupping one hand protectively around the other. He didn't seem to inhale the smoke, nor did he take it out of his mouth to knock off the ash. The cigarette clamped between his lips made it appear as if his head was the statue of an idol with incense being burned in front of it.

'In Germany, my son, you're experiencing the death throes of a Utopia, which must be terribly painful.' He swept the air powerfully with the edges of his hands, as if practising karate. 'It's all over!'

'Christopher Walken!' said Niklas Kalf.

'That's right.'

'In that music video. Who was it again?'

'A music video?' Christopher Walken was baffled.

'Yes, of course. You flew in it.'

'In the video?'

'Yes.'

'Really?'

'Yes. If I could only remember who the musician was.'

'OK, OK.' Walken nodded seriously.

He spat the cigarette out onto the ground and stamped it out. Then he flew. He folded his arms across his chest, closed his eyes and lowered his head as if listening inside himself. Then he floated, at first only a few inches off the ground, finally all the way over Kalf's head, opened his eyes and spread out his arms. Niklas Kalf shielded his eyes with his hand and blinked up at him.

'Don't worry.' His voice was suddenly very loud and intimidating. 'You'll see the world as if you've just woken up, and you'll see to your surprise that everything's back where it should be. You'll be bewildered at how much you have split the present from the past. Understandable: the desire to sever the connection with fascism. But it just can't be done. You'll see how beneficial it is in the end to rejoin the historical continuum.'

'We would never have imagined politics becoming important again.'

Slowly Christopher Walken floated back down to the ground. He lifted his nose into the air and with great concentration collected snot in his mouth for a moment, moved it from one cheek to the other and then spat it out with a short, violent movement of the head.

'I know.' He pulled a face. 'Now someone's got to explain: that means war. And this thing means interest. And this one means power. And that one over there is hunger. But I'm a person you can trust!'

There was something drawling, lazy about his voice that Kalf liked listening to. Everything he said struck him as completely illuminating. Trust had been the last word, and he thought he could still see it trembling about the old man's lips, which looked moister than they had a moment before, and fuller than Christopher Walken's had ever been. He thought of the wind blowing across a still lake and wrinkling the surface of the water.

'And who's that?' asked Niklas Kalf, suddenly afraid.

The old man's yellow eyes lay deep in their sockets. The skin around them was shaded as blue as if it was wet, and run through with veins, as though endlessly cool, blackish blood was flowing right beneath the epidermis.

'That's me, you fool.'

All kindness had vanished from his voice. And although Kalf's whole body was trembling, he still forced himself to laugh.

'I don't think so!'

'Don't you like me, or something?'

The old man looked offended and turned away. Took his hat and put it back on. 'I still think it's a thousand times better than De Niro, the fool, in that film with an egg. You know the one I mean?'

'The one where you have those disgusting long finger-nails and use them to peel the egg?' The anxiety eased again.

'Yes, exactly. But that isn't De Niro and it isn't me. How many times do I have to say it?'

'That was *Angel Heart*. With Mickey Rourke.'

'Who wasn't bad, by the way. Much better than De Niro.'

'I don't know about that.'

They both fell silent for a moment.

'You're somehow a person of the Eighties, aren't you?' Kalf observed.

'All for you! It's all just for you, my son.'

He thought of Dostoevsky and understood what the old man meant. A trick, that's all. *That's not bad for the devil.* He looked out into the prairie. Staying here, he knew, would be the temptation. Always to be part of this country. And he knew that for that to happen, Liz's life was what it would take. Could he still trust himself?

'You aren't Catholic, are you?'

Kalf shook his head.

'You can tell, if you don't mind me saying so, my son.' The old man studied him closely. 'You really believe that man is essentially good.'

He was surprised. His generation had never concerned itself with morality. Somehow its concepts seemed con-taminated. They had only ever talked about art, and he had to think a long way back, to his puberty, to find a point when he had actually thought about whether man was good. Of course man was good.

'Of course,' he said, 'man is good.'

'And you believe that? Or is that just a belief that's been forgotten, so to speak? Still intact, but useless?'

The old man's voice was very soft as he asked the question.

I don't know, thought Kalf. Do I still believe that? That man need only be given the freedom withheld from him, for evil to disappear? At some point? No, I don't believe that any more, he thought, feeling the cold flowing from his fingertips into his body. He had to admit that he hadn't really believed that for a long time. For a long time he had believed in the seashells that protected the soft flesh of freedom. My freedom, he thought. And my flesh. Wolfman Man.

'*Homo homini lupus.*' The old man laughed. 'Or not?'

Niklas Kalf nodded.

'And the rest, youth? *Perdu?*'

Yes, he thought with a shock: *perdu*. That was what was different. And he didn't know whether he yearned for the ideals of his youth, or only for youth itself. And at the same time he didn't know whether he was only repelled by those ideals, or by the way he had been. He stared at the old man and felt how unprotected at that moment his soul lay before him. With the few, endlessly practised movements of an oyster fisherman he had opened the shell! Nothing, he knew, prevented the old man from slurping it down, fresh from the sea, in a single gulp.

'The thought remains,' he said quietly, 'that everything

could be different. And that becomes all the more precious the more the world becomes a single place.'

'Well said, my son. But it must be clear to you that all that nonsense about blindness lost its meaning long ago, now that the globalized world, as you quote McNeill so elegantly, is just *a single place.*'

'Yes, you're right,' he admitted. 'The only thing that can be said is that every other place must necessarily be the place of a transcendent experience. Although I'm surprised that you of all people should bring up that idea.'

The old man sniggered with joy.

'Quite. I completely agree: today the glowing heart of Utopia is to be found once again where it was once preserved and nurtured. In what Meister Eckhart called the little spark of the soul.'

He laughed all over his wrinkled face. Then he looked mockingly at Kalf and said, 'Shall I tell you, my son, how I cured the old Magister of his cough?'

Now he was Al Pacino. Small and agile. Kalf told him so, and the old man looked at him with the big eyes of Pacino, wide with horror.

'Which film?'

He knew. '*Scent of a Woman.*'

'Yes.'

'You're sentimental!'

Pacino laughed again. 'All for you! All for you!' Then he took off his hat and wiped his wrinkled face with his whole hand. Brushed back his straggly black hair.

'It was 1327, I think, or 1328.' For a moment he stared as lifelessly ahead of him as only Pacino can. 'A terribly cold, wet winter, anyway. I found the Magister when he was about to set off for home from Avignon. There was a terrible draught in the wretched wooden box of his carriage, the rain was dripping in, and the carriage bounced violently about on the bad road. Eckhart was about seventy at the time, and could hardly sit down for haemorrhoids and gout. He had spent almost two years waiting in the corridors of the Papal Palace in Avignon, being sent from pillar to post, and finally almost being arrested as a heretic. Which would, I must admit, have been very flattering to me. Such a clever man! They say he recanted at the end. Or at least that's what John XXII boasted, servant of the servant of God, in his bull *In agro dominico*, but it isn't true!'

He seemed to be pursuing another thought for a moment. Then he scratched the corner of his left eye with the long nail of his little finger.

'But that's another story. At any rate: Eckhart was cold and coughing his soul up, so to speak. I comforted him. They buried him right at the side of the road.'

Al Pacino stopped, and blinked at Niklas Kalf as though waiting for applause. 'Yes, the little spark of the soul! You're quite right. But that doesn't mean you don't need to look after yourself, sonny.'

The last word hissed sharply through his narrow lips.

He turned away abruptly and tramped back to the car. Kalf had to hurry to catch up with him, and the engine was already running when he pulled open the passenger door. As they went rumbling down the hill in silence, and the leaf springs of the old pickup creaked with every bump in the road, it began to get dark. The old man was smoking again, and the glowing end danced in front of his lips.

WHAT WE ARE MADE OF

'And Liz?' Niklas Kalf asked quietly.

The old man didn't reply. Held the steering wheel with both hands and kept his eye on the road. Then he suddenly looked at him from the side, with De Niro's crooked grin, the mole twitching above it. His voice as raw and broken as Kalf expected. *GoodFellas*, he thought.

'What do you want to know?'

'When I'll see her again.'

De Niro pursed his mouth as if he had an acid stomach. 'I mustn't say anything.'

'But how is she?'

'I mustn't say anything.'

'Tell me!'

'I mustn't.' The old man bent down to him and his eyes flashed conspiratorially. 'But anyway I have the feeling that Liz died for you long ago.'

Kalf shook his head in horror. As he did so he noticed he was blushing.

De Niro gave a gurgling laugh.

'Isn't that right? I have the feeling you've settled in very nicely to your new life. Maybe you're quite pleased to be rid of her? And that kid she's carrying?'

'No!' Kalf yelled at him.

'Ah.'

He stared back out of the window and tried to calm himself. 'I still don't know what they want from me,' he said quietly, without looking at the old man. 'Tell me: what's really going on with Eugen Meerkaz?'

'Meerkaz?'

'Yes. What's his secret?'

'Meerkaz, yes! I knew him well, your Eugen Meerkaz. Very well, in fact, my son.'

Kalf was desperate. He knew he was close to the answers he'd been seeking for months, but no one would give them to him.

'What am I going to do?' he asked, resigned.

But the old man said nothing. And when Kalf finally turned to look at him, he was staring into that terrible face. Yellow eyes, set deep in their sockets, returned his gaze. Cold black blood flowed under the pale, densely veined skin of that ancient man's face. His lips trembled, moist and full.

'Don't move! Stay here,' he gurgled quietly.

Kalf, rigid with horror, couldn't turn his eyes away.

'Stick with the girl.'

'Who do you mean?' he stammered, wondering at that moment which name occurred to him. 'Asia?'

'That one?'

The old man laughed as though that possibility greatly amused him. 'No, no, not your sweet, pale beast. Not that one! Just wait!'

Another one demanding that he wait: *don't move!*

Niklas Kalf was silent for the rest of the journey. The gas station had long been aglow in the white light of the EXXON sign when they got there, and the sky above it was black and deeper than it had been for ages. The old man stopped right next to Kalf's car, which stood just as he had left it, and when he got out he clearly heard petrol being pumped through the hose and saw the numbers clicking on the old-fashioned mechanical display of the pump. Then it stopped. The display showed $4.38.

'Look after yourself, my son!'

The old man's voice dragged him out of his amazement and he turned to look at him. Just saw the Stetson and the thin collar tips of the worn-out shirt. A cigarette between his thin lips smoked itself. The old man tapped his hat and set off. And before he joined the traffic on Highway 10, he sounded his horn. Niklas Kalf hung up the nozzle and closed the tank.

'Four thirty-eight,' said the squat Mexican girl behind the till.

He paid and drove home.

CHAPTER FOURTEEN

Rome

Asia lived in an old camper van in the western part of Marfa, where there was also an abandoned ice factory, the rodeo arena and, still further out, the loading gate for the railway tracks. The plot of land around the camper van was cramped. The gate to the corral consisted of T-shaped bits of metal fixed to concrete pipes that someone had once painted bright colours, the struts alternately red, yellow and blue. Although the paint had flaked off long since and rust was swallowing the rest, the fence reminded Niklas Kalf of a brightly coloured fairground stall from his childhood, the frame of an old motor scooter or the entrance to a ghost train.

At the end of the dusty grounds stood a horsebox, its hatch folded down, filled with straw. Sometimes, when it rained, or when the wind was particularly cold at night, Kalf heard the mustang slowly trotting towards it. Most of the time it stayed between the horsebox and a dried-up tree, ten feet tall and completely stripped of bark, stretching its white branches like fingers into the black night sky. The horse's preferred place was under that tree, which was no protection against anything at all, and it was there that it stood when he watched it from the little window by the bed in the camper van, when Asia was asleep or away.

'It isn't a mustang!'

'I know.'

'It's a Quarter Horse.'

'Yeah, I know.'

Asia had explained it to him time and again. The thoroughbreds of the English settlers had been crossed with the ponies of the Indians, which had in turn evolved from Arabs and Berbers, the animals of the Spanish conquistadors. The result was a horse that was very good at sprinting, ideal for American horse races which, since there were no real racetracks, they had been forced to run on the main streets of the towns, and which finally developed into the standard racing distance of the quarter mile.

'That's why it's called a Quarter Horse. It isn't too big, but short and compact, with very powerful shoulders and hindquarters. It can carry heavy men as well as loads over long distances. It can put on spurts and take tight bends. The Quarter is ideal for herding and catching cattle. It's good for ranch work.'

The horse's coat was a deep, rich brown. It had a black tail and black pasterns, and its nostrils were black too, but its soft skin always glistened damply and had those small, pale spots that dogs have on their lips. When Kalf stood by the gate and offered it a carrot, the nostrils first opened wide like little probosces sniffing in all directions, before the horse bared its teeth, which were long and black at the gums, and with a tentative lower lip drew the carrot in.

The horse was a young stallion, and Asia said it had

been born on her father's ranch. The arched brow, like the front of an old car, and the bulging blood vessels, meandering just under the skin, showed the whole of the animal's strength. Kalf had never studied the broad muscle bed of a horse's hindquarters as closely as he did now, when it paced up and down in the corral, and he imagined what spurts of energy, what perseverance those muscles were capable of on such slender pasterns. It was the hesitant, prancing hoofs above all that let you forget time and watch for hours the tremendous care with which the horse took each step on the sandy ground, even though it was completely level and utterly familiar. Sometimes the creature nodded its head, as though agreeing with an invisible interlocutor. Kalf had a sense of looking into a strange realm in which the horse alone was visible to him.

It often stood there completely motionless, as if stuffed, its head not relaxed, but in an attitude of stretched rigidity, its legs precisely parallel, only the long tail whipping alternately to the left and the right and back to the left, although there were often no flies there at all. And just when he didn't know whether what he saw was an expression of composure or of unbearable tedium, the horse would nod three or four times and stiffen again, only lifting one rear hoof for a moment.

Sometimes it rolled in the dust, seldom during the day, and then just for a few minutes. First of all it lowered both forelegs, as though testing out how lying down was done, then the back legs, and then it lowered itself hesitantly first to its knees and finally its rear. It usually stayed in that sitting posture, only lying right on its side very briefly, when its long neck was completely relaxed, and its head rested calmly on the ground. Only now did one see how massive that body was, all its elegance suddenly gone and the horse just a herbivore like any old cow. But soon it straightened up again to gain some momentum and throw itself right on its back, its legs with their gleaming hoofs slightly bent and stretched upwards like a toy animal. Usually it rolled spiritedly several times from one side to the other, rubbing its back in the dust.

Then when it had, with a great deal of effort, heaved itself back onto its hoofs, it had a good shake as if it were not only a matter of getting rid of the dust, but also of shifting its internal organs, displaced by the unfamiliar position, back into the right place. As it did so it made itself quite stiff, stretched its neck as far down as it could, bared its teeth and snorted.

During the night, when the whistles of the two locomotives of the goods train had woken Kalf at about two o'clock and the container wagons had slowly crossed the town with a dull rumble, and when a ghostly gleaming strip, watched by no one, had disappeared into the prairie, he was the first to hear the grinding noise of horse jaws.

'Go to sleep!' murmured Asia, when he turned round to the little window above the bed and, huddled on his elbows, looked outside. 'Go to sleep!' she repeated. 'Ignore it.'

And although he did lie down again and even tolerated her hand on his chest, as he went back to sleep he couldn't help thinking of the horse's eyes. Sometimes it took up a position with its head at one end of the horsebox, as though it wanted to hide them, the way we put our faces in our open hands. Otherwise, one always saw the open gaze of the enormous eye domes, on which appeared the gleaming smears of lachrymal fluid, just as bubbles glisten with the weightless motion of rainbow-bright soapy water. He was frightened by that indifferent gaze, which went straight through one, as if one wasn't there, as transient as everything else and not worth remembering! At the same time that gaze made him think strangely of his child, and he calculated again. It was now nearly seven months old. As he slept he ran his fingers through Liz's hair.

The night of their first kiss at the Mystery Lights, Asia and he had parted almost without saying goodbye. The dust had risen icy cold with each of their footsteps as they walked to the car. Hands in the pockets of her jeans, she barely said a word as he drove back to Marfa. Finally they agreed to meet the next evening at Maiya's.

Maiya's was run by a New York artist, Maiya Keck, who came here, like everyone else, because of Donald Judd. Kalf often ate there when he could no longer stand being in the hotel any more. On his first visit he had thought the high-ceilinged room, with the little tables, the white tablecloths, linen napkins and candles, the waiters and waitresses in long white aprons and everything just as it would be in a European city, was a mirage. Niklas Kalf felt chilly on the short walk along Lincoln Street and past the town hall, and hurried to get to the restaurant. Stopped by Asia's table, rubbed his cold hands together and grinned at her. He could hardly make out the expression in her almost transparent blue eyes.

'Glad you could make it.'

'Yes,' she said.

The moustachioed father at the next table, who had laid his white Stetson on the chair next to him, ate a steak in introverted silence, while his wife and daughter curiously studied the other guests, young people in European clothes, drinking San Pellegrino and Prosecco: Marfa's tourists, mixed up with the very earnest members of the local art scene, most of whom he now knew by sight. Kalf ordered a bottle of Sangiovese, and they ate grilled radicchio and savoury tart with caramelized fennel, then pasta and, for dessert, little tarts with fresh cranberries, toasted walnuts and vanilla ice cream. Asia talked about her life here, without mentioning Frank. She wanted to know how he liked America, and he described what it was like coming to New York for the first time. Not a word about Liz. Instead: the idea of Empire. Rome. The restaurant closed at ten o'clock, and they were the last guests by a long way. They stepped carefully out into the silence.

That evening she brought him back to hers. She trembled at their first kiss, and when he tried to hug her she pulled away, although she didn't stop kissing him, roughly and with her eyes closed, as if snapping for him, her tongue small and her teeth unusually round and smooth. Her cold, small hand grabbed him by the back of the neck, but when he tried to put his arm around her waist again she pushed him away.

'What's going on?' he asked, pressing himself against her.

She took a step back. He let his arms drop. She walked up to him again. Pulled his head down to her and kissed him again. Stepped back again. Behind her the darkest night he had ever known, black and velvety, and cold. A wind had risen, and there wasn't a star to be seen. He didn't understand what she wanted. Her breath was white in front of her mouth as she looked at him as if wondering what to make of him.

She's so young, he thought, the taste of her lips staying with him.

'Are you coming?'

'What about Frank?'

That was her business. The wind tore the words from her face. She was incredibly beautiful.

Liz, thought Niklas Kalf.

'Of course,' he said and couldn't help laughing because she was suddenly so serious. And he noticed that he was, too. How long it had been since he had thought of Liz! It was only now, when the memory of their last night together in New York filled his senses with the distant heat of that summer, that he realized how long it had been since she had gone missing. And again he saw her resting her hand on the high-arched belly in which she carried the child. She was lying beside him again, and then she brushed the heavy blonde curls out of her face and looked at him. Tired and happy. And he looked at himself in her eyes, doubly reflected in her gaze and her expression.

Asia turned abruptly away and went to her car. It took a moment to emerge from the memory, but then he followed her and was surprised at how unquestioningly he did so. They drove through Marfa and finally along a dark farm road where only isolated, low houses stood, and finally stopped at the metal fence surrounding her plot of land.

Asia was bony, and when he held her in his arms she curved her back. He felt the vertebrae in her neck and her heartbeat in the cervical artery under her thin skin. She had strikingly small ears, and her eyes were small, too, and so pale blue that Kalf often thought he couldn't see the pupils under her white-blonde lids and eyebrows.

When they slept together, they had to shut the windows of the camper van and draw the curtains so that the horse didn't hear them. Kalf always protested, because the heating in the camper van couldn't be turned off, so it soon became unbearably hot. He held on tight to her bony hips, the places that stayed dry the longest, and firm. But on their first night he didn't notice the horse, although he later thought he remembered hearing the stamping of hoofs. Once he thought he saw a big shadow in the red and green light from the little lamp with the brightly coloured Tiffany shade, which fell outside like melting ice cream. But she drew his head down to her and he closed his eyes as they kissed. He was surprised by her white skin. Her breasts were very small and, with the delicate, dark veins that ran through them, almost translucent, but when he kissed them carefully and licked her tender skin, she pressed against him with all her might.

'Hm, good!' she murmured. 'Like that! Just like that!'

'I want to sleep with you,' he whispered.

'Oh yeah, fuck me.' Asia grinned. 'Fuck me nice and hard.'

They made love somehow nervously, silently and without glancing at one another, with very fleeting kisses. It didn't last long, then it was over, and they were lying side by side, and she told him how long she'd been living here in the camper van.

It had something to do with her father, from whose ranch she had fled. Kalf asked her about her childhood, but she just shook her head.

'And what about Frank?'

'Shut up!'

He fell silent, and she looked at him across the broad mattress that filled the whole rear area of the camper van. It was so stiflingly hot that they couldn't bear a sheet. Her pelvic bones rose up, high and sharp. The blonde fluff of her pubic hair was barely visible, her vulva glistened pinkly.

'Yes,' he said and couldn't help thinking about Liz again. Again the memory came to him unexpectedly, and again it was that last night in New York that he couldn't escape.

Liz kissed him as tenderly as you kiss someone when you've known each other for a dozen years, full of devotion, but also with that indifference that alone is capable of defeating time. He understood less than ever how he could have found himself so far away from her, and tore himself from the memory only with a great effort of will.

Asia looked at him for the duration of an infinitely slow blink of the eye. Then she grinned. 'Want to fuck me again?'

'Sure!'

He crept over to her and she sat down expectantly in front of him, like a gambler taking up position.

'Let's see if we can shorten your recovery time,' she said with a smile, and grabbed his cock.

When he kissed her on the shoulder and his lips wandered up and down her neck behind her ear, she suddenly let her head drop with a humming sound. He bit her, very gently, at the place in the nape of the neck where the sinew of the muscles divide, and at that very moment he felt her fingernails on his thigh, and boring tenderly into the skin. Now her lips opened wide, and they licked out each other's mouths, and Asia didn't take her mouth from his even when she lowered herself onto him, her cunt slippery from his sperm and pulsing wide open.

He only rubbed himself briefly against the cool wetness before plunging in. Immediately they began to move evenly, as naturally as if they'd known each other for a long time, and she took him into her as far he could go, let go of his lips and straightened up with her eyes closed and an almost triumphant laugh, her hands behind her back on his thighs. He too closed his eyes, and for a long time they moved together without any loud moans or a single word until Asia finally fell forward.

She lay heavily on him as though all her muscles were suddenly paralysed, he instinctively froze, and they moved together just long enough until the stimulation began to hurt. But at some point she took a deep breath, her slender torso swelled in his arms and very close to his face he heard her swallowing as if waking from a long sleep.

'Want you to come deep in my pussy,' she moaned in his ear, breathing heavily. 'Fill me.'

He kissed her for a long time and started moving hesitantly inside her again. He thought of Liz and their child, and at that very moment he came. It took a long time, and she watched him as it happened.

They never met anywhere else. It simply didn't suit her to leave what she saw as her territory. In fact she seemed, when they slept with each other, to dissolve in a strange kind of way, and the fact that the horse went berserk when they did had something to do with it. It was as if the animal could sense his strangeness. And once Asia cuddled up against him and asked, 'Why are you here, Niklas?'

'I mustn't say anything.'

He kissed her on the forehead. He couldn't lie any less.

For a long time neither of them spoke, and he thought she was already asleep when she suddenly murmured sleepily, 'Tell me more about Rome.'

It had started to rain again, and the horse, which didn't like rain, whinnied and stamped on the wooden planks of its shelter. Niklas Kalf didn't know what to say. He ran his hand over her short hair and thought. Rome, he thought. Rome is the blonde in her forties at the fountain with the antiques that she's dug up from God knows where. She's shivering in her thin white lurex dress with the chain straps, smoking hungrily. What should he tell Asia? About those flats near San Pietro in Vincoli that no one ever talked about, whose doorways open behind narrow cast-iron grids, or the young men in the bar at the Hotel Hustler that the Japanese girls are so fond of. Rome is the priests in their cassocks, Africans and Indians, hurrying across the glowing Piazza San Giovanni in the summer, their crucifixes knocking against a stone shell in which they have just dipped their fingers.

Paiata, he thought, the intestines of baby lambs, herds of which drift with long, soft hair across the Sabine Hills, hot-roasted like little nests or soft-boiled with rigatoni. Tripe in one of the restaurants in Testaccio, the mountain of amphora shards beside the former slaughterhouse. Pan-fried sheep's brain and artichokes from the Sicilian colonies that flood Rome in the spring. Rome is the crazed locust from North Africa on a travertine window-sill in Via Giulia.

Rome, thought Niklas Kalf, is the Mithraum under San Clemente where the figure of Mithras still gleams, forcing the bull's throat to its knees and slicing its throat through. Nearby gurgles the watercourse of the old aqueduct that has led for two thousand years to the Cloaca Maxima. A thin little tree, by the light of a cellar lamp, grows down there from a crack in the wall in a flower bed of green, slimy algae.

'Rome?' he asked Asia quietly, and she opened her eyes again.

'Yes,' she whispered and smiled at him. 'Tell me about it.'

'I don't know.' He thought for a moment. 'Have you seen *Gladiator*?'

'It's set in Rome, isn't it?'

'You remember when Russell Crowe is on the way home and he runs his hand through the corn?'

'Why?'

'Do you know what marble feels like?'

'Friends of mine have a marble floor in the bathroom.'

'After two thousand years marble steps look like old sofa cushions, smooth and soft.'

'The mountains here are old too.'

'You're right. Rome's a bit like Marfa.'

'You're nuts!'

'No, I'm not. Rome's a place in the desert, too, just like Marfa. A place in the desert of time.'

She looked at him curiously. 'Explain that to me.'

'A friend of mine had her child in Rome.'

'Yeah, and?'

'The hospital she went to is on an island in the river that flows through Rome. The Tiber. And there's been a hospital on that island in the Tiber for as long as Rome has existed. Can you imagine what it means to have a child there?'

Asia ran her hand over her face. 'What are you trying to tell me?'

He laughed. 'That's Europe.'

'What do you mean, Europe?'

'If you drive a few miles out of town you're somewhere where in all likelihood no human being has ever been. Here every child is the first child in the world.'

'And Rome?'

'Rome means sleeping with ghosts. In every room where you spend the night. And with every woman you kiss.'

Asia looked at him for a long time, and it was only in that gaze that he knew he was right. It held no ghosts. He leaned forward and kissed her.

'And what about the sea? I read there was a sea there?'

'Yes, that's right.'

The stallion stamped in the rain.

'The sea is everywhere in Rome. The marble plaques in the squares are as soft as ebbing waves, and all the women smell salty. And there are seagulls.'

'In the city?'

'Yes.'

'That's beautiful,' whispered Asia, closing her eyes again.

He stroked her cool, very white body for a while. But when his hand tried to snuggle between her legs, she pushed him away.

'No, honey, I'm too sensitive now,' Asia murmured. 'Better get some sleep.'

And she really did go to sleep shortly after that, behind him as always and embracing him as he lay awake for a while. Liz was infinitely far away, and with her the life they had had together. He didn't have the feeling of being unfaithful to Liz in the arms of this pale, translucent girl that he didn't understand. But he knew that this girl, whose breath blew evenly against his nape, protected him in some inexplicable way from that mysterious old man who was increasingly swathed in Kalf's memory in the smell of petrol.

And yet he still had to get away. It was high time to follow up the information that Elsa Meerkaz had given him. *Palm Springs*, she had said, and: *Ask Pinky*. A week had passed since his phone call to her. Day after day he put off his departure because of Asia. He snuggled up against her, closed his eyes and tried not to think that he was betraying Liz.

He heard the casual, rather shuffling step of the horse. He had often noticed how the movement seemed to flow step for step from the lowered, bobbing head into the body, with that empty, lid-lowered gaze. He imagined the stallion stretching out a leg and taking a step forward, making the leg quite straight and then bending down to gnaw its own hoof or its pastern. Sometimes, not often, it suddenly set off from a standing start to a gallop, hardly anything more than a crashing sequence of steps was possible in the pen, and already he had to brake at the gate and would fall into a trot as fast as the cramped space allowed, for two rounds or three. Then the stallion always stopped as if frozen, as if waiting for the result of its explosion of strength. And whenever Niklas Kalf watched the creature and sensed the rigidity of that expectation, he thought, something's going to happen now. But nothing ever did.

CHAPTER FIFTEEN
Christmas

On Christmas Eve it snowed. A layer so thin that the grey asphalt and the yellow and white road markings gleamed through it. Damp, soft, feeble snow, but he was woken by the sound of treadless tyres spinning with bright surprise somewhere in the neighbourhood. The snow gleamed blue as sour, watery milk beneath the low sky, and Niklas Kalf decided to wait one more day before setting off for Palm Springs. He still hadn't told Asia that he planned to leave Marfa.

He spent the day at home and only went out late in the afternoon to drop in once more at the bookshop. There he had a latte and one of the side-plate-sized chocolate cookies with which Marvin filled a jar right next to the PC day after day. As he did so he read *Spiegel Online*.

Night was falling. Kalf stared outside and saw that it was beginning to snow again, heavy flakes sucked full of damp wetness. The snow fell crookedly, from right to left, across the big rectangle of the window. He saw the movement and imagined that faint fizzy prickle, a hissing smack as the falling flakes covered the ground.

At some point the phone rang, and Marvin picked it up. Kalf only registered the fact when he called his name.

'Nick! It's for you.' The sentence took a painfully long time, as Marvin was agitated. 'It's a Mrs Smith, asking if she can meet you at the airport.'

The thoughts tumbled in his head. Had Lavinia betrayed him? But if Venus Smith really was here, that probably meant that Elsa Meerkaz had talked to Gallagher. Anxiety welled up, while all the things that made up his life here fell to pieces at the same moment. There is a small airport in Marfa, used by local airlines that travel between El Paso and Houston and the smaller towns. He had never yet been out there. He wondered what he had to offer her. And would she have Liz with her?

'Venus Smith?'

Marvin nodded violently.

Kalf looked out into the snow again, how it fell diagonally from right to left across the window. 'Tell her I'm coming.'

Marvin murmured something into the receiver before he hung up, and Kalf reached for his down jacket. He had arranged to meet up with Frank and Marvin this evening. He grinned nervously at him. 'We'll meet up at my place as usual, yeah?'

Then he hurried through the snowy rain to his car. The thought of Liz, a longing for her that constricted his throat, took control of him as it hadn't for a long time. In less than an hour it would be completely dark. The Beetle with its back-wheel drive and its narrow summer tyres, long since bald, barely held the line on the light, mushy snow, and it was over a quarter of an hour before Kalf cautiously turned into the short access road that led to the airfield. On the corner a single dim arc lamp burned, casting a very narrow circle of light that the Beetle bisected before coming to a stop by the airfield.

The headlights didn't reach far into the white, completely untouched surface from which two cold chains of light cut a gangway that seem to him to disappear only at the horizon. From there, where the road collided with the sky, a black, three-lane track led almost to the hangar, ending at the small wheels of a Learjet, whose pointed nose jutted towards him. The twin-engine plane was dark apart from the red and green navigation lights that blinked rhythmically on the winglets.

Kalf stopped about fifty yards away and wondered whether he was afraid, but he felt nothing but tense expectation. Almost at that very moment the door swung open and became a flight of stairs leading down to the airfield. Soft light fell across the red carpet on the steps onto the snow. Kalf got out of his car. He waited beside the Beetle while a man in a chauffeur's uniform carried a folded wheelchair down the five steps and snapped it open. The man pattered quickly back up and disappeared into the plane. Carrying Venus Smith in both arms, he then came slowly down the steps and set her carefully in the wheelchair.

The white gauntlet gloves hesitated only for a brief moment above the gleaming chrome hand-rims, then she gave the wheels a single synchronized push and they rolled, leaving a delicate trail behind them, close up to Niklas Kalf.

'Well, fucker?'

Venus Smith was wearing a white ski anorak and black Chanel sunglasses, the gold logo big on the wide arms. Red, high-cut Puma boxing boots. Kalf couldn't help thinking about New York, and how he had climbed the steps in front of her. He noticed that he was in fact strangely pleased to see her. Until his dream occurred to him again. Her breath a soulless cloud of condensing steam.

'What do you want from me?'

She laughed and licked her lips.

'Aha! And all this time I thought you wanted something from us.'

Her voice sounded almost disappointed. She swung her wheelchair powerfully around him and out onto the taxiway, still talking as she did so. 'How about your girlfriend's skin intact? Her unharmed eyes? All ten of her fingers?'

With each swing of her arms the tyres, breaking through the damp snow that had begun to crust over, made a noise that sounded like srrreee, srrreee, srrreee.

His hands were in the pockets of his jacket, and he watched after her until she stopped with her back to him and looked out into the black night. The sky, now that it had stopped snowing, was clear and filled with stars.

Very quietly she said, 'Nice here.'

'Yes,' he said.

'Have you ever seen the way a plane leaves a shadow on a solid blanket of cloud when it passes under the moon? Between the moon and the cloud bank?'

'No.'

'And the way that shadow – in which you can make out the outline of the plane much better than you can in the uncertain flickering of the red and blue lights through the cloudy haze – seems to hurry after the plane, so eager and quick that it makes you smile?'

'No, I've never seen that.'

He saw her nodding. Then the wheelchair performed a half-turn on the spot.

'I grew up in Inglewood.' She looked at him closely. 'A part of LA where you wouldn't last a night. There's hardly anything there but the bodies of aeroplanes flying over you. It's beautiful the way the shadow overtakes the plane when it passes under the moon.'

He nodded, and she went on studying him.

'Inglewood, you get that, motherfucker?'

He shrugged.

'Shit.' The wheelchair swung around, and she stared back into the black, star-twinkling sky. 'Do you actually plan to stay here for ever?'

He didn't reply.

'I can understand that, I'd even say I understand it very well,' she said. 'But what about Liz? I just mean we think it's a little strange how little you seem to care about a woman who is, after all, bearing your child.'

Naked rage flared up in him, and he had to control himself not to walk the five paces separating them and knock her out of her wheelchair. But strangely he had the feeling he knew exactly what was going on, which meant that in the end it wasn't really hard for him to regain control of himself. Elsa Meerkaz must have revealed that he'd come across Hans Holdt, and there was something hidden behind that German soldier, something that Venus Smith probably assumed he now knew. With a few swings of her arms she was beside him again, looking at him as if she'd read his mind.

Without hesitating he crouched down in front of her. She smiled.

'I still don't know what you want from me,' he said quietly. Her smile, he thought, is incredibly beautiful. The red boots gleamed new and inviolable.

'We know that isn't true. You are in possession of very special material about Eugen Meerkaz, and we want it.'

He ran his hand over one of the tyres of the wheelchair which immediately, like a nervous animal, retreated a little. She reached for the chrome hand-rims and stopped the chair.

'How is Liz?' he asked quietly.

'I think you've seen the pictures. As you've seen, nothing's happened to her that can't be healed.'

'And the child?'

'The child!' Venus Smith looked at her boots, and her smile disappeared.

'What do you want to know?' he asked tonelessly and got to his feet again.

'Meerkaz. We're just interested in Meerkaz. In his time at Caltech in the late forties he had access to certain projects.'

'What sort of projects do you mean?'

'Rocket technology. The John Parsons department.'

'I don't know anything about that,' he said and stuck his hands into his jacket pockets. Unfortunately it was the truth. In his diaries Meerkaz mentioned Parsons's research into jet propulsion, but he never went into any detail. He was sure: what he knew wasn't enough to save Liz.

She looked at him very carefully for several minutes, as if she wanted to give him as much time as possible.

'Shame,' she said finally and rolled back slightly. 'I'd really hoped you'd see sense.'

With wide swings of her arms she brought the wheel-chair back to the plane. Srrreee, srrreee, srrreee. The chauffeur was still waiting, his arms folded over his belly, by the steps.

'You're wrong!' he called after her. 'That research isn't anything special. It was all published ages ago.'

'Fuck you!'

Once again the wheelchair swung round, and Venus Smith looked at him. 'Fuck you!' Finally she took off her sunglasses. Her eyes were dark and cold.

'What about Liz?'

The smile was unchanged, like a billowing sail across her face.

'Merry Christmas, Nick!' she said very softly, just as the chauffeur lifted her out of the wheelchair.

That's a warning, thought Kalf, although he wasn't sure: is it a warning? The steps slipped gently up, then the fuselage of the plane was as smooth as if there had never been an opening in that perfect form. But the Learjet didn't start. Kalf made out shadowy movements in the cockpit, but the engine wasn't turned on, the headlights stayed in darkness, the plane with its three little wheels stayed where it was, at the end of a dark three-lane track that stretched back to the horizon. He waited for a few minutes, then drove home.

Why, he wondered as he drove, had Venus Smith actually wanted to speak to him? When he found the door to his apartment unlocked and saw a man sitting on the sofa, calm and with a grin on his face in the midst of absolute devastation, he knew.

A white woollen coat lay over one corner of the sofa. They hadn't found anything, because there was nothing

for them to find. That, he thought, was why this man
was still here. That was why the Learjet was still motionless on the airfield. And that was why the big black guy,
his hair woven into a single plait that lay on his head like
a knitted cap, was shaking his head with a smile.

'Hi, motherfucking poet! Nice to see you.'

He studied his gloves for a moment as if wondering
what needed to be done. 'That's enough now, you
understand?'

'I don't understand what you mean.'

'You don't?'

'No.'

'You really are a piece of shit, man, aren't you?'

The guy got to his feet, picking up a baseball bat of
gleaming polished aluminium that Kalf hadn't noticed
before. His right hand slipped along the metal to the handle. 'Listen, man, I'm going to beat the shit out of you.'

He said that completely calmly, and Kalf shut the door
behind him without thinking. It didn't occur to him to
run away. The first blow from the aluminium hit him
in the stomach and he immediately fell to the carpet. Then
a shoe caught him in the head, and he felt something in
his forehead exploding. Then another blow to the
shoulder. In front of his eyes red streaks passed through
the light, and strangely he saw, in slow motion and
without sound, the door opening and someone hesitantly
coming in. With all his strength he tried to haul himself
up again and to his surprise recognized Frank Holdt,
who seemed to be yelling at the black guy, because both
their mouths were snapping, and their eyes were wide
open, although Kalf couldn't hear a sound.

He saw Frank, his face red with agitation, pushing the

other man in the chest, while he, still as silent as if behind glass, picked up the baseball bat with the same movement and attempted a quick blow at Frank's head, but the bat struck only air. Kalf, who could hardly breathe, tried with all his might to get to his feet and help his friend. And when he had finally hoisted himself up and was leaning against the wall, Frank was suddenly holding the bat, which landed in the shattering sofa lamp with a crash that pierced the swirling silence in Kalf's ears. Then Frank hit his adversary in the face, the man held his mouth, spat blood and stumbled towards him. Thank God, thought Niklas Kalf, it's over now.

But as soon as he was within range the black guy, shoulder to shoulder with Frank, suddenly put his hand in his trouser pocket, and something leapt gleaming in his hand, a greedily sniffing point. Frank was already groaning, his face filled with surprise, as his hand whipped frantically over his body, feeling for the handle of the knife as if it wasn't all far too late. Blood dripped from his fingers as he did so, but he didn't notice. Slowly and softly, as if he had neither bones nor weight, he slipped to the floor. Kalf saw Frank's right hand die twitching on his blood-drenched belly, unable to grip the handle of the knife through which his life was draining faster than he could breathe.

But when the black guy finally bent over him with a bloody grin, Frank's left hand suddenly darted upwards, as if he had only been waiting for that, and plunged his index and middle finger into the other man's eye. A horrified, shrill cry, then everything was suddenly very quiet. Kalf looked into Frank's face, from which all warmth was draining. He had felt an affinity with him from the first moment. What they had shared was a fear of death. For the first time he felt sorry that he had slept with Asia. But then the other man started groaning, and Kalf knew he had no time to lose.

He walked the two paces over to him and sat down on top of him. The black guy reared up furiously beneath him, but Kalf gripped both his hands and pressed them to the ground. As he held him like that, his legs beating uselessly, the man's face was right in front of his own, and his one still-open eye stared at Kalf with the vacant madness of a panic-stricken pig, while his other eye, straining with exertion, went on streaming watery blood that smeared over his face and around the bloody wound of his mouth.

As if he was experienced in this kind of thing, Niklas Kalf waited calmly until the other man's hands twitched less and he reared up less powerfully, before letting go of his wrists and instead swiftly and without hesitation grabbing his opponent's throat. The black guy had a muscular neck with a pronounced Adam's apple. Kalf's thumbs found purchase there and he pressed it hard to the sound of a shrill scream. The hands now twitched like those of someone delirious, and brushed his skin here and there but without managing to reach him, as unthreatening as the hands of an air guitarist. The globe of the one wide-open eye stared fixedly at Kalf and looked, without its companion, strangely unimportant.

At some point the Adam's apple stopped twitching against his two clasped thumbs, then the arms, which had still been flapping as if they could anchor themselves in the air, grew limp, and finally the uninjured eye, buried under a layer of blood and jelly from the injury to the other, was extinguished too. Still, Kalf didn't let go of his grip until the black guy's skin began to get colder. He struggled to his feet and dragged himself over to the sofa. Every breath was painful. Frank is dead, he thought. And the last thing he thought about was the smell of death. Death smelled damp and metallic, like heavy, wet earth.

CHAPTER SIXTEEN

Easy peasy

The first thing he was aware of was Marvin, who supported him, brought him to his car and loaded him onto the passenger seat. And that was exactly what he felt like: a painful parcel, incapable of movement on its own. When they set off, he closed his eyes with a groan. They left the town and soon, too, the asphalted road, the pickup crashed ever more heavily through potholes and over bumps, and his head beat unbearably against the headrest. His lips, which felt like swollen sausages, refused to move. His ribs hurt with every breath he took. He saw the headlights quivering across the pale desert sand, back and forth between two deeply sunk ruts through which Marvin navigated his long-legged car, steering into the skids and skittering and sliding over the powder-white subsoil, only just avoiding rock formations that pierced the sand like tortoiseshells.

Then the car's vacant double vision suddenly caught the dirty front of a mud hut, and froze. Two small windows, between them a door, and a narrow veranda with a porch, from which two steps led down into the dirt. It was all covered with a thin layer of snow. The engine died and, along with the quiver in his head, the tremor of the headlight beams.

The next thing he saw was a cat. It sat on the veranda on the lower edge of the left-hand beam and was the colour of the bleached stopper of a preserving jar. With enormous pupils that collected the night, it stared across at them as he cautiously got out and Marvin took from the bed of the truck the bag in which he had hastily packed his barest necessities.

Kalf dropped with a groan into an old rocking chair by the door. Marvin looked at him sceptically. The cat acted as if they weren't even there.

'Can you manage here without me for a few days?'

He struggled with the sentence, and Kalf couldn't help remembering the first time he had seen him in the bookshop. Back then he couldn't have imagined them becoming friends. He nodded to him, but Marvin no longer seemed convinced that bringing him here had been the right thing to do.

'I don't think it would be good for me to come back here all that soon.'

'Of course,' said Kalf quietly, breathing as shallowly as possible to keep the pain from searing through his lungs more than was absolutely unavoidable. 'Not a problem.'

He struggled to make no unnecessary movement. The rocking chair wobbled a little more, then stopped. Marvin brought a blanket and laid it over his knees. Then lit the lamp that hung on a chain from the porch. The cat, still turned towards the black night on the edge of the veranda, looked round at him for the first time. At least its eyes, which could just as easily have passed right through him, fell in his direction for a moment. Then it began lavishly licking its fur, and its eyes narrowed pleasurably into thin slits.

'Is Frank really dead?'

Marvin nodded.

'And the black guy?'

'Him too.'

So he was a murderer. He stared at Marvin and waited for that certainty to change something, but nothing happened.

'I'll sort it all out,' said Marvin reassuringly. 'I reckon we ought to keep you out of it. It's just better if you don't ask a stranger too many unnecessary questions.'

The cat's ears pricked up towards the desert night. Kalf was glad that Marvin was taking control of things. Tried just to breathe in and out.

'Are you sure you don't need a doctor?'

'Quite sure. Don't you worry about me.'

Marvin studied him sceptically again, then wished him goodnight and walked to the car. The headlights flared up, and Kalf saw the cat's eyes clench. Then the lights wheeled into the void beside the hut. Kalf imagined Marvin setting the gearstick to 'D'. The pain grew so intense again that he couldn't suppress a groan. He wasn't sure whether the cat was watching after the car. At least its eyes went in that direction, and its fur shimmered for a moment longer in the floating fingers of the headlights that darted away across the cacti and the white shadows of the thin layer of snow that had formed particularly in the dips and by the sharp edges of the sand dunes.

The pickup drove slowly down the slope away from the hut, and disappeared behind the hilltop. Nothing remained but the sound of the quietly, evenly hissing mantles of the gas lamp, which drew a narrow disc of light beyond which lay the uniform blackness of night. Kalf listened for animal noises, but everything seemed to be completely silent, and he was reassured to see the tips of the cat's ears moving ever more slowly from side to side. Nothing to fear, he thought, registering with relief that the pain when he breathed seemed to be easing a little.

'*Bedenke immer Katze*,' he whispered in the cat's direction, '*daß du bald niemand und nirgendwo sein wirst.*'*****

He was sure he wasn't badly injured. Nothing but a few haematomas that were starting to make room for themselves under his skin. He poked his dirty, blood-crusted finger in his mouth to feel the dragging pain in his swollen cheek, which was making the whole left side of his head pulse with the rush of blood. Spat a little blood on the dusty boards of the veranda and wiped his finger on his shirt.

'Marcus Aurelius,' said Niklas Kalf, and the cat turned its head as if listening to him. Another sentence occurred to him: '*Bald wirst du alles vergessen haben, und bald werden auch dich alle vergessen haben.*'******

He tried to sit up a little. The cat's indifferent gaze followed his movements. Its chest and nose were white, and a white strip like a necklace ran around its tiger-striped neck. He imagined it setting its soft paws with dreamlike certainty and infinite caution on the hot sand, some burning noon now or five thousand years ago, here or in the cast shadow of the Nile. Death nothing but a dried-out leather grimace in the scorching sand. Long-legged and industrious, it stalked over as only lowly gods do.

'Oh, cat, just keep still.'

And it did, a metre from the rocking chair. Placed both white forepaws chastely side by side and looked at him with a gaze so indifferent that it passed straight through him as if he barely existed. And as he listened to the pain in his body slowly slumbering, for a moment he forgot to ask himself how he was to rise from this rocking chair and make his way to bed. For the first time in ages, the thought of Liz filled him completely.

'Cat,' he whispered, 'tell me what love is.'

The cat stretched and yawned, and the night with all its stars hung above it. They had landed in early September, in a summer that had been over now for almost four months. He was sure that the cat knew more about love than he did. And that he himself was just starting to understand what it might mean to love.

'Easy peasy,' he murmured and pushed himself painfully up on the arms of the rocking chair to go inside.

The cat watched him without moving. The empty night over the desert looked too threatening for him to bear being in it any longer. He was glad to know there was a roof over him. Barely had he opened the flyscreen with the cheeping creak of the old spring and the roughly constructed door behind it, than the cat silently and in a single flowing movement darted from the veranda into the dark house. Had the black guy dealt with Liz in the same way? Kalf saw Frank dying again. There was nothing he could have done but watch.

It was a few days before he could breathe in again without his ribs sticking into his lungs. He spent almost all his time sitting on the veranda with the blanket over his knees, watching the snow melting in the sun in the course of the morning. In the little dip where Marvin's hut stood it was as silent as in the dunes. At night it snowed thin flakes, and the cold wind clattered the panes in their old, dried-out putty. But in one corner of the hut there was an iron stove, dry firewood stacked beside it, and several blankets lay on the bed. There was a table and a box of groceries and a stand with mirror and bowl.

When he had struggled to undress on the first evening, he had inspected, as best he could, the already crusted wound to his forehead and his swollen mouth, and the haematoma on the left of his bottom rib, where the blood seeped thickly into the tissue. There was another fairly big swelling on his left shoulder blade.

The box contained orange juice and sliced bread, peanut butter and a big piece of Cheddar, beer and unsalted crackers. The privy was behind the house, as was the pump, above which a wind wheel scraped. What he missed most was the computer. It was only now that he understood how much the course of his day had been defined by going online, always in search of stories and strange lives. Now he finally finished *The Brothers Karamazov* that Marvin had stuck in his pocket, and after two days he started walking around among the head-high mesquite bushes, the fat-trunked yuccas and the paper-dry, long-feathered grass that grew everywhere here in little clumps. As he did so, the cat attentively followed each of his movements from its favourite position on the veranda. Sometimes, for no reason that he could perceive, it disappeared with a leap among the grass.

He tried to come up with a plan for what to do next, and could think of nothing. He longed for Asia and often imagined her blue, glittering eyes and her small, greedy kisses, the nights in the camper van and how she had snuggled up to him. He knew that with Frank's death all that was over.

Nonetheless he was disappointed that it was April, in the end, whom Marvin brought with him the next time he came. He didn't like her seeing him like that, but finally she persuaded him to have his wounds examined, and as Marvin went out to fetch fresh water, he took his shirt off and lay down on the bed, and April studied his bruises. With that elegant gesture that he knew from before, she wound her heavy hair around so that it didn't fall into her face. She had some ointment which she carefully applied, and for a moment they were as close again as they had been that Sunday when he had gone with her and her son to the cemetery. She sat down on the bed next to him and asked with a smile how he was. Would he tell her what had happened?

'I can't.'

For a moment he was afraid she would threaten him with the police, but April only nodded. That was all. He knew she wouldn't betray him. But he also knew that everything between them had been said. She mentioned that Dave had asked several times when he was going to come and see them again, and he asked her to say hello to the boy from him. Her lips were the matt red of a candle.

When they heard Marvin's footsteps on the veranda, April said, 'It's time for you to get out of here.'

He knew she was right. They would look for him and find him. The sheriff, Marvin said, was looking into a break-in that Frank had tried to prevent, and in which both Frank and the burglar had lost their lives. He, Marvin, had been there, and had told the police everything that had happened. There wasn't a trace, he said, of the foreigner to whom Frank had rented the house.

'And Asia?' Kalf finally asked quietly, when they were alone together for a moment.

'She doesn't want to see you.'

They had never talked about it, but at some point when Kalf was on his way back from her place, Marvin had said something in the bar that made it clear he knew.

'Never again, she says.'

'Yes,' replied Kalf, and there wasn't actually anything more to say.

He understood her, even if it hurt. And when the two of them drove away and April waved to him one last time, he knew he would never see her again. What had felt like a new life was over.

CHAPTER SEVENTEEN

Happy New Year

The sounds of dying engines, car doors slamming. Footsteps on the wooden veranda, then there was a knock at the door. Marvin didn't knock. Marvin called before he came in. Another knock. The fear was there again.

'Coming!'

He hauled himself out of the chair and went to the door. The bruise on his belly was by now yellow and brown and still hurt, although it was almost ten days since they'd fought. Hesitantly he opened up. A young woman, almost just a girl, stood in the doorway. The first thing he noticed was her thin brown hair, which she repeatedly brushed from her face.

'I'm Imogen.'

He didn't understand. 'Imogen?'

'Yes, Imogen Engel. I think you know who I am.'

Niklas Kalf froze. This was impossible.

The girl laughed and attempted a joke. 'Hi, I'm Imogen from Oklahoma!'

'Imogen from Oklahoma,' he repeated blankly, and the memory of his first evening in New York was clear and distinct in his mind. Albert Snowe, who couldn't stop talking about Imogen Engel on that first evening.

'Imogen Engel,' he said, studying the girl suspiciously.

214

It really was the same sulky child's face as in the photographs of her arrest, which he had seen at some point on the Internet. But you could see that she'd got older. She must have been twenty by now, he reflected, and saw the chewed-off fingernails when she brushed her thin hair from her face. She wore a green army jacket and cargo pants. Who, he wondered, had sent her? And how had she found him?

'Happy New Year!' she said and grinned at him.

She was actually right.

'*Schönes Neues Jahr!*' he replied.

She smiled as if he'd paid her a compliment. Then she pushed her way past him into the house. Considered in passing the wound on his forehead, the bruise on his chin, and shook her head.

'We haven't much time. It isn't safe here any more. You've got to get out of here.'

He watched after her. She climbed over the old newspapers that covered the floor, pushed the used plates on the table aside and looked at the stones that he had collected. The cat, which had been sleeping on the mattress, leapt up and vanished behind the trunk. I've got to get out of here, he thought agitatedly. He'd been waiting for that. When Marvin came in and threw the New Year edition of the *New York Times* onto the stack, he looked at him with surprise. New Year's Eve celebrations: the crowd in Times Square, the fireworks over the Petronas Towers in Kuala Lumpur and over the Acropolis. ARMY ACTS TO ADD THOUSANDS OF GIs TO ITS GULF FORCE.

'She said she knew you,' Marvin said apologetically, and he barely stammered as he watched the girl prowling through the shack picking everything up.

'Yes,' said Kalf tonelessly and followed Marvin's gaze. Somehow that was true.

'*The Brothers Karamazov*,' Imogen read, looking round at them both. 'By Fyodor Mikhailovich Dostoevsky.'

She lowered the book. 'How did that happen?' she asked, pointing at Niklas's forehead.

Kalf asked Marvin to explain, and Marvin told her about the phone call on Christmas Eve.

'What phone call?' asked Imogen.

'Someone wanted to speak to me. Out at the airport,' Kalf explained. 'A Mrs Smith.'

'Venus Smith?' Imogen looked at him closely.

'Yes.' Somehow he wasn't surprised that she knew the name.

Marvin went on with the story. He and Frank had gone over to Kalf's house. He had waited outside in the car, because they had planned to go straight to Joe's Place. Then he had heard noises from the house.

'And?'

Marvin hesitated for a moment. At first he hadn't dared to go in. He was so sorry.

'We've got to go,' said Imogen, without looking at him again. 'I'll wait outside.'

Niklas Kalf started packing. Marvin had brought him everything that could still be found in the devastated apartment. He took the toothbrush from the washbasin and put it in the bag along with everything else.

'Asia came to see me,' Marvin said quietly.

'And? What did you tell her?'

'That you'd left suddenly. That I didn't know where you'd gone.'

Kalf nodded.

At that moment the cat reappeared and rubbed against his legs. At some point in the night it had slipped into his bed and woken him up. Since then he had been allowed to stroke it. He bent down and stroked its fur one last time, then put on his jacket and laid the bag on the bed. Picked up *The Brothers Karamazov* and took out his bookmark.

'Will you return this, please?' He held the book out to Marvin. Marfa Ignatyevna had turned up again at the end, and her question still echoed in his ears. *I understand what duty means, Grigory Vassilyevitch*, she had said, *but why it's our duty to stay here I never shall understand*. Time to go.

'I've kept it a bit too long.'

He grinned at Marvin. 'I'm afraid there'll be a bit of a fine to pay.'

'That's OK.'

Marvin pulled a bundle of dollar bills from his trouser pocket and held it out to Kalf.

'What's that?'

'For the car. It's all I've got.'

Niklas Kalf nodded.

'That'll be enough,' he said and put the money away. Then they hugged, he picked up his bag and they went outside.

Imogen sat in her car, a battered GMC 1500 with a martial-looking radiator grille and matt olive-drab army paint. As soon as he had thrown his bag behind the seat and climbed in, she started the engine and turned. In the rear-view mirror Kalf saw Marvin waving at them, then the dust swirled up and they juddered along the cart track. The bruises on his ribs no longer troubled him much. When they reached the road, Imogen stopped.

'So? Where are we headed?'

He looked along the road and wondered. His heart suddenly thumped in his throat, and already he couldn't begin to understand why he had stayed and waited in Marfa for so long.

'I've got to get to Palm Springs,' he said then.

'Why Palm Springs?'

'There's someone I've got to find.'

'Who?'

The engine gurgled dully in neutral. He shrugged. 'We've got to turn left,' he said, without answering her question.

Imogen set the gearstick to 'D', stepped on the accelerator and took Highway 90 westbound. On either side of the blacktop, low fences with parched earth behind them, ground smooth by the wind. For the two hours to Van Horn they didn't speak a word to each other. Niklas Kalf watched her from the side as she drove, the way you look at a taxi driver. She looked as calm and concentrated as if she were doing a job. When they took a break in Van Horn and had a coffee at the bar of the same burger joint where he had stopped for breakfast on the way there, he asked her what she wanted from him. Imogen lit a cigarette.

'Nothing, nothing at all,' she said, smiling at him wearily.

'And who sent you?'

'Who sent me? Albert Snowe said I should look after you. He told you about me, didn't he?'

Kalf nodded.

'Al visited me in jail and then he sorted out an apartment for me, and a job and so on.'

'And your parents?'

'No contact.'

'I see.'

But how did Al Snowe know he was in Marfa? Had Lavinia given him away after all? But why did Imogen show up only now, so late and so soon after Venus Smith? The tension climbed his spine. Everything that had happened over the past few months seemed to be coming together now. Imogen's story had been the first thing he had learned in this country. She was a murderer, and for the first time he was able to accept that he himself had murdered someone. But there was no emotion attached to the fact.

'What was it like to kill somebody?'

Imogen gave him a disparaging look. 'That's what everyone wants to know.'

'No, you don't understand,' he said, but he didn't know how to explain to her what had happened to him.

She smoked and looked out the window.

The television above the bar showed the picture of a satellite. They had tried to make contact with Pioneer for the last time a few days ago, a presenter reported, but the probe hadn't replied. Finally a very faint signal had reached NASA's Deep Space Network four weeks ago. The engineers were working on the basis that the probe's fuel had finally run out. Although Pioneer 10 was only conceived for a mission lasting twenty-one months, the probe had held out for thirty years. *So you can say*, the presenter added with a smile, *that it was worth the money*. The camera showed the gilded plaque with the drawing of two people that had been fastened to the probe.

Niklas Kalf took a sip and looked at Imogen, who ignored the television. 'The thing has been flying at thirty thousand miles an hour since it started in 1972. You've got to imagine that.'

Imogen blew out smoke and looked at him with a shake of the head. Asia occurred to him, and the fact that clearly he always had to tell stories that no one could make head or tail of.

'Pioneer 10 will reach Aldebaran in two million years, the red eye in the constellation of the Bull.'

'You're nuts.'

He smiled and looked at her. They were the only people sitting at the bar of the diner. They ate blueberry muffins. Imogen Engel had ordered a decaf hazelnut latte, he a latte with an extra shot of espresso. He had asked where she'd come from, and she had told him that in 2001 she'd been released from Spofford Juvenile Center, where she had served her sentence. When he asked what she'd been doing since then, she had just shaken her head.

'Aldebaran. That reminds me of something,' he said.

'What?'

'I can't remember, But it'll come to me.'

'We've got to go!' Imogen wiped her mouth and scrunched up her napkin.

He smiled scornfully and swung his half-full cardboard cup around until the foam had mixed completely with the coffee. 'Why are we actually in such a hurry?'

Imogen didn't smile.

Aldebaran, it occurred to him, was the name of Phil

Gallagher's production company, the guy Venus Smith worked for.

'I promised Al I'd look after you.'

The sky was cloudless, but a milky blue. He thought of the clear days in Marfa when you felt you could see out into the universe, and noticed that he already missed the place. There, it suddenly seemed to him, he had been safe. Imogen switched from Highway 90 to Interstate 10 West, put her sunglasses back on and filtered into the traffic, which flowed much more densely here.

About two hours later they were in El Paso, from where he had set off back then, and as they approached the city he pulled his cellphone out of his luggage and turned it on. A short time later he heard the message-received tone. As Imogen drove through El Paso, whose Mexican twin Ciudad Juarez grew up the mountain as a collection of white huts beyond the Rio Grande, he heard first the voice of Lavinia, who had already left him a message shortly after he left New York. Then came a dozen phone calls from Germany, his mother and Liz's father repeatedly asking them to call back. In between, calls from friends who wanted to know when they would both be back in Germany, and a call for Liz from her office. All those voices sounded so alien that Niklas Kalf simply endured them motionlessly, staring out of the window.

Then he erased them all and switched the phone off again. He would call as soon as he had found Liz. But till then that old world, the one they had left together, didn't exist for him.

The road took a wide curve along the river, and it was a moment before he understood how the city on the other bank differed so fundamentally from the one on this side of the border. Beyond the river a thin pillar of smoke rose from each house, and that pale glade of thin cords of smoke reminded him more of paintings by Bruegel or refugee camps in Kosovo in the winter than of a modern city.

They set off again towards Las Cruces, but before they reached it Imogen repeatedly checked the rear-view mirror, accelerated, slowed down, changed lane.

'Are we being followed, or what?'

He didn't mean the question seriously. Tried it out ironically like dialogue from a thriller.

'I think so.' Imogen took her eyes off the mirror. 'But don't look round!'

He stared straight ahead as if paralysed. At the junction of Interstate 10 with Interstate 25, Imogen switched to the west-bound lane before suddenly sliding close by the yellow marker barrels to head north. The long-legged, leaf-sprung pickup swayed dangerously under the quick steering manoeuvre.

'And?'

Imogen went on looking in the rear-view mirror. 'Shit!'

Kalf looked round at the black Pathfinder, which was staying a painfully precise distance from them. Then Imogen switched to the far-right lane and eased off on the accelerator, making the Pathfinder, which had understood the manoeuvre, drive so close behind them that he could make out the outlines of two men behind the darkened glass of the windscreen. Imogen suddenly took an exit that he hadn't even noticed. The Pathfinder sped past them.

'Cool!'

Imogen grinned at him.

'But surely they'll be back?'

She shook her head. 'They'll see it as a diversionary manoeuvre and drive back onto Interstate 10 to intercept us. They think we want to head west.'

'But we do.'

'Yes. But now we'll take another route.'

The road led into the desert, and at some point they went past the ghostly dune mountains of White Sands that rose straight out of the plain. He saw on the map that they were close to Roswell, the place where UFOs had first been supposedly sighted in the 1950s, and in the middle of the white of an empty landscape he read the name Trinity Site, next to a little pink circle. That was where the first atom bomb had been tested. Late in the afternoon they reached Alamogordo. Blinking traffic lights and enormous car parks, the Sacramento Mountains very close, barren, like sanded-down rock formations, a few clouds drifting above them. They had burgers for dinner and drank beer, and then Imogen drove to a Holiday Inn Express. A thin green strip surrounded the low building, watered so industriously that the whipping salvos of droplets from the lawn sprinklers ticked at the windows.

Their room was big, two queen-size beds. Imogen dumped the bag and disappeared into the bathroom without a word. Niklas Kalf lay down on one of the beds and closed his eyes, heard the sound of the shower and almost fell asleep to it. When Imogen came back out of the bathroom, water glittered all over her skin and hung in the tips of her strands of hair, which she blew out of her eyes as she attended to her bag. She was pale, and her skin looked as smooth as a freshly opened yogurt. A tattoo on her right shoulder blade. As he tried not to stare, he wondered what it represented. She stood up and stepped over to the bed.

'Oh, that.'

She seemed to think for a moment about what else there might be to say on the subject. Her shaven vulva was that of a child. 'That's from jail.'

For the first time since Marvin had taken him out of Marfa, he felt hot water on his skin. He stood for a long time under the jet in the narrow cabin and then in front of the misted mirror. Ran his hand over the bruise beneath his ribs and looked at his back. Wiped the condensation from the glass and tried to remember what he might have looked like six months ago. His skin was surely more suntanned than ever before. Were the wrinkles beside his mouth deeper? He wore his hair longer than he had in Germany, and for the first time in years he had bought a wet-shaver and started shaving regularly. And his eyes? Don't eyes change?

When he came out of the bathroom she seemed to be asleep already. The fan of water passed across the window every minute. But no sooner had he turned out the light than he heard Imogen getting up, slipping under his duvet and snuggling up into his armpit. Immediately his heart thumped in his throat. He tried to breathe calmly.

'Tell me what they want from you,' she asked him quietly,

'I don't know.'

What had Venus Smith said? *Rocket technology. John Parsons's department.* 'It's something to do with John

Parsons, an explosives chemist who worked on rocket fuels. Meerkaz and Parsons were killed in an explosion.'

'Meerkaz is the one you're writing a book about.'

'Yes, how do you know that?'

'Snowe told me. And he told me about Elsa Meerkaz. They know each other.'

'Yes.'

'Do you know her?'

'Elsa Meerkaz? No. But she's a well-known figure in the Los Angeles immigrant community. Photographs always show her in long robes, with her thin white hair tied tightly back in a bun. A severe-looking face. She's over ninety.'

'What did you actually do all that time in Marfa?'

'Nothing,' he murmured and stared at the inert television, whose huge black screen seemed to absorb the faint light of the room so that, although it was nearly dark, it reflected the beds and, in ghostly form, the two of them as well.

He hadn't actually experienced anything in particular, he told her. 'Apart from the business with that nameless guy.'

'What guy?'

'I don't know. An old man. He talked to me at a gas station when I was about to go home. And then I helped him feed his calf.'

'You did what? Fed a calf?'

'Yes, we drove out to a field. He talked about all kinds of things. But most of all he did strange things.'

'What sort of things?'

'Oh, it doesn't matter, forget it.'

Niklas Kalf slept badly. He heard her breathing through the drumming of the sprinkler, and a few times headlamps twitched through the narrow gap between the heavy curtain rails, their light straying across the ceiling. Her breathing entered his dream, an incredible sky of very bright blue, completely cloudless and of such a pastel, unshaded colour that Kalf almost failed to see the point where it met the sea. He could only just make out the horizon by the shimmering of the waves in the endlessly wide bay, which he was looking down upon from above. And right up in the dome of the sky there was something transparent, something radiant about that blue. Like the white of the eye, he thought in his dream, in which the sun was just setting and a fine golden dust lay upon everything.

Two palm trees, their tall tips tirelessly nodding in the sea breeze, bathed their bright green in the sun for one precious moment longer than any of the things around them. And as he watched their whipping pennants, from which the warm light slowly dripped, an aeroplane entered his field of vision. It had crossed the powdery sky behind him, to appear now above his right shoulder and fly between the palms towards some vast city that broke in a bay down below and ebbed away in the sea, as if the city was itself a huge light-gleaming wave of streets and houses.

Suddenly he knew where he was, and struggled to wake and tell Imogen. They had to get there. But he couldn't do it, and when he woke up the next day he had forgotten the dream.

Next to the television, on a kind of sideboard that served as both desk and kitchenette, there stood a coffee machine and an ice bucket wrapped in cling film. A little bowl with the usual assortment of sugar sachets, sweetener and coffee whitener. They set off without breakfast and spent the whole day on minor roads, bought mineral water at a filling station and ate chocolate bars. Shortly after midday they took a break at a diner in Socorro, then crossed an Apache reservation on Highway 60. The road was deserted and the journey was desolate: it was almost four hundred miles to Phoenix, and would take them until far into the evening.

'And Liz?' Imogen asked at some point.

He shrugged. And Liz? he thought. Did she even still exist, or wasn't it more that she'd disappeared from his life long ago, and he just hadn't admitted it to himself? 'I don't know.'

The sun had set an hour before, and twilight was quickly falling over the land.

'I'll help you find her.'

Phoenix lay under a glittering foam of red and blue lights when they got there somewhere between nine and ten. This time Kalf slept very well and didn't dream at all, and when he woke up early the next morning Imogen lay rolled up like an animal on her side of the bed. He looked at her for a few minutes without moving, then she opened her eyes.

They had pancakes and filter coffee for breakfast in a cafe with an enormous pink doughnut on the roof. Outside the big windows the traffic passed along Interstate 10, which they met up with again here in Phoenix, and he noticed the many trucks decorated with airbrush painting and chains of lights. At around midday they crossed the Colorado River near Ehrenberg. A California

Inspection checkpoint ran across the highway. NO
FOOD, NO ANIMALS. The blue of the sky was dark
and cold, as if the protecting membrane against the
universe had melted away. Imogen drove the whole way
at least twenty miles an hour too fast. Just before Palm
Springs they stopped for the first time at a Mobil gas
station. The wind blew dry over the cracked asphalt. It
was very near here, Imogen said as she got out, that Jay
Smith was killed.

'Who?'

'Pinky.'

The name hit him like one of the gusts of wind that
swept across the desert.

'Who?' he asked again, agitatedly, in the hope that he
had misheard. He came quickly round the car.

'Pinky,' repeated Imogen. 'Don't you have that in
Europe? The Little Rascals?'

She stuck her credit card into the machine on the
pump and blinked over to an American flag that fluttered
between the toilets and a white petrol tank.

'How do you know this Pinky was killed?'

He heard Elsa Meerkaz's voice in his ear again: *Ask
Pinky!* Of course he knew the Little Rascals. Pinky must
have been at least ninety, he reflected. And once, as a
child in the twenties, he was a silent movie star. Pinky
with the freckles.

Imogen Engel brushed from her face the thin strands
of hair that the wind repeatedly blew over her eyes. He
waited for her finally to answer him, but instead she took
the nozzle and started filling up. She avoided his eye. But
after a moment in which they both listened to the grind-

ing sound of the fuel pump, she started to tell him. So quietly that he could hardly hear.

'It was painless. The black Ford Cherokee that he had bought two years before gleamed in the heat. The paint shimmered like new, because he'd just had the car washed. Although I don't think Jay particularly liked the car. Perhaps because he didn't like any cars made after the early seventies.' Her gaze darted uncertainly up to him.

'And what happened then?'

'He tilted his head slightly. Just far enough for his left temple to touch the red dust which, he registered, was pleasantly soft, and the sun appeared in the black, gleaming paint. A black sun without power or any light as we know it. Its glow was as dark as the world from which it shone across to Jay.'

Imogen looked at him seriously, her face frozen. 'Jay closed his eyes and tried to breathe more calmly. Then he was dead.'

Pinky, thought Niklas Kalf. 'Why did he die?'

Imogen tried to find words, but nothing came to mind. She shrugged. 'Al said I should quiz him.'

'Quiz him? What about?'

'About Parsons and Meerkaz. And about the explosion that killed Meerkaz.'

Suddenly Kalf understood. 'He was there. Pinky was there!'

Imogen nodded.

He looked at her in disbelief. 'So? Why did he die?'

The tank was full, and the pump stopped. Imogen took the nozzle out of the hole and hung it back up.

Then she looked at him like a child annoyed with the stupidity of adults. 'That has nothing to do with you!'

He shook his head. He couldn't make room for his fears. The crucial question now was what they should do next.

'Pinky was the trail I had.'

'Pinky?'

'Yes. Elsa Meerkaz said to me: *Ask Pinky.*'

He took a few steps away from the gas station. As soon as he stepped out from under the roof, the sun burned hotly down on him. The American flag snapped in the wind, which tugged at him, too. He walked out onto the empty highway. The central reservation drilled its way towards a distant vanishing point like a honey-slowed arrow in time, and passed right through him. A bird of prey hung motionless in the air for a provoca-tively long time, right over his head, as relaxed as the trucker who let his arm fall in slow motion into the cold sun as he hurtled past him, and the shrill horn cut through Niklas Kalf. They had no option but to drive on. To the place where this road ended, after crossing the whole of America, to bump into the ocean at some point or other. He remembered the dream he had had, with the palm trees and the plane and that city plunging like a wave into the sea.

'Let's go,' he said, when he stood next to Imogen again, who had been waiting for him.

'And where do you want to go now?'

'To LA. Where else?'

'You're a weird guy,' she said slowly.

'What do you mean by that?'

The wind still blew those thin strands of hair across

her eyes, and she carefully brushed them out of her face again.

'I'll put it this way,' said Imogen quietly, and the wind swallowed her voice almost entirely. 'You don't belong here, somehow, do you?'

CHAPTER EIGHTEEN

Standard

Another perfect day. The sky so deep that he had the feeling it was pulsating over him, when he sank back into the low upholstery and stared upwards. The sun was still circling the roof terrace of the Standard Downtown and shining on the surrounding skyscrapers. Niklas would have liked another iced tea, and as he looked round for a waiter it struck him that he was almost the only guest present. The staff at the bar, all wearing red shirts and sports pants, were chatting under the video wall, which was showing a baseball game. The music was as loud as ever, but clearly they'd programmed ambient music for the afternoon, which vanished in the void above his head. He hated this hotel. And that was the first thing he said to Imogen when she was back from shopping and suddenly stood in front of him, over her left forearm the fluffy coloured cords of several gleaming, unwieldy varnished paper bags.

'I hate this hotel! I hate it. I hate it.'

Imogen didn't ask why, just nodded and went to the room to unpack her shopping. He stayed on the roof terrace and finally ordered his iced tea. Shortly afterwards the sun disappeared behind the skyscrapers, and gas flames were lit on the propane heaters that stood at regular distances in the middle of the grey upholstery landscape on the red carpet floor. They had been here for almost a week. He rang Elsa Meerkaz every day and left messages in which he urgently requested a conversation. Either she wasn't at home, or she kept putting him off.

She would call. Nice that he was in town, soon they would be able to meet up. No, today wasn't good.

Once he also phoned Lavinia, who sounded very surprised that he should get in touch. He told her nothing of all that had happened in Marfa, and stayed silent about the fact that they were now in Los Angeles.

Was there any news of Liz?

No, no new pictures, no message, nothing at all.

Hesitantly he asked if she'd told Snowe he was in Marfa. She vehemently denied mentioning it to anyone, but he didn't know whether he should believe her.

'Where are you now?' she asked.

'I can't tell you that.'

'And what are you going to do?'

'I don't know.'

'Anyway, be careful,' she replied, disappointed, and he said how glad he had been to talk to her again.

Imogen had explained to him that the Standard was the most desirable hotel in the city. A red sofa snaked in endless twists and turns across the reflective black marble. A DJ had his desk in the middle of the big room through which machine-like beats crashed incessantly. 'The little goggle-eyed lights are by Verner Panton,' said Imogen. The seats were by Pierre Paulin.

'Aha.'

'Flower Pods. That's what the lamps are called.'

The twelve-storey building, with all its marble and

aluminium, had been built as the headquarters of the Superior Oil Company in the early fifties, right in the banking and business district of Los Angeles. One relic of that time, apart from the narrow 'S' on the door handles, is an old electric clock next to the lift shafts, whose green-backed folding panels show the time not only in Los Angeles, but also in Denver, Houston, Chicago, New York, Caracas, Rio de Janeiro, London, Teheran, Calcutta, Hong Kong, Tokyo, Sydney and Honolulu. In the minibar there is vitamin-enriched water and face cream made of cactus fruits. He hated the hotel from the first moment.

A plane settled into a long orbit and showed its belly. It vanished slowly behind the black AON skyscraper and it was a long time before it reappeared. Sunset started very quickly. In the upper storeys of the skyscrapers there were rows of windows whose lights suggested they might be apartments. Was it candlelight you could see from down here, or just the flickering of light in atmospheric diffusion? He imagined apartments in the skyscrapers, each as big as a house, with stairs and vaulted cellars, terraces and halls and narrow corridors for the staff. Box rooms everywhere, and framed photographs, and discreet little bathrooms behind forgotten bedrooms, in one of which someone with black hair on the back of his hand holds his neck under cold running water for a very long time. Silence by a window on the thirty-eighth floor. Not even pigeons on the windowsill. And all of time's leftovers, the dark wood and the old linen, the silver-framed photographs and the yellow roses. He saw a hand reaching for an old-fashioned telephone whose speaker and receiver hung like two fat and faded wads of flowers. A face studying itself in the mirror. A vow, a letter, a child, and troubled sleep. Someone clears their throat.

This was where Los Angeles was founded. Kalf had climbed Flower Street to Bunker Hill, still covered with Victorian villas until the late forties, and back down Bunker Hill Steps to the Central Library, from the twenties, and on to the Biltimore Hotel, where the Oscar award ceremony used to be held, and which J.F. Kennedy made his election headquarters. In the 50s these old Victorian villas were demolished. The old families of the city, the Otises and the Gettys and the Hammers, made good money from the sale, but at the same time they ripped out the heart of LA. Instead the Business District was built, a skyline of banks and office skyscrapers, like a jewel in a setting of three eight-lane freeways, because the automobile meant you could finally leave the old centre of power.

Sunset and Hollywood Boulevards and Wilshire and Pico and Melrose Avenues are the trails of that flight, and Kalf had followed them. He particularly liked Sunset Boulevard, which pushes its way in a soft series of meanders from the sea past Santa Monica and into the city, repeatedly touching the canyons that open up to the sea. Past the Getty Center and through the house-high hedges of Bel Air, past the UCLA campus and down to Beverly Hills. Hollywood begins where it crosses Fairfax Avenue, and at the point where the hill gets going it is one of the most beautiful streets in the world. It is euphorically overlaid by billboards with house-sized faces from the television, then it glides past Chateau Marmont and into Hollywood, eking out such emotion as it has to offer, the desiccated glamour of old motels with their neon signs, the eternal regular haunts of the stars, Il Sole, Spago, and white Bentleys. And on the horizon, Downtown gleams behind a wall of dust and smog like the city in the clouds.

While sunset waits above the sea at the end of Sunset Boulevard, Mulholland Drive leads into the night in a completely different way. Kalf had repeatedly driven along the countless twists of that line with which the city borders death. LA is an island on land, and Mulholland Drive runs along its coast, but no one here looks out across the desert sea. All the villas that cling to the steep, eroding slopes with stilts and concrete plinths stare at the city lights as though enthralled. Behind them lies darkness, and where the irrigation ends, life ends.

The kingdom of the coyotes is not of this world, and the weirdest sound that Kalf had ever heard in this city was their howling at dawn, before it was drowned by the perpetually swelling sound of cars. Once on Mulholland Drive he had come upon a whole pack of coyotes, suddenly standing in his headlights, their eyes flashing stones. Kalf stopped, turned out the light and let them pass. Between two villas they switched direction down into the city.

He couldn't get their eyes out of his mind as he watched the blue glitter of the pools, with their underwater lighting, reflected in the metal panels of the bar, and the Saturday evening party slowly got under way. The waiters in their red sporty outfits had gone; the night shift wore latex costumes that were supposed to look like the uniforms of the Highway Patrol. The illuminated windows of the surrounding skyscrapers flickered in their mirrored shades. The zips at the bottoms of their bodices.

A fantasy emerging from the obsequiousness of the staff, the waitress's smile suddenly a fixed mask of unattainability. He closed his eyes and wished more than anything never to have to open them again, so that they could finally stop recording things, so that the film of observations might snap, that film that failed to show the only person who mattered.

Sometimes he thought about how he would explain to someone what he had done after Liz's disappearance. He couldn't understand why he hadn't found the situation unbearable. But he was sure that he was engaged in a kind of hunt, and he had to stay cold-hearted. And sometimes he even believed he would only get Liz back when he forgot her completely. He wiped his eyes with his hand.

The lift spewed out guests as if they had suddenly been conjured up out of nowhere. Beneath a purple neon light, two gorillas, one in shaggy brown fur, one in black, checked the blue wristlets required for entrance. Most of the people pushing their way to the front were Asian, many with their hair dyed blond, more men than women, hardly any male Latinos. A man with a blue spangled cowboy hat, whose partner, a tall, dark-skinned beauty, wore gloves the same colour. A black man with a shining bald head, a delicate blonde pressed up against him, barely reaching his armpit. Since they had been in LA he kept wondering what would happen if Venus Smith suddenly appeared here. He was scared that she might, but at the same time it was the only thing he was waiting for. He had just realized that he was slowly getting drunk when Imogen came out of the lift.

She held out her right wrist, the one wearing the

bracelet, to the gorilla, but didn't look at him, instead spotting Kalf and waving like a schoolgirl with a little gesture of her left hand. She wore a black tube dress and white snake-leather boots, which he didn't see until she was standing in front of him. The dress revealed her thin, moon-pale shoulders.

She said something that he didn't catch, because a helicopter was coming in to land on a nearby skyscraper. All that could be seen at first were three navigation lights approaching as the aircraft descended, but now the hard, dry cackle of the rotor blades cut through the musical backdrop, and the black shadow came down towards them with a deafening noise. Shortly before it touched down, it shivered on the spot for a while, as if taking measurements of some kind.

Imogen sank into the white sofa next to Kalf. For a while they sat in silence watching the hustle and bustle around them, but at some point he leaned over to her and said very loudly, close to her ear, that he wanted to know what it had been like in jail. She laughed as if she had been expecting that question. She had, she told him, often had visits there from people who wanted to write up her life story. Wasn't it weird always being preoccupied with strange lives?

'No,' he said, shifting close to her. 'In Marfa I sometimes thought I could start a new life. And that's what my work's like, too. You put on a stranger's life. A lovely feeling. That's the biographer's quirk. He escapes into strange lives.'

'But why?'

'I never wanted to write a novel. People always think

I'm a writer, but that's not true. I don't want to make anything up. I want to know what we're made of.'

Imogen didn't seem to understand what he meant. One of the waitresses bent down to them, smiling broadly behind her mirrored shades. Kalf ordered wine for them both.

'And what are we made of?'

He shook his head and didn't reply. Liz's hand in front of her belly. The empty bed. The coyotes' eyes. Kalf held his breath and let them pass.

'I don't know,' he murmured.

At that moment the waitress arrived with fresh glasses, red napkins and a new bowl of nuts.

They drank and watched the other guests, and at some point they went over to the pool. There was no one in the water, but in the cabanas round about, the bright red gleaming cubicles, people were whispering and laughing, and just as Niklas Kalf lost himself in the sight of the glittering reflection of the water, a wave lapped up, a small, trembling wave that stopped right where they were standing. He followed it back to its source, and saw something that he couldn't at first believe. At the other end of the illuminated basin a very fat, bald-headed man was squatting on one of the white recliners, feeding imaginary ducks from a big silver bowl of scraps of bread.

'That's Marlon Brando!' said Niklas Kalf tonelessly.

'Yes,' said Imogen.

Brando was wearing a white towelling bathrobe that fell open over his chest, and elegant Turkish slippers in fine dark grey leather that contrasted strongly with his white calves. With the silver bowl in his arm he stared after the bits of bread, which he was scattering in the water like a sower. But when they were standing right in front of him, he looked up and grinned at Imogen. She bent down, and he kissed her on the cheeks, let the silver bowl clatter onto the floor beside the recliner and put both hands on her bare shoulders. Kalf saw his soft breasts falling from the opening of the bathrobe, saw the thin white hair on his chest and his small, hard nipples.

'This is Nick,' said Imogen. 'A German writer.'

'Biographer,' he said, realizing how drunk he was.

Brando nodded and silently held his hand out to him, his grip powerless and indifferent. His feet in their oriental slippers were far apart. Kalf couldn't help thinking about Pinky, and felt ill. They sat down, and he watched as the pieces of bread which, like a family of ducks, a herd, a swarm, a school, he couldn't find the right word, slowly scattered across the pool.

The thought of Liz sobered him up for a moment, but her image was too faint to occupy his mind for long. He struggled to calculate which month of her pregnancy she was in now, but couldn't come to a certain conclusion. Instead he registered with panic that he was feeling more and more ill. Why didn't he say anything? He had to say something. He urgently wished Brando would run his huge hand over his head, as he had done in *Apocalypse Now*. But he didn't.

'I don't feel well,' groaned Niklas Kalf and hurried to the toilet.

That night Imogen jerked him off. At first he resisted, because he was actually far too drunk, but then he let her open his trousers and masturbate him. When he came, she placed her hand over his glans in such a way that it caught all the sperm, and with the other pulled a Kleenex from the box on the bedside table and wiped herself clean. Then she took out a cigarette.

'You're very deft!' he murmured.

'You learn a few things like that in jail,' she said, the cigarette in her mouth, and switched on a smile.

Everything blurred in vague, ice-cold dreams, above which Imogen's face hung like a moon cold as a light-emitting diode.

CHAPTER NINETEEN

The wind from the Pacific

Two palm treetops, warm light slowly dripping from them. Coming into view, a plane that had crossed the sky behind him, heading between the palms towards the city that ebbed away down below in the bay as if it were itself nothing but a wave of houses. Los Angeles, he thought, and thought of Barcelona, the Roman ruins under the cobblestones and all the detritus of the ages.

The side rudders of the big passenger plane were gold in the evening sunlight. On either side of the wings the pin-bright navigation lights flashed. He watched the plane descend over the city, and it occurred to him that he had seen it all before in a dream. In that dream the sky had been a very bright blue, and there was something transparent about that blue right up in the dome, where the universe weighed particularly heavily on the firmament. Like the white of an eye. Everyone enters America first in his dreams, Niklas Kalf thought.

He was waiting on the terrace of Elsa Meerkaz's house, looking down into the bay. Below him in the hills gleamed individual white villas, Sunset Boulevard snaking between them, and beyond the tip of the mountain the expanse of Venice Beach could be seen. From up here the roaring waves were only white strips that painted regular patterns. High sails filled the bay. He knew; this was the end of the journey. This was the point where the past flowed into the present. He had no expectations now. Relentless the endless breath of the waves as they roll in and break, then surge up the beach in all their white spray. They seem to stop, as though breathing in, before dragging the sand back with them in a greedy movement, while the next wave falls on the beach to tear at it with a loud, high hiss, incessantly grinding away at the coast.

The garden clings to the slope, on the left a little fountain in a low basin, a huge pine right at the cliff edge of the plot, where the lawn ends in a gravelled rim behind low, scrubby box trees. The trunk looms far out beyond it, must surely be more than three feet in diameter and divides six feet above the ground into two massive branches whose growth and deformation make it look like a primeval lizard, a two-armed colossus, high as a house. One of the two branches has grown almost vertically down, as though to balance the other, main branch that reaches out far above the abyss.

As Kalf studied the tree, he discovered against the grey of the bark a bird of a similar grey, which plummeted just at that moment and with a few quick wingbeats flew past the terrace to land in a giant eucalyptus. With one last, resolute beat of its wings the narrow grey bird vanished from Kalf's field of vision, while only a cackling sound could be heard from the pine tree. Kalf spotted the nest, and then saw the bird as it flew back and, as if it was the easiest thing in the world, caught in its claws one of the yellow hummingbirds that whirred in the blossoming bushes. And now he spotted the little piles of yellow feathers, as if they'd been swept together, on the unbelievably lush lawn, trimmed twice a week, he was sure, by Mexican boys.

The drive from Downtown to Pacific Palisades leads via the 110 South and the Interstate 10 West and then to the Pacific Coast Highway, which runs between the sea and a steep length of coast, a sandy, muddy wall whose deep washed-out cavities are overgrown with scrub. Above and between them little white wooden houses with panoramic windows and, right by the sea, tall, narrow beach villas, almost windowless on the side facing the highway.

Kalf had come at the agreed time to the address that Elsa Meerkaz had given him, 520 Paseo Miramar. A winding road high above the sea, all the houses hidden behind head-high hedges and walls. An old woman came to the cast-iron gate, and at her first word he recognized her as the Austrian housekeeper he had spoken to so often on the phone. Carefully, slowly, she walked in front of him down a narrow flight of steps to a little patio. From there they passed through a heavy wooden door into the house and out through a sitting room to the broad terrace. As he waited, he wondered what it meant that he had already seen this garden in a dream.

'It was supposed to be three, I think,' said a cool voice behind him, and Elsa Meerkaz, whom he looked round in surprise to see, added with a smile, 'the young falcons, I mean.'

Niklas Kalf nodded. He hesitantly gave a little bow when she gripped his right hand with her own warm, dry hand. Even if he didn't admit to himself that he hoped that this conversation, for which he had waited so long, would solve everything and Liz would soon be free again, his heart still thumped when she looked at him now for the first time. She had pulled back her grey hair with a tortoiseshell comb, from whose nacreous shimmer the afternoon light seemed to drop. And a white veil lay over her pupils like the light lipstick around the outline of her mouth. They both looked down at the sea, and her smile was expectant.

'Are they really falcons?'

'Certainly. I love watching them.' She looked at him almost confidentially.

Kalf nodded. The afternoon heat lay over the sea like a heavy perfume.

'A wonderful view,' he said. 'Almost like the Mediter-ranean.'

'Somebody who came here once said: It's a little bit like your house in Sanary. And it's true, the sunset really is like the ones in France in those days.'

'Did you like it there?'

'It was like an island. It took us half an hour on foot to get to the village.'

'But you had a car?'

'Of course. I had a little car, a Renault, which was I don't know how old. It was one of the first cars ever built, I think, and it was in terrible shape. Oh, yes, it occurs to me: I must tell you the story of the shooting stars.'

Niklas Kalf said nothing.

'Once I wanted to drive some friends back to Sanary after a dinner, and just as we'd got into the car we saw countless shooting stars. It rained meteors. It was a beautiful, clear night, full of stars, and the meteors rained down. I still remember, it was November 1933. It never happened before, such a rain, such a shower of meteorites. Big meteors. They didn't hit us, because they were consumed before they reached the earth, but it was all around.'

'They landed near you?'

'No, I told you, they didn't, because they *verglühten*, they were burned up. It happens very rarely that meteorites actually reach the earth. It was more like fireworks, you know. We'd never seen anything like it. I parked the car, and we got out, and someone said, "Let's go down to the beach!" Down there we weren't disturbed by the lights of the houses. I quickly ran back up to the house to fetch Eugen, and the two of us went down the hill, down the very steep road. And when we had reached our friends, the car suddenly set off.'

'I don't understand.'

'It just moved. It rolled directly towards the three men. So I jumped on the running board and turned the steering wheel to the other side. But one of the wheels caught in a rut, the Renault flipped over and rolled over me. I touched myself: I didn't feel anything at all, it seemed good. But suddenly there was blood everywhere. My hand was full of blood. In the hospital they discovered my wrist was broken into twelve pieces.'

They went on standing on the terrace, looking out at the sea. And when Kalf didn't reply, she led him down into the garden. A table with four wicker chairs was set there, a jug of lemonade and two glasses stood ready, and a plastic napkin dispenser. Elsa Meerkaz laid a white paper napkin next to his glass and poured lemonade into both glasses. She sat with her back to the sea. A hummingbird settled behind her on the top stem of a bush that whipped bright green in the wind. Niklas Kalf cleared his throat and took a sip. So here they were at last. He felt his rage at this woman.

'One question.' His heart pounded. 'Why did you betray me?'

She gave a thin smile. 'Betray you?'

'Of course. Or what should we call informing Venus Smith of my whereabouts?'

'That's not true. I don't know anyone called Venus Smith.'

'But you do know Phil Gallagher.'

'Yes. A film producer who's interested in your book.'

'Nonsense. What he's interested in is your husband's secrets.'

'I don't know what secrets those might be.'

Kalf shook his head. 'Someone tried to kill me in Marfa. My wife's been kidnapped. I've had evidence that she's being maltreated. Be honest with me at last!'

'I'm really very sorry about all that, Herr Kalf, but I have no idea what it could possibly have to do with me.'

'I can tell you. I've told you on the phone that I met someone in Marfa whose father you will remember. A German soldier who came to Los Angeles after his release from a prisoner-of-war camp: Hans Holdt.'

'What did you say the man's name was? Holdt?'

'Hans Holdt, yes.'

'No,' she replied, 'I don't know that name.'

Elsa Meerkaz poured him another glass of lemonade. He watched her and said nothing. The lemonade was very sour and cold.

'And Parsons?'

'What about Parsons?' Her voice now had an irritated undertone.

'Did you know him well?'

'John Parsons? Not at all!'

'But he worked for Theodore von Kármán, like your husband. I haven't found anything about him in the documents you sent me.'

'Exactly. We had no contact with Parsons whatsoever. Listen: Parsons was considered a bit strange. When my husband got his job in 1941, Parsons was working on a rocket project that von Kármán was in charge of, sure, but Parsons actually did what he felt like. And he was little more than a student, at least ten years younger than my husband. Where the JPL stands today, the Jet Propulsion Laboratory, there was nothing but desert in those days. It was there, at Devil's Gate, that Parsons carried out his rocket experiments.'

'And you never met him? You were living in Pasadena too, at the time.'

'No, never. Parsons was a loner.'

'Hans Holdt mentions occult practices in connection with his name.'

'I don't know anything about that,' said Elsa Meerkaz and smiled at Kalf. 'There were always rumours, though.'

'What kind of rumours?'

'Oh, summoning the devil, things like that. After the war people were very susceptible to that kind of thing. Just think of the anti-Communist witch hunt.'

'But your husband never mentioned anything like that?'

'Never!'

'So how come he died in John Parsons's house?'

The silence in which Elsa Meerkaz studied him for a long time and without any noticeable emotion immediately gaped wide open. It didn't look as if she was thinking, or as if she was surprised at his remark. Her expression was merely dark and empty. Kalf heard the cries of the falcons. It grew cooler, and he noticed that the sun was slowly disappearing. In his dream, he now remembered, it had gone down. He took another drink of lemonade and set the empty glass down carefully.

'How did you end up with this house?' he asked calmly.

A smile darted across her face. 'When we came to LA someone told us that just about every house in these hills was for sale. And in those days there were hardly more than a dozen houses. That was during the war. People who had their business downtown didn't have enough gasoline.'

Did she mean petrol was rationed?

Yes. Her husband had never had any problems with that, because his job was important to the war effort.

'It was built for Clara Bow, the famous actress. I was told she found an old castle in Spain, near Seville, and she didn't just find the castle, she also found the blueprints. And she built the house here exactly according to the blueprints.'

'Did you never actually want to go back to Germany?'

She dabbed the corners of her mouth with her napkin.

'I know people who even tried not to fly over Germany when they went to Austria. And I've known people who had to go to Germany for some kind of business, and never spent the night there. They stayed in Switzerland. And there are people who stopped speaking German. They forgot their German almost.'

'Did that happen to many?'

'No. Very few.'

He saw her seeming to collapse into the wicker chair, behind her the silent hummingbirds and behind them the sea. The two old ladies after the reading in New York came back into his mind. That was on the twelfth of September.

'Have you ever been to the canyons?' Elsa Meerkaz asked suddenly, pulling him from his thoughts. 'For example, if you continue down this road, at some point the villas end. Do you know what comes next?'

'No idea.'

'Nothing. The water supply ends at the fence of the properties. A metre away from the lush lawn that the automatic watering system sprays every evening at seven o'clock precisely, there's nothing but red dust.'

He nodded.

'You know,' she went on, 'everything here is a little paranoid. Everyone's copying something. Now it's Tudor, now it's an English cottage, now the Southern states, now a Mexican pueblo. But all these dreams are directed entirely inwards, because you can't trust anything outside. Armed response. In the event of danger the call goes straight through to the security company.'

'And?'

'Fear. There's fear everywhere.'

'*Waiting for doomsday conscious unconscious*,' quoted Kalf.

'What's that?'

'A poem:

Die Bäume verneigen sich
Vor dem Wind vom Pazifik der Bescheid weiß
Über die Dauer der Millionenstadt
Waiting for doomsday conscious unconscious
Of its fate rising from past and Asia.'*******

'That's lovely. Who's it by?'

'Heiner Müller.'

'Don't know him.'

He nodded. 'Where's Liz?'

'I don't know. I really don't know.'

Every day on Ocean Boulevard in Santa Monica the moment comes when the joggers, whose eyes were gazing into the void a moment before, slow to a standstill and glance up. And the tramps who have been camped there all day in large groups, tirelessly moving their possessions from one bag to another, all pause. Some of them struggle to their feet and walk over to the makeshift balustrade along the cliff-lined coast that slides year after year into the sea. The couple in flip-flops stop, and the redhead with the pinched mouth and the pensioner with the brightly coloured shirt and the gay couple. Below them the broad sandy beach, deserted now and a dusty brown barely distinguishable from the grey-painted lifeguards' huts that line the whole bay at regular intervals to Malibu.

At around this time people sit in traffic jams on the Pacific Coast Highway, drivers stare out of their SUVs across at the sea and their eyes are lost, like everyone else's eyes, in the place where the sky flashes red each evening.

At that same moment Niklas Kalf, too, wound his window down and smelled the salt. Very slowly the shock of having learned nothing was easing. All hopes of Hans Holdt being the key to that secret in the life of Eugen Meerkaz that he still didn't know, had been quite in vain. In vain he had spent weeks waiting for that conversation. No idea what he was supposed to do now. His memory of Liz was assuming a hopelessness that was starting to smell stale. Far out on the sea he saw the black shadow of a tanker on its way southward. The sky behind it shimmered in shades of red that slowly melted along the horizon.

That glow that made the joggers pause, and for which many people were said to come from the city to the beach to see and be reflected in it, lasts only a few minutes. And as Niklas Kalf wondered what to do now, the sky grew dark and dull, and everyone hurried on their way to escape the night that can be nowhere as cold and bleak as it is out there on the western horizon, once the light is gone.

CHAPTER TWENTY

Bad man from Bodie

It was nine in the evening, and the car park in front of the Standard was almost empty, but the music pumped up from the bar as it did every day. In the skyscraper opposite, an uplighter in every room and reflections of scattered light from the other office buildings in the floor-to-ceiling glass panes. Office cupboards and desks, house plants and blurrily shimmering green EXIT signs. The yellow-lit junction of Hope Street and 7th Avenue deserted but for one black SUV whose rear lights cast red trails on the wet road. Kalf looked up to one of the skyscrapers above the top floor of which, on a wide concrete frieze, ONE WILSHIRE shone in white lights. The start of Wilshire Boulevard.

Imogen had already been lying for an hour in the huge bathtub that stood open in the room. The walls of the hotel room light grey, the carpet dark grey, the heavy curtain over the strip of window that ran the whole width of the room, the same glowing orange as the upholstery of the couch. When Niklas Kalf walked over to Imogen she slipped so deeply into the white foam that her shoulders disappeared.

'What did he say?' he asked and sat down on the edge of the tub.

'I've told you three times.'

'Tell me again.'

Imogen groaned and dipped under the water. A lapping, white field. Air bubbled up, then her head reappeared. She wiped the foam from her face and lay on her side.

'He said he was Phil Gallagher, and it was about your wife.'

'And?'

'As regards the current situation no one has anything. That's why he wanted to talk to you.'

He nodded. 'But how does he know we're here?'

'No idea,' said Imogen, stroking the foam from one of her legs, which she stretched out of the water and studied closely. 'Perhaps from Elsa Meerkaz.'

'Yes. But she doesn't know we're staying here.'

'No idea,' she said again.

He felt himself starting to mistrust her. He was frightened that Venus Smith had found them here, because he couldn't understand how she could have done. There was something wrong about this appointment. But the thought that everything would soon be over was so enticing. That was the only reason he had come to Los Angeles. But he knew he had nothing to offer Gallagher. He got to his feet. Anything could happen.

'I think the car might be there already,' he said, not looking at her. 'See you later!'

'See you later.' He heard her voice and felt her eyes on his back as he closed the door behind him.

Outside the hotel he looked for a moment longer at the illuminated sign on the roof of the neighbouring skyscraper: ONE WILSHIRE. Phil Gallagher's address was 5608 Briarcliff Road. Imogen had told him that was in North Hollywood. Quite a good address, she had said.

The black limousine that was supposed to pick him up was waiting in the hotel car park. It was a Lincoln Towncar, one of those big hire cars that he had seen time and again in the city, with the characteristic sequence of numbers in white foil letters on the bumper. Smiling, the Japanese chauffeur opened the rear door to him, but just as Kalf was about to get in, he suddenly felt a dull blow and then a piercing pain in the back of his head, his hands were pulled back, cold metal closed around his wrists and he was pushed into the soft leather of the car seat. He didn't manage to defend himself, and even if the blow hadn't almost knocked him out, he wouldn't have done so. He felt a kind of consent, even to the pain.

The car set off, the lights of the night passed grey and matt through the tinted windows, Kalf lost consciousness and didn't come to until they stopped. He had no idea how much time had passed. The handcuffs cut firmly into his flesh. He managed to struggle upright, and in the car headlights he saw a white obelisk, perhaps twelve or thirteen feet tall, with Japanese characters. Where the wind had blown aside the snow, Kalf could see graves. They were decorated with shells and coins, toy figures and little American flags made of plastic foil, sweets wrapped in brightly coloured paper and carefully stacked pyramids of little stones, the head of a doll, a wreath made of white paper swans and countless origami figures threaded into garlands.

The whole setting reminded him of the prisoner-of-war camp in Marfa, and now he could also see lines in the night-time scrub, in which one might have imagined huts. Particularly under the thin snow there was something of an abstract pattern about the geometrical layout, a blueprint; the plan of the camp was the very thing that had been preserved here in the desert. A playing field where all the dead who doubtless belonged here could have been revived to go on playing.

Behind the obelisk a mountain range rose in the moonlight, its summits pointing into the night. The Japanese man bowed. When he came back to the car, taking great strides and holding the collar of his uniform jacket closed over his chest, Kalf fell back exhausted into the upholstery and lapsed into unconsciousness again.

He didn't wake up until the vibration of the engine died away. The driver's door was opened and slammed shut again. Through the windscreen of the Lincoln Kalf saw the Japanese man stamping through the snow until he reached a figure on horseback. It was morning. The rider was wearing a white Stetson and a red and blue checked jacket with a lambswool collar. He said something, and the Japanese man waded back through the snow to the car. His breath hung like a little cloud over his head. The car door was wrenched open and Kalf pulled outside. The steel bands cut painfully into his swollen wrists each time he moved. How cold it is, Kalf found himself thinking as he made an effort to pull himself upright. The glare stung his eyes. The rider pranced quickly over, and the horse trod snow. The man had a rifle at an angle on the saddle in front of him.

'Mr Kalf! Pleased to meet you after all this time. I'm Phil Gallagher.'

Niklas Kalf blinked up at the man, who showed no

signs of dismounting. He curiously studied the producer's fleshy face under its wide-brimmed hat. Small eyes and soft, droopy cheeks. A mouth that reminded him of the pointed beak of an octopus.

'I'm sorry you had to take this long journey, I wanted you to come out here. You see: this is the real America. I'm here almost all the time. My farm is just beyond that hill there.'

'Where is Liz?'

Phil Gallagher laughed. 'First things first.'

Kalf nodded. 'I need to pee.'

Gallagher gave a sign to the driver, who took a key from the breast pocket of his uniform and lifted Kalf's arms, reviving the stinging pain. Then the steel clasps were removed, and Kalf carefully brought his painful wrists in front of him.

'But hurry,' said Gallagher, resting the Winchester on his left forearm. He was wearing thin leather gloves.

Kalf registered that the Japanese man kept the engine running so the heating would work. The Lincoln puttered away quietly to itself in neutral. Niklas Kalf turned round and walked a few paces away. The wind blew dry snow which lay on the sharp edge of the boot ledge, forming a tiny dune from which something was constantly trickling down in the lee of the wind.

He stopped and tried with numb fingers to open his trousers and pee. On the opposite side of the valley, which now lay in morning sun, he could make out a few huts, piles of rubbish, rusted machine parts in the snow. He identified a flywheel that must have been six feet in diameter, several big gear wheels, connecting rods and something that looked like the remains of a kiln. Between the knee-high bushes a path ran down to what must once have been a city.

'You know *Giant*?' Gallagher called over to him.

Why *Giant*, of all things? What made him think of that film?

'Great, isn't it? I wish I'd made that movie! The landscape in Texas is truly unbelievable. I was told you were down there for a while?'

Kalf turned round and nodded as he stamped back.

'I really wish I'd known that before, Kalf. You've certainly tried my patience.'

The producer laughed. The horse tossed its head and pranced on the spot with surprise for a moment. Gallagher leaned low over the pommel to Niklas Kalf.

'Southern California "is today, as England was two centuries ago, the westernmost outpost of Nordic civilization".' You know who said that?'

Of course he knew the quotation. But he shook his head.

'Robert A. Millikan,' said Gallagher, '1923. *The California Institute of Technology: Its Directions, Aims, Accomplishments, Needs and Financial Condition*. Why did you refuse to work with Venus?'

'I haven't the faintest idea what you want from me.'

'I don't believe you. And you know what? Your stupid game of hide-and-seek has cost us a lot of time. If you'd cooperated straight away, your wife would have been free long ago, and you'd both be at home right now.'

'So tell me, at long last, what's this all about?'

Gallagher shook his head as if he was very disappointed by this answer.

'OK, then,' he said quietly. 'When was the explosion in John Parsons's house?'

'June, 1952.'

'And do you know what Parsons was doing that day?'

'I assume he was experimenting with rocket fuel.'

'And apart from that?'

'That's all I know. It's in the Caltech publications.'

Gallagher laughed. 'Sadly only half the truth. Of course it was about fuel. More precisely: a revolutionary rocket fuel. But it was also about an occult ritual.'

'I don't know anything about that.'

'I know that you do.'

'Rubbish.'

'Of course you do. There must be some documentation of the experiments that were carried out at the time. And Eugen Meerkaz kept those documents. You know what OTO is?'

'No.'

'I don't believe a word.'

Gallagher looked attentively at Kalf. 'In 1939 John Parsons, the co-founder of the Jet Propulsion Laboratory, was made chairman of the American section of the Ordo Templi Orientis, which had fallen under the spell of Crowley a considerable time before.'

'Aleister Crowley?'

Gallagher ignored the question.

'By day Parsons worked for Theodore von Kármán, carrying out research into rocket fuel on the Caltech test site at Devil's Gate. By night he organized rituals along the guidelines that Crowley issued from London. Incantations, chanting, that kind of thing. Black masses. And Meerkaz was there.'

'So?'

'Meerkaz was a reasonable man. I don't believe he had anything to do with that esoteric stuff. He was interested in something quite different.'

Phil Gallagher leaned forward, one forearm across the pommel, the rifle barrel resting on it, aiming dangerously, and waited.

'Cold?' he asked finally when Kalf remained silent.

'Yes.' Kalf clasped his arms around his torso. 'What's happening to Liz?'

'That's entirely up to you.'

'I don't know anything.'

'Asshole.'

'I don't know anything.'

The producer looked around as if awaiting agreement from somewhere. But there was no one there. Just this valley with its empty hills, dully, monotonously covered with snow. 'Do you know where we are, by the way?'

'No.'

'This is Bodie. Bodie was a gold-rush town, and the mine back there was one of the most productive in the whole of California.' Gallagher pointed to a collection of wooden cabins and an old shaft tower.

Kalf had heard of ghost towns, most of them old gold-mining settlements that had grown into big towns over just a few years and had mostly been abandoned when the mines were exhausted. He saw Phil Gallagher moving the rifle's safety catch.

'There was so much crime here that everyone in the West knew the bad man from Bodie.'

The producer paused, as if he was just saying all this to give Niklas Kalf one last chance to tell him what he knew. As if he was waiting for the crucial word. And now, as he eyed Kalf contemptuously, his patience seemed finally to run out.

'You stupid asshole!' he murmured to himself at last. And casually he fired.

Only when Niklas Kalf was already falling did he hear the incredibly loud shot that stung his ears, and only when he was already lying in the snow feeling with both hands for the intense pain in his left thigh did he scream. Then he heard a second shot, which only missed him because Gallagher's horse shied at that moment, and reared up whinnying. The producer had trouble reining it in: he cursed and shouted at the Japanese man to see to the German. Then he pulled the horse round, and Kalf, who was writhing with pain, caught another furious glance from Gallagher before he rode away. As soon as he was part-way up the hill, Kalf struggled to his feet and ran off.

He knew he had no time left. Heard behind him the Japanese man, who clearly hadn't expected the wounded man to have the strength to run away. But at first the wound barely hurt at all, he was just scared by the blood that was steadily pulsing out above the back of his knee and soaking his trouser leg. As long as Gallagher didn't turn round and come after him! He had reached the first cabin, and was out of sight.

He looked with surprise down a wide road with log cabins on either side, and hobbled over as fast as he could to a church, the Gothic wooden portal five steps up, to hide there. Now the pain was digging through his leg for the first time, and it took him all his self-control not to cry out. He saw with horror the bloody tracks that his flight had left in the snow. The church door was open, but a chicken-wire fence closed off the space. PRAISE WAITETH FOR THEE, O GOD, IN ZION in gold letters behind the altar. A small organ beside the altar and a stove, a stack of hymn books next to it, dust everywhere. All he could smell was dust, and in the air he shivered.

The cold crept up his leg until he simply couldn't walk any further. Instead he studied the old pews. He would have liked to hear the preacher's voice and from outside all the noises of the real town when the hills here were scattered with mines and shafts, countless heaps of earth as the tunnels were dug, wooden towers and sheds, roughly cobbled huts and shelters, stove fires and scrawny donkeys, braying and yelled at, beaten and spurred, pulling iron tubs out of the mine into daylight on ropes thick as your arm.

Niklas Kalf couldn't have told whether moments or minutes passed before he finally shook away his thoughts and hobbled back down the five steps. There was the shop, its panes almost opaque, and the dress on the tailor's dummy a greenish grey. In the hotel opposite, the big billiard table with the lion's-claw feet, the cue stand, the mirror behind it. Kalf had to catch his breath again in front of the school. Toys and schoolbooks behind the windowpanes, a microscope on a windowsill and a globe that was now nothing but a wooden sphere, its paper skin having vanished long ago. A faded American flag with the wrong number of stars. A pumpkin shrunk to the size of a fist with wide-set eyes and a toothless mouth. Kalf heard footsteps and just managed to duck into a side street when the Japanese man appeared on Main Street with a pistol in his hand.

He hurried to get up to the slope behind the town, where Bodie's cemetery had once been, to seek shelter among the gravestones. He knew that if the Japanese man spotted him halfway he would make an excellent target. But he had to stop breathlessly by an enclosure around a grave, sun-weathered bars, white and gnawed away by the wind. What had once been fenced in here was long gone now. He saw the Japanese man appearing behind the last house in the town, quickly hobbled a little further and dropped with a groan behind a gravestone. Behind a low embankment that hid him from the town, he found the Lincoln. The Japanese man was searching the area, and it was a moment before Kalf worked out that the leafless bushes hid his trail.

If he stretched out his left leg it didn't hurt so much. He wasn't sure he would have the strength to get through the snow to the car, and above all to be quicker than the Japanese man, who would inevitably spot him if he came out from behind the stone.

MARY

WIFE OF

B. BUTLER

DIED NOV. 14 1878:

AGED 30 Y'RS 8 MO'S 8 DS.

He was touched that none of her days had been forgotten. He was cold, and it was getting colder and colder. The marble was still just as white as it might have been in 1878, but sand and rain had weathered it. There was a verse under the name.

THUS STAR BY STAR DECLINED,

TILL ALL ARE PASSED AWAY,

AS MORNING HIGH AND HIGHER SHINES,

TO PURE AND PERFECT DAY.

For a moment Niklas Kalf watched the crows circling with heavy wingbeats over the valley, then he pulled himself up and limped off. He didn't look round. But almost immediately he heard the Japanese man's voice behind him. The powdery snow sprayed beneath his hobbling feet when the first shot rang out, echoing from the surrounding hills. And he was over the embankment and out of range at first, but soon the Japanese man would be up the slope. With the last strength in his body, Kalf reached the car and pulled open the driver's door. A second shot ricocheted off one of the nearby rocks. The sudden warmth in the car, its engine still running, almost took his breath away. In the same movement with which he shifted the gear stick to 'D', he threw the door shut and put his foot down.

The Japanese man appeared in the corner of his eye, very close now to the slope near the car park, while the tyres of the Lincoln spun, but then the snow chains had eaten their way through the thin snow and the gravel flew up behind the car. Kalf swung the wheel round, and the Lincoln lurched towards the exit. The Japanese man, clutching the pistol in both hands, aimed at the tyres, but when the shot whipped through the valley Kalf was already at the first bend and concealed by the high, snow-covered hills.

The road, which swept widely downhill, was covered in deep snow, but it had plainly been ploughed not long before. The edge where the ploughshare had carved its track through the snow was sharp, the snow on either side of the road a good three feet high. Kalf had no idea where he was, but after about ten miles the unsurfaced road led to a highway.

With a great effort he removed the snow chains and sank breathlessly, teeth clenched, back into the driver's seat. He carefully opened his trousers and pulled them down to his knees. The entry wound was quite a way up his left thigh, a reddened, frayed hole in which the blood sat glistening and, like a fountain, spilled repeatedly over the edges. The bullet must have come back out on the other side of his leg, because he felt a much more intense pain there, and it was from there that most of the blood was pouring onto the leather of the driver's seat. Kalf took off his shirt and his T-shirt, which he tore into several strips that he pressed firmly onto the wound. The pain paralysed him for a moment, and he groaned loudly, then pulled his trousers up carefully over the provisional bandage.

He decided to head down the road, which soon led past a lake, from whose milky water there jutted unreal rock formations which he knew from travel guides: Mono Lake. The towns of Lee Vining, Crestview, Tom's Place, Bishop. On the left the mountains loomed high. Los Angeles started appearing on the road signs. For hours he drove through desert until he passed by that white obelisk again and the remains of barracks, camp roads and barbed wire where they had stopped during the night. His leg was less painful when he kept it still.

Mojave Junction. An enormous parking place for aeroplanes whose silver bodies gleamed in the desert like landed scaly fish, with covered cockpits and yellow protective casings over their turbine mouths. Fuel tanks, a railway line, billboards at the side of the road, another hour to L.A. Wooden pylons with whirring wires.

ROSAMOND	6 miles
LANCASTER	17 miles
L.A.	88 miles

Edwards Airforce base and the NASA Flying Research Center. The freeway pulled wide apart, a strip a good thirty feet wide between the lanes, with grey bushes, the asphalt cracked and repaired with strips of tar. Those strange desert trees with one trunk divided into two, three branches, a wreath of green leaves on the top. Sequoia? Palmdale. The Mojave Desert Information Center.

Suddenly the exits from Avenue A to Avenue R, an alphabetic countdown to the city whose true boundary no one knows. The Aqua Dulce Canyon Road. Mountains of rubble, trailer parks, farms with white fences and green, irrigated land. Rock formations like piled-up ice floes, pushed high and frozen. Soft hills that look like a folded woollen plaid blanket. Oilfields with bobbing pump-rigs. Highway 5 to Los Angeles. Motorway bridges, solid-cast streams of traffic, the Pasadena Freeway 210 turn-off, the 405 turn-off, palms and eucalyptus trees on either side of the road. Antelope Valley. Niklas Kalf switches to 170 Hollywood Freeway South. The pain twitches through his leg every time he moves. Burbank airport. The 170 becomes the 101 South. Echo Park. Hollywood Bowl exit.

The Downtown skyscrapers appear on the horizon, it's half past three, and unbearable thirst sticks his tongue to his gums when he takes his foot off the accelerator and joins the afternoon traffic jam. He stops and shuts his eyes for a moment. What is he to do now?

CHAPTER TWENTY-ONE

Fever (Hollywood)

First Niklas Kalf drove back to the Standard. As blood welled from the wound each time he moved, they coolly told him at reception that Miss Engel had already checked out the previous day. No, no message. And no luggage. So she'd betrayed him. He wondered what he should do now, asked for a glass of water and took small sips from it. He mustn't leave a single clue. No one was ever going to betray him again. First things first, thought Niklas Kalf. First he needed bandages.

In a drugstore in Downtown he bought plasters, bandages and aspirin, in a shop next door a new pair of trousers. In the changing room he lifted the blood-drenched strips of fabric from the wound, which immediately started bleeding more heavily. Nonetheless he managed to apply a kind of pressure bandage to it, and pull the new trousers over the top. He looked for an ATM and withdrew as much as possible, bought something to eat and a bottle of mineral water and drove around without knowing exactly what he should do now.

Finally he left Downtown via Wilshire Boulevard, eventually reached Hollywood and started looking until he discovered a sign advertising furnished apartments. An unadorned, run-down apartment block. It was a quarter of an hour before someone came to show him the apartment, a room with a kitchenette and a tiny bathroom, sofa and folding bed on the first floor above a garage where he could hide the Lincoln. There were bedclothes and towels. The television worked, the phone didn't. He paid for the rest of the month and the next and pulled the door closed behind him. The bed smelled stale and it was cold in the apartment.

Even so, Niklas Kalf slept for twelve hours, and when he woke again he didn't have the strength to get up. Just lay there and recapitulated once again the evening two days ago, when Imogen had told him Gallagher wanted to speak to him. Gradually he ran through all his experiences, until finally he remembered Snowe's story. He recalled his suspicion before he left the hotel room, and the way Imogen had stood in front of him in the hut on the first of January. And Pinky's murder. How could he have believed he wasn't one of her victims? But could it really have been Gallagher who had sent her? He remembered that night on the roof of the Standard.

Over the next few days the pain eased when he didn't strain his left leg too much, but with every careless movement the wound opened up again. Even so, he managed to go shopping. But he spent most of his time in bed. He heard cockroaches behind the kitchenette. He changed the bandage several times a day, and at some point it stopped bleeding. He watched the play of shadows from the dirty palm trees on the wall behind his bed and in the afternoon slept an uneasy sleep full of dreams that he couldn't remember afterwards. Towards evening he usually hobbled to a Chinese takeaway in Franklin Avenue and ate fried noodles.

On the way there he discovered an Internet cafe where he stopped because his leg was throbbing too hard. He slumped onto a bar stool in the window at one of the screens, although the messages from an alien world had nothing at all to do with his life. Semen banks had offered soldiers who were being sent to the Gulf region free storage of their sperm for a year: a service as a sign of patriotism. He tried to ignore the loud music. Glass phials had been washed ashore on the Dorset coast. They contained anthrax vaccines. Possibly they were from a British ship on the way to the Gulf to protect the UN inspectors and the Western troops in Iraq, who were looking for biological weapons there. Kalf wearily clicked the browser window closed and hobbled to the counter, paid for his time online and two mango lassis and headed back.

The Pakistani behind the till was the only person who looked him in the eyes. The people on the street, who came towards him or walked past him because he was so slow and had to take lots of breaks, gave him as wide a berth as possible and didn't even look away, just through him. He stopped when he noticed that he was starting to shake with weakness, and when he had finally managed the two blocks up the hill and across Franklin Avenue, sweat was pouring into his shirt.

From his apartment, 2037 Grace Avenue, you looked down on Hollywood, all the old hotels, the dustily tousled palm trees and the fallow land in between that is sold by day as a car park to the tourists, ten minutes for two dollars. Nothing to see but tattoo parlours and cheap boutiques for latex and leather. The evening sky was almost always that expectantly glowing desert orange that he knew so well from Marfa, and which he remembered every evening with the same feeling of longing.

At some point at the end of January he read a two-page list of signatures in the *New York Times* under the heading NOT IN OUR NAME, and spent an hour studying the list of names, some of which he knew, Laurie Anderson, John Ashbery, Judith Butler, Brian Eno. Then when he changed the bandage he had to admit that his injury wasn't healing as he had hoped. Presumably an internal inflammation had developed, because the scabbed wound was swollen, the edges were red and tense, and the scab itself was seeping.

The attempt to buy iodine ointment from the pharmacist cost him an unexpected effort, every step hurt more than ever before, and he felt himself getting weaker and weaker. It took him twice as long as usual to cover the two blocks, and he nearly had to leave the two bags of groceries behind. He'd bought far too much for fear that he might not be able to leave the apartment again. He looked into the sky, wiped his sweaty forehead and took another few steps. At home he crept shivering into bed and slept a deep and dreamless sleep. It wasn't until he woke again in the middle of the night that he had the strength to apply the ointment and then cover the wound only with a loose gauze bandage.

The cockroaches usually disappeared as soon as he got up and turned on the light above the kitchenette. Then they quickly darted behind the sink and the cooker. They were only reluctant to abandon the bin, even if he took out the rubbish. But they didn't, as he had established with relief, come anywhere near the folding bed. Their armour would have made no sound on the soft carpet, but he never discovered a single specimen on the floor or the sofa table or between the sheets. At first he hadn't been able to identify the sounds they made, and the clicking of their chitin on the metal of the sink and the rustling from the trash had only been the background noises to his pain, but since he had found out what they were those sounds had acquired a special power over him when he lay awake at night, and now that fever was setting in, their volume increased as his sense of time fell into abeyance.

The pain always kept him just above the line of sleep. His eyelids trembled, and he listened to the metal hiss behind the cooker and the fridge. Waited to see what the pain would do and felt the fever spreading inside him. Shivers alternated with outbreaks of sweating, his leg throbbed with pain that was getting worse and worse, whether he put weight on it or not. He slept badly, his sleep disturbed and shallow, and he felt as if an even, soft whirr was quietly and constantly tugging at him all night and finally pulling him slowly out of his sleep. How hot his face felt! He pushed aside the thin, narrow duvet in its threadbare cover.

When he woke late in the morning there was a light rain, and the wound pulsed painfully. An old newspaper lay next to the sofa. Pale in the grey light the quivering, almost searching trail of the exploding spaceship. SHUTTLE BREAKS UP, 7 DEAD. He remembered how lasciviously the boy had lain across the world, a shadow, on their flight to New York. The shaved nape, the tanned skin. He wished the war would finally begin. Colin Powell presenting evidence from the Secret Service to the UN Security Council, supposed to confirm the production of weapons of mass destruction in Iraq. An address by Bush in front of the White House. Times Square in the rain. Passers-by with hoods. Police with machine guns. THE NATION ON HIGH ALERT. An aerial shot of Mecca in a live report on CNN. Kalf followed the immeasurable mass of white-clad pilgrims in their swaying, halting, staggering motion in a circle.

He was no longer sure whether the gloom meant that night was coming or day. When he took off the bandage to apply fresh ointment, he was afraid of the pain, which had sharply increased, and tried to feel the exit point. He could clearly feel it swelling more and more under the scab, the skin tense and palpitating painfully.

When he could no longer bear not knowing what the wound looked like, he removed the bathroom mirror above the washbasin with the help of a steak knife, and set it next to the sofa in such a way that he could get a glimpse of the back of his thigh. He was horrified by the red, inflamed, severely swollen wound. He went uneasily to sleep in front of the television and woke up shivering again in the night. He hadn't been hungry for days. The pain made him sink deeper and deeper into a special kind of freedom that very slowly released him from the world like a ship leaving the jetty. Under the cotton-wool darkness of sleep and fever a gleaming cold shell grew, so that at some point it was too late to call a doctor, regardless of what happened next. He was as lonely as anyone could be, lonelier than he could have imagined in Marfa, but the pain was his home, and there were moments when he enjoyed the way the poisonously throbbing wound assumed control.

And sometimes in that state of shivery half-wakefulness he allowed himself to think again of Liz, and of their child. At some point now it would be born. Would have been born. Always that hammering headache. He took three aspirin and tried to sleep. Heard in his dream the rain-drenched, slow ticking of drops that fell into the plastic tube of an infusion, into the completely clear water surface of a medicine that quivered with each new drop like a vibrating guitar string. The liquid ran slowly, very slowly through the tube and the hypodermic on the back of the hand and into the veins that zigzagged along beneath the dark skin, bluish and swollen as a river in the rainy season. The drops of antidote were the only sound in the dark room.

He knew it was Liz who lay there. Bent over her and slowly moved the arm with the infusion, laid it carefully around her shoulders, reached beneath her back with one arm, the other under her knees, and lifted her out of the hospital bed into a wheelchair. The smell of vanilla enveloped him. With some difficulty he pulled the drip stands over and, in the semi-darkness of the room, whose size he couldn't gauge, checked that the medication was still flowing. Slightly adjusted the syringe in her hand, and for a moment the pain twitched around her lips. She had to get out of here. He was looking for her shoes, but then he woke up. The pulsing pain in his left thigh moved along his hips and into his abdomen. How can I explain to her what's happened? Where I've been all this time?

One morning, when the throbbing in his leg started to move to his groin, he struggled to his feet in spite of the pain and hobbled, on a long-handled brush that he found in the bath, and whose bristles he wedged under his armpit, the two blocks to Hollywood Boulevard to buy an antibiotic, although they wouldn't let him have one without a prescription. He felt ill as he tried to persuade the salesgirl, but she just shook her head and looked at him as if he was a tramp. He had trouble staying on his feet. He had thrown up several times in the past few days. Couldn't remember when he'd last had something to eat.

On the way home he bought chocolate, pear juice and ready meals for the microwave. People avoided him in the street. His whole leg throbbed ready to burst, and when he came home he could no longer lie on his back because the wound was so swollen. Sunday 16 February *New York Times*. Pictures of the global anti-war demonstration. FROM NEW YORK TO MELBOURNE, CRIES FOR PEACE. Idiots, he thought, and dozed off again.

At some point the abscess opened all by itself. After he had eaten too much chocolate and then taken some aspirin he had to throw up again, and when he knelt by the toilet bowl and made one of those careless movements he'd been trying so hard to avoid, he felt the wound bursting open. He immediately had a terrible stench in his nose, stronger than the sour smell of vomit, a mouldy sweetness, but associated with a feeling of relief as the palpitating pressure on the spot subsided.

He felt with horror that the scab had come away from the wound canal, taking a great bung with it, and carefully inserted his fingertips into the crater, which was no longer painful and bleeding as the fresh wound had been, but numb, strangely hardened tissue. A round, swollen opening, from which flowed something damp and sticky. He looked at the pus on his fingers, yellow and creamy, and the nauseatingly sweet smell took his breath away. He struggled up, tore open the window and immediately washed his hand. Then he dabbed at the wound with a fresh towel until nothing was seeping out.

Now the pain quickly eased. That same night he was able to lie on his back again and wasn't kept awake by his throbbing leg. Instead he sank into an even sleep from which he awoke the following morning, he was relieved to notice, with less of a fever. The swelling around the rim of the wound subsided, both at the entry hole, where the reddening around the scab disappeared, and at the place where the abscess had opened. Kalf rinsed the open wound with clear water several times a day, then applied iodine ointment. The discharge gradually became lighter and thinner. Soon he felt strong enough to get up and take a few steps. The vertigo eased. He realized with surprise that it was already late February.

That meant the agent would soon be coming by for the rent, so he needed money. Kalf also noticed that he was hungry. But before he risked going out he mounted the mirror above the washbasin in the bathroom again, and looked at himself for the first time in weeks. Of course he had registered in the corner of his eye that by now he had a dirty-blond beard that almost completely hid his lips, but he was still surprised at how sunken he was, how scrawny, his eyes bloodshot and dull. His hand trembled when he tried to straighten his hair and wipe the dandruff from his stained shirt. It was the same shirt that he'd been wearing the evening he said goodbye to Imogen. He calculated. Six weeks had passed since then. His top shirt button was missing, both sleeves were torn. Bloodstains everywhere, and traces of vomit. He saw the dried blood and the pus on his trousers. He had clearly wet himself, too, although he couldn't remember that. So first he decided to clear up, took out the trash and washed shirt, trousers and underwear in the washbasin, dried the things over the arms of both chairs, and only then did he dare to venture outside.

And when he had actually reached Hollywood Boulevard without fainting, and without his wounds opening up again, Kalf rewarded himself with a mango lassi in the Internet cafe he had last visited weeks before. The Pakistani behind the bar served him as indifferently as ever, but even he, Kalf thought, showed repugnance at his dilapidated condition.

Niklas Kalf was glad that the agent didn't ask how long he planned on staying. He wouldn't have had a reply. When that became clear to him, he lost the sense of lightness he had felt since the fever subsided. He sat helplessly on the sofa and looked at what he still owned, the wallet, the passport and his mobile phone, which he hesitantly switched on. The battery was almost empty, and his phone book had disappeared along with everything else. He scrolled through the list of calls. Lavinia Sims was the last person he had spoken to. Without thinking he pressed redial. She answered immediately.

'Lavinia?'

'Niklas?'

'Yes,' he said and didn't know how to go on. Too much had happened and everything he was supposed to do was past. He had done none of the things he had hoped to achieve in New York. Liz had probably, because he had proved useless to his blackmailers, lost her life long ago.

It was a long time before Lavinia answered the question that he finally asked.

'No, I didn't give you away.'

'And Snowe?'

'I didn't tell Snowe where you were. You've got to believe me. Do you hear me?'

'Yes,' said Kalf, then the battery was empty and the connection broke off.

He looked at the palms whose shadowy outlines wiped the wall behind his sofa. Fetched a newspaper, beer and fried noodles from the Chinese. DISARMING IS NOT ENOUGH. A picture of the shuttle crew a few minutes before the explosion. At an electronic-junk dealer's on Highland Avenue he found a suitable charger. His posture was more bent than before. His skin was dark. He might not even have recognized himself, he thought as he unpacked his shopping. Then he plugged in the charger, and an hour later the phone rang. As if they'd been waiting until he could be contacted again.

'Yes.'

'Niklas?'

He had to think for a second before he knew whose voice it was. 'Hi, Asia. How are you?'

'Can I drop by? I've got something for you.'

He was surprised by Asia's question, but his heart beat quicker at the thought of seeing her again.

'Now?' she asked. 'You're in LA, aren't you?'

'Yes. But how did you know?'

'I hoped you were. I've just got here.'

Half an hour later the doorbell rang.

She hugged him at the door before he could say a single word, and he let her hold him tight for a long time, even though his leg still hurt when he stood up. He felt how much he had missed her and how much he longed to go back to Marfa with her. She brushed the hair from her face and sat down on the sofa, from which he had removed the bedclothes, throwing them beside it in a bundle. She set a shoebox on the table and looked at him for a long time with her light blue, transparent eyes.

'You're not looking good,' she said at some point and smiled as if she was the one who had to apologize.

'Frank,' he began and cleared his throat.

'It's OK.'

'I'm very sorry.'

'It's OK.'

'I didn't know what would happen.'

'I know.'

He lost himself in the lightness of her eyes as she stroked his hair. 'I couldn't reach you,' she said quietly.

'I know,' he said.

'But there's something I absolutely had to give you.'

Asia pulled the box towards her. Looked at it once more as if wondering whether Kalf was ready for what she planned to show him.

'I found this in Frank's belongings.'

'What is it?'

She shook her head and pushed the box over to him. 'Take a look. I think it would have been better if Frank had given it to you straight away.'

Niklas Kalf saw how eagerly she was waiting for an explanation. She wanted to know at long last why he had come to Marfa and why her boyfriend had had to die. And why Kalf had then disappeared. He couldn't help thinking of the camper van again and how they'd made love and the clattering horse at the window and Marfa's endless sky and those lights the night of their first kiss. She went on waiting for him to start speaking, but he said nothing.

'Then I'll go now,' she said at last, and he nodded.

He supported himself against the door frame so that the pain in his leg eased slightly. 'Nice of you to come.'

'Yes,' she said and didn't ask what his plans were now. Or whether they would see each other again. She leaned forward instead and kissed Kalf on the cheek. And he took her by the waist, drew her to him and smelled her again, felt again her firm body and the breathing in it and how everything moved under her thin skin.

CHAPTER TWENTY-TWO

Müssen wir tüchtig sein

The music sounded like an organ, but in amongst it he heard drums and bells, a deep roar and then again something penetrating and shrill like an ensemble of piccolos. It had taken him more than an hour to get to Pacific Palisades after Asia had gone, and the journey had taken more out of him than he had expected. He felt weakness everywhere in his body again, and in passing he looked at his face in a little gold-framed mirror that hung over a little Empire table in the corridor. His cheeks seemed even more hollow than before under his straggly beard, his shirt still had stains that had resisted washing, and his limp was more pronounced again. The housekeeper who had opened the door to him waited by a small flight of steps. He walked past her into the sitting room.

Heavy, richly carved and painted ceiling beams spanned the long, hall-like room which opened on one side with three arched windows to the terrace and the sea. On the opposite side was a massive fireplace. Carpets on the gleaming, dark red terracotta, armchairs, a sofa, a low table. The fire wasn't lit. The organ crescendo, accentuated by the drums and bells, was clearly coming from this room, although there seemed to be no one in it. Suddenly the noise broke off.

'Mr Kalf!'

He turned round and saw in a small room beside the stairs Elsa Meerkaz, who swung round on a piano stool, behind her an organ with registers and pedals, a confusion of control cables and bellows and sound holes in the wall that connected the little chamber with the sitting room.

'A cinema organ,' Elsa Meerkaz explained and rose with difficulty. 'I think I told you the house was built for Clara Bow, the silent-movie star.'

'Yes.'

Elsa Meerkaz sat down on the sofa and Kalf in the armchair opposite her. He was glad he didn't have to stand any longer. He wearily put the box on the table.

'How are you? Quite honestly, you look a bit the worse for wear. Much worse than on your last visit.'

'I know,' he said.

A moment before he hadn't known how he would meet her. Did he hate her for what she had done to Liz and to him? Did he still hope she would help him? He ran his hand over the box, which not only contained the precise record of the experiment in which Meerkaz and Parsons had lost their lives, but also speeches, essays, letters from and to Eugen Meerkaz, Parsons, Aleister Crowley and Cameron, Parsons's wife. But above all plans and detailed calculations, formulae and diagrams.

He took off the lid and pushed the box a little further over the table towards Elsa Meerkaz, who looked at him suspiciously.

'That's what Phil Gallagher's looking for.'

She nodded gravely, and silently began to spread the

various documents out on the narrow table. The letters, lab books, Gestetnered memoranda, whose greenish type was already very faded. Sketches for experimental structures, a few postcards, handwritten poems which, as Niklas Kalf knew, were by John Parsons. She flicked through them, set some aside, bent low over the pages.

Niklas Kalf gave her time. But at last he said, 'Tell me, finally, what happened. So that I can save my wife.'

Elsa Meerkaz looked up.

'Gallagher came to me, again and again, urging me to let him have certain materials. But I didn't have what he was looking for.'

'But you were afraid it might exist?'

'Eugen had left some hints. I could imagine what Gallagher wanted.'

'And you didn't want your husband's memory to be sullied.'

Elsa Meerkaz nodded and smoothed her white hair with the palm of her hand. Her mouth was grim, as if the memory hurt. He understood: she had known what it was all about, but found nothing in Eugen Meerkaz's personal effects. Clearly Parsons had placed greater trust in the other German he knew, Hans Holdt.

'Hence me.'

'Yes. Your book would confirm that there was nothing to discover. That Eugen wasn't involved in these rituals.' She looked at him, embarrassed, and added, 'I knew you had no idea.'

He nodded. He had long since given up worrying what she thought about him.

'But why did Gallagher not blackmail you?'

'Of course he did!' Elsa Meerkaz gave a thin smile. 'He's insane. That was what first gave me the idea of commissioning you to do this book.'

'I don't understand.'

'I simply told him you had all the material. I told him it had all been in Germany for ages.'

Elsa Meerkaz hesitated for a moment before she went on. 'In the end, I hoped, your ignorance would prove there was no secret that I could have revealed to him.'

'You mean if Liz had died because I didn't know anything, your husband would have been left whiter than white, and Gallagher would have left you in peace.'

She nodded.

'And that was why Imogen gave me a way to Gallagher.'

She nodded again.

He thought for a moment. 'And what about Albert Snowe? What did he have to do with this whole affair?'

'Snowe? Nothing at all.'

She shook her head disparagingly. 'Snowe guessed there was something in Eugen Meerkaz's life that might be interesting to him. So I promised him your book if he'd look after you in New York.'

'You mean he was to make sure that I didn't go to the police?'

'Yes. When he told me that Phil had kidnapped Liz, I begged him to keep you from going back to Germany. Where the police would certainly have sent you. You were to stay in the United States.'

'As bait.'

'As bait. Of course.'

Elsa Meerkaz looked at him motionlessly. He remembered his conversation with Snowe in the Goethe House and how the publisher had begged him not to involve the police. He had a trustworthy informer. Niklas Kalf shook his head angrily.

'And then? Where did Imogen come in?'

'Snowe sent Imogen off to protect you when Gallagher found out where you were.'

'So you didn't tell Gallagher?'

'No, of course not.'

He was surprised. He remembered Lavinia assuring him of her loyalty in her last phone call. 'Lavinia Sims?'

'Yes. But unfortunately we noticed too late.'

'I don't understand. It couldn't have mattered less to you whether Gallagher caught me.'

'Of course. But it did matter to Snowe. He still thought you were going to disclose Eugen Meerkaz's secret.'

'And he thought Imogen would do whatever he liked.'

'Yes.'

'But that wasn't true.'

'No, it wasn't.'

Niklas Kalf just looked at Elsa Meerkaz for a moment. Then he said, 'Tell me where Liz is.'

She shook her head. 'I think your wife has been dead for a long time.'

That sentence struck him like a blow. The wound was throbbing worse than it had for ages. Elsa Meerkaz had suddenly managed to touch that one spot where his whole person had healed over the past few weeks, and it almost seemed as if the pain was tearing him in two again. *Inner and outer world* ran through his head. How he hated this woman.

'No,' he said then.

'Don't be stupid.'

Her voice sounded compassionate. 'Since it's been clear to Gallagher that you don't know anything, Liz is just a potential witness, and therefore a danger.'

Kalf slowly shook his head. 'No,' he said again.

Elsa Meerkaz studied him expressionlessly. He would have to be strong now. It was too late.

'You have to show me now,' she said, without taking her eyes off him, 'what you're made of.'

What we're made of. The phrase resonated inside Niklas Kalf and held him prisoner: *What we're made of.* He remembered. That, he had said to Imogen, was what interested him about people. But did he know what he was made of? Had he not, since he had been in this country, lost everything he thought he consisted of? All of his certainty and, if Elsa Meerkaz was right, all of his future, too. Without Liz, what was left of him? What was he made of? He stared at Elsa Meerkaz until he suddenly thought of an encounter he had forgotten a long time ago.

'In the early nineties, shortly after the opening of the borders, I went to Auschwitz for the first time.'

Elsa Meerkaz didn't take her eyes off him. Her expression was abrasive and cold.

'And?'

'I talked to a salesgirl in a little kiosk at the entrance to the museum complex. In German. She said she thought it was funny that the younger visitors always spoke English. The kiosk was stocked with all the current brands: Pepsi, Marlboro, Magnum, BonAqua.

'Through the window you could see the gate with the

cast-iron inscription in that strange arch. The black and white posts, the tower and the double row of barbed wire. How small the gate is, I thought. The wood of the barrier burned in the heat. On the high-voltage warning signs the painted, almost entirely faded death's heads. The lustre of the porcelain isolators. And suddenly that curiously tender desire to extend a hand. The salesgirl smiled at me and said she could always tell the Germans. And how funny she found it that they always spoke English. She said "funny". I bought a bag of Fisherman's Friend.'

'What does that mean? What sort of story's that?'

He didn't know. He tried to find words.

'If they're too strong, you're too weak.'

Why did he tell her that? Niklas Kalf didn't know. But he suddenly felt an unexpected sense of peace. Because now that all the things that had constituted his life were gone, all that remained was Liz. There was no room for doubt. Perhaps I really do understand what I'm made of, he thought, and cleared his throat.

'I come from a Europe that's in the process of forgetting itself.' He tried to explain what he meant. 'How they built chapels on the arches of the Roman roads when the cobbles had sunk into the mud. How people simply forgot that the same language had once been spoken in England and Sicily. And how that forgetfulness had broken Europe, was still breaking it today. It's crazy: just as its unity is being evoked, it's collapsing. The botanical gardens of the universities are being abandoned, newspapers are firing their correspondents.'

'What do you mean? What are you getting at?'

He didn't answer her question, asking instead, 'Didn't you have problems associating with a former German soldier?'

'Hans Holdt? Not at all. War sometimes gets the best out of men. It gives them access to their spirituality.'

'What do you mean?'

'Hans taught us all a lot. In Africa he'd come into contact with ancient wisdom that was very valuable to Parsons and all of us.'

'You were there!'

Suddenly he understood everything. He could hardly believe it himself, and said it again. 'You were there, back then.'

Elsa Meerkaz remained expressionless.

'It was a Monday,' she began. 'Parsons had invited us to his house in Pasadena.'

'But the explosion happened on 17th June 1952, and that was a Tuesday.'

'Certainly,' she said quietly and looked at her hands. 'But the ritual began on Monday night.'

'What ritual?'

'That has nothing to do with you. What you need to know is that it lasted until the following morning.'

'There are letters from Aleister Crowley to Parsons in those papers. Did you know Crowley, too?'

'Not personally.'

'But they celebrated rituals from his secret lodge.'

'I said I wouldn't tell you anything about that. Anyway, I wonder why I'm telling you all that so willingly. Just this: we went to bed fairly exhausted when our task was done.'

'Who's we?'

'Cameron, that was Parsons's wife, and me. Hans and Pinky.'

'Pinky?'

'Yes. He was part of our circle.'

'And that's why you had him killed.'

'Phil Gallagher was on his trail,' she said apologetically.

'And apart from that?'

'We slept the whole next day.'

'And your husband?'

'The men went to the laboratory at some point.'

'Did that often happen?'

'Yes. At any rate Pinky brought us breakfast in bed in the afternoon. And then the explosion happened.'

Niklas Kalf took an old newspaper clipping out of the box. 'That was at eight minutes past five. The explosion could be heard a mile away in Pasadena. The lower storey of the house on South Orange Grove Avenue, it says here, was completely destroyed, the doors torn from their hinges, two walls collapsed, there was a hole in the ceiling, and the windows were shattered in the house next door.'

'Yes. It was indescribable. The three of us were incredibly lucky.'

'Parsons, it says here, was still alive. The ambulance took him to Huntingdon Memorial Hospital. That was where he died.'

'He looked terrible.'

'And Eugen?'

Elsa Meerkaz looked at him, and for one brief moment a smile of reminiscence darted across the old woman's frozen face. 'He didn't suffer. He was already dead when I got to him.'

Now, he knew, was the moment for the crucial question. And again he asked, 'Where is Liz?'

There was a long pause before she replied, her voice as toneless and indifferent as if in her thoughts she was still lost in the events of the past.

'I don't know where Liz is.'

'But you told Gallagher where he could find me.'

She gave a faint nod.

'Then help me now. You owe me that. Where is he hiding Liz?'

Elsa Meerkaz stood up and walked through the room as though weighing up what she should do. She stopped in the middle of the carpet, turned round to him and said, 'The LA Theater. I don't know what Gallagher does there, but he bought it a year ago, and there have been rumours since then.'

'Rumours?'

'Yes, rumours. I can't say more than that.'

'And what is the LA Theater?'

'An old cinema. When Eugen and I arrived here, that was where all the great films were shown. Then at some point it was closed, like all the cinemas in Downtown.'

Niklas Kalf started putting the papers back in the box. Elsa Meerkaz watched him.

'Don't bring him the material,' she said imploringly. 'Who knows what he'll do with it. There's no point letting him have it, you won't save your wife now. I'm sure Liz died long ago.'

'No.'

He was in a hurry now, and it didn't occur to him that Elsa Meerkaz might want to keep him from going. He quickly put the lid on the cardboard box. He felt himself getting dizzy when he got to his feet. Took a deep breath and saw outside, beyond the wide-open doors to the terrace, the sea.

He remembered the dream in which he had looked down into that bay and felt he was at his journey's destination. For the first time in ages he seemed to be getting closer to Liz. Now I know what we're made of, he thought, and was about to turn away from the section of sky when Imogen came in. Slowly and without looking at him she stepped out of the afternoon sun, one hand in her almost white jeans. She made no move to greet him. Only when she slumped onto the sofa did she look at him blankly.

He sat back down and avoided her gaze.

'How was Pinky involved?' he asked Elsa Meerkaz instead.

The widow nodded.

'I managed to persuade Imogen to cooperate with me rather than with Albert Snowe.' She smiled at the girl who sat expressionlessly on the sofa. 'The young lady had started to find Snowe a little tiresome.'

'What has that got to do with Pinky?'

'After Gallagher found out where you were hiding, there was the danger that he would find Pinky, too. Particularly after I'd allowed myself to be carried away and mentioned his name to you.'

'And?'

'It was a matter of damage limitation. Instead of going straight to you, as Al Snowe had wanted, Imogen took a little detour to visit Pinky first. And she actually managed to get to him before Venus Smith did.' Elsa Meerkaz snapped off the light in her face. 'Sadly not in your case, Mr Kalf.'

'Are you saying Imogen murdered Pinky?'

Her lip curled. He had known it for a long time. But the thought still made him shudder, and he had to struggle to stay calm. And only now did he doubt whether he would simply be allowed to take away all those documents, given that Elsa Meerkaz had gone so far as to have someone murdered for them. But he was far too tired to feel afraid. He looked at Imogen, and now the girl returned his glance, making him shiver. He didn't even care about his own anxiety.

'Why did you just leave the hotel?'

'You were supposed to have been killed by now,' she said calmly.

The widow watched attentively for his reaction. Of course, thought Kalf. After his visit here Elsa Meerkaz had betrayed him to Gallagher. And Imogen had seen to it that his suspicions weren't aroused. He picked up the blue book that lay on the table next to his cardboard box, which he'd been looking at all along without being aware of it, a blue cloth edition. And now, too, he also understood the German words that he had been reading for so long, without really reading them. GOETHE'S FAUST, GESAMTAUSGABE. He flicked the slim volume open at random, and the thin pages fell silently apart, as lascivious as an almost faded blossom. ENGEL CHOR, he read, out loud,

> 'Was euch nicht angehört
> Müsset ihr meiden,
> Was euch das Innre stört
> Dürft ihr nicht leiden.
> Dringt es gewaltig ein
> Müssen wir tüchtig sein.'*********

Niklas Kalf paused and looked up to Imogen, who now wasn't taking her eyes off him. She didn't understand a word, she protested. What was it supposed to mean? He couldn't help smiling at her indignation. How strange those German words sounded, particularly where they rhymed. How strange, he thought, that he had happened on that precise passage, the choir of angels, and slowly and emphatically he read out the last two lines:

> *'Liebe nur Liebende*
> *Führet herein.'**********

He had to look at her once more. He knew it would be the last time. Now he remembered how Albert Snowe had first mentioned her name, at that dinner in New York. Imogen Engel. The story of a murderess no one could understand. And how she had gone on to turn up in Marfa. An animal, not particularly alien, but alien as animals are. Niklas Kalf looked at her, and now he knew that he would never be able to see the lie in her eyes.

'Do you know the story of the *Angel of the Waters* in Central Park?' he asked, paying no further heed to Imogen. Elsa Meerkaz was still standing at the window. 'I mean the Bethesda Fountain?'

'I don't know. It's so long ago. What's it about?'

'You know, I think Liz is still alive. There's a passage in the Bible that says: *Wer mein Wort höret, der kommt nicht in das Gericht, sondern ist vom Tode zum Leben hindurch gedrungen.'***********

'I don't understand what you're getting at.'

'It was the name of a Biblical pond near Jerusalem: Bethesda. That's what the fountain in Central Park is called after, the one where they found the corpse of the man killed by this girl here.'

He smiled over at Imogen, who looked blankly at him.

'Bethesda. Sick people gathered by that pool, because every now and again an angel went down to the water. *Welcher nun der erste, nachdem das Wasser beweget war, hinein stieg, der ward gesund, mit welcherlei Seuche er behaftet war.*'************

'So?'

'One of the cripples had been waiting there for thirty-eight years. *Da Jesu denselbigen sahe liegen, und vernahm, dass er so lange gelegen war, spricht er zu ihm: "Willst du gesund werden?" Der Kranke antwortete ihm: "Herr, ich habe keinen Menschen, wenn das Wasser sich beweget, der mich in den Teich lasse, und wenn ich komme, so steiget ein anderer vor mir hinein. Jesu spricht zu ihm: "Stehe auf, nimm dein Bett und gehe hin!"'*************

Niklas Kalf stopped speaking. Everything seemed to be coming strangely together. What we're made of, he thought, is nothing but a breath. He set the blue book back down on the table, picked up the cardboard box and got up. Elsa Meerkaz looked at him quizzically, but he merely shook his head. Then, without a word of farewell, she went out onto the balcony and for a moment he watched her standing against the pulsating sea of lights in the bay, over which night was now falling.

By the time he reached the Lincoln, which he had parked under a tall eucalyptus tree, the sky was spilling out its most poisonous orange. The city gave off light as a jogger gives off heat in winter.

CHAPTER TWENTY-THREE

Devil's Gate

Between Flower and Hill Street, Downtown is still defined by the art deco office temples, which loom between car parks and the old clothes factories, mostly dark and uninhabited, but tiled in gleaming green or yellow, with recessed facades beneath a tower, often with an aerial tip of the kind familiar from old sci-fi movies. Wild crossovers of Stalinism and mission style, where the First and the Third World merge. Here, in its innermost core, LA reveals itself as a Mexican city, whose centre is Broadway. In the twenties most of the world's premiere cinemas were here. Only a few isolated examples remain, with neon signs that jut far into the street, the cinemas themselves converted into department stores thirty years ago. The whole street is now a cheap shopping area where large families stroll up and down stocking up on shoes and clothes, CD players and burritos in hand.

In the middle of this, between 6th and 7th Streets, is the LA Theatre, and since it was never converted, a black and white photograph still hangs behind the rusted snake fence of the portal, showing Charlie Chaplin with Einstein, both in tuxedos, coming out of the premiere of *City Lights*.

Niklas Kalf looked at the old picture. The fear that Liz might be long dead sent his heart pounding wildly. Nervously blinking, the neon signs of the department stores drew the eyes of the passers-by into their dark arcades. Cars bumper to bumper. Hawkers whose bootlace panels stood around them like angels' wings. In the cinema entrance hall it all seemed far away, although Kalf would have had to take only a step to be back in the middle of the hustle and bustle. He was scared by the idea of getting still further from the noisy presence out there on the street, but he had no choice. He tapped into his mobile phone the number that Elsa Meerkaz had given him.

Gallagher answered almost immediately. He was surprised when Kalf said his name and told him he was, so to speak, outside the door.

'What do you want?' Kalf thought about it.

He was there to give him, at long last, what he was looking for.

Kalf heard Gallagher breathing.

'I want my wife.'

A short time passed, then the wide front of the former cinema entrance, which was nailed together with wood, opened up. He saw not a glimmer of recognition in the Japanese man's face. The door fell shut again, and Kalf was standing in a vast hall, its size at first impossible to guess in the gloom. Walls with mirrors and gold rococo ornaments, on the red carpet individual groups of seats, heavy armchairs, delicate tables and standard lamps with pleated fabric shades. Glasses that looked as if they'd been drained decades ago. A chair pushed back with a gesture from another age. Niklas Kalf felt how weak and tired he was. His wound throbbed so violently that he wondered if it was about to burst.

'Come. Along here.'

The Japanese man was already waiting by a staircase that clearly led down to the basement of the building, and Kalf, when he followed him, managed only a glance into the auditorium.

The space, vaulted over with the gentle oscillation of the first balcony, rose up to house-height. In a perfect slope the stalls, torn out in places, fell gently towards the screen, which was flanked by columns and caryatids. Only a few rows of the very flat, wide seats remained complete. He thought of *Greed*, and Murnau's *Sunrise* with the studio landscape of lake and tree and reeds and the lights of the big wheel. *The Passion of Joan of Arc*, Asta Nielsen and Pola Negri's eyes. He had to overcome his reluctance to follow the Japanese man. In the mezzanine down the stairs there were no lights on the walls, the floor creaked, and the worn red carpet felt so frail beneath Kalf's feet that he was afraid he might go through it.

'Please come.'

Another floor down, his feet carefully feeling their way along the pale marble of the steps, which glowed fleshily in the darkness, and step by step the sense grew that he was not alone on these stairs. As if other steps were following him in the same rhythm. Laughter and whispers, pale and incorporeal susurrations as black and white as the films that had once been shown here, prisoners of screenings long extinguished, shadows without light and as dead as the faces from which they once were carved. But the closer he came to the last step of the stairs, which flowed with a solemn sweep onto the marble floor of an illuminated subterranean room, the more those other footsteps retreated, and the whispering fell silent.

The space looked as if it had once been a dining room, presumably the cinema restaurant. It was in the shape of an oval, with a matching milk-glass ceiling by which the room was lit. And although some of the panes were broken and you could see the lamps behind them, not many of which still worked, that down-lighting still blinded you to the fact that you were two storeys underground. All around in the head-high wooden panelling there were vitrines and swing doors; Kalf recognized pictograms for telephone and toilet in the crystal glass. The symmetrical rows of tables that had once filled the room had been broken up, crammed together in the middle, forming a big table for computers and plotters and models that made Kalf think of strangely shaped rockets. Extension cables snaked from the wall to the tables, supplying the electronic equipment and the big standard lamps with electricity.

Just as Niklas Kalf saw Gallagher's broad face again, and felt his little eyes observing him as he walked up to him, his exhaustion and dizziness vanished. He tried very hard not to limp and to hide that he was wounded. Strange to meet someone who wanted to kill you.

'That OK?' asked Gallagher, pointing to the leg.

'It's OK.' Kalf stopped by the table.

The producer nodded to the Japanese man, and Kalf listened to his footsteps on the stairs. I'm not a threat to him, thought Kalf.

'What have you got for me?'

'The material you're looking for. All about John Parsons's experiments.'

Gallagher's eyes flashed. 'Did you know they called a crater on the moon after him?'

'After Parsons?'

'Exactly. The guys at NASA probably got a guilty conscience at some point: anyway Parsons's Crater is 37 degrees north, 171 degrees west. And you know what that means?'

Kalf shook his head.

'The goddamned crater's on the dark side of the moon!'

Gallagher snorted. But as quickly as his own observation had filled him with mirth, another thought sobered him. 'OK then: let's see it!'

Niklas Kalf put the cardboard box on his side of the table and opened it. He took out a small, narrow envelope and fumbled a sheet of paper from it. Thin, almost transparent, with the writing in red ink. He read: '*We prepared ourselves magically for this communication and built a temple by the altar, with the analysis of the key word. Parsons was dressed in white, carrying the lamp, we in black, with hoods, chalice and dagger. At his suggestion we played Rachmaninov's "Island of the Dead" as background music. At about eight o'clock he started dictating; Meerkaz wrote down exactly what he heard, as he heard it.*'

Kalf handed Gallagher the letter across the table, and Gallagher looked at it carefully before putting it back in the envelope.

'That matches my information,' he said slyly. 'According to my research the Rachmaninov recording is the one made by the Philadelphia Orchestra in 1929. Sergei Rachmaninov himself conducting. A 78. It lasts exactly eighteen minutes.'

Niklas Kalf took out another letter.

'Here's a letter from Aleister Crowley to Parsons: *Start four hours before sunrise. A time in which all hostile influences are extinguished. Complete perfection. Wear black. Cut the red star from your breast. Renew the blood. Spread out a white cloth. Put the blood from the birth upon it, as SHE is born of your flesh and through your mortal power on earth. You should recognize through the sign: Babalon is born! That is rebirth, all things are changed, the signs, the symbols, everything! With the Muse's help you are to write a suitable invocation to Babalon, and this you are to consign to the flames now burning.*'

'You got this from Meerkaz, didn't you?' Gallagher asked excitedly. 'I was right.'

'No, you're wrong. It's not from Meerkaz.'

'Where, then?'

Instead of answering him, Kalf read him the text in which Parsons recorded the ceremony with which he joined Crowley's OTO sect: '*I, who in the outer world am called John Whiteside Parsons and in the inner Fra. 210, herewith in the presence of Fra. 132 deliver this oath of a Magister Templi, which is for me the oath of Antichrist. And I swear that my name is Bellarion Armilus Al-Dajall, Antichrist, come to fulfil the law of the Beast 666.*'

'Where did you get that?'

'*Dear Hans, the purpose of the invocation of Babalon was to externalize the Oedipus complex; at the same time, because of the forces involved, it produced extra-ordinary magical effects. However that may be, this operation is completed and concluded.'*

'Who's Hans?'

Niklas Kalf was no longer afraid. He ran his hand along the edge of the table as if he could already touch Liz. Nothing would happen to him now. Nothing would hurt him. The secret in every life changes the world. And the one who knows about it is in possession of a key.

'Hans Holdt,' he said.

Gallagher stared at him and seemed to think with great concentration.

'I should have worked that out,' he whispered then. 'That means Holdt survived.'

'Yes.'

'Did you know that Parsons's last words are supposed to have been: *I hadn't finished*?'

The producer thought. 'I find it strange that Holdt survived.'

'What do you mean?'

'No idea. We don't know exactly what it was that exploded.'

'Wasn't there an investigation?'

'Yes, of course. The 58th Army Explosive Ordnance Disposal Unit was even called in from Fort MacArthur to discover the source of the explosion.'

'And?'

'They found traces of mercury fulminate.'

'And that doesn't suit you?'

'No, in fact it does. That's how I got into all this in the first place.'

'I don't get it.'

'I'd been offered a screenplay about Parsons. A biopic with a lot of occultism and rocket research. And in the documentation I found that report from the *Los Angeles Times*. Parsons, it said, had been on the trail of a completely new explosive.'

'I can't believe you kidnapped my wife just because of an explosive.'

Kalf tried to stay calm. He thought of all the calculations, formulae, outline sketches of experimental arrangements that lay in the box. He might have solved the mystery more quickly if he'd known something about chemistry and maths.

'I assume this will help you,' he said, and pushed the box across the table.

Gallagher immediately started going through it. Kalf was repelled by the producer's greed. It was as if he was seeing for the first time why Liz had had to suffer.

'Parsons,' murmured Gallagher as he read, 'did quite astonishing work in the field of liquid rocket fuels. He was the first to work with nitric acid as an oxidizer.'

'Means nothing to me.'

'Later he hit on the idea of testing aniline. Red smoking nitric acid and aniline. Self-igniting. NASA were still using the mixture for the Titan rocket.'

He agitatedly pulled out a few documents and pushed them across the table. Kalf read United States Patent Office, patent number 2693077 and the heading REACTION MOTOR OPERABLE WITH LIQUID PROPELLANTS AND METHOD OF OPERATING IT. The patent had been issued on 2.11.1954.

'But Parsons had been long dead by then!'

'Yes. He was dead. But I still think he did it.'

'What do you mean?'

'You know,' Gallagher said, 'rocket fuel isn't about formulae, it's about mixing, stuffing, testing. I know that Parsons was very close to his goal out on the test site at Devil's Gate, while his elegant colleagues, von Kármán and Malina, were having lunch with Einstein in the Caltech Athenaeum. And I think that day in South Orange Grove Avenue it finally worked.'

'What did?'

'A completely new rocket fuel.'

Arms spread wide, Gallagher pointed at what was in front of him: plans for a spaceship, calculations of the hyperbolas of trajectories, circuit diagrams, flow charts, outline diagrams of all kinds of technical equipment.

Niklas Kalf looked at him, baffled. 'And that's it? I mean, that's what all this has been about?'

'Yes, of course. That's what it's about. It's about the right of every free man to fly to the stars. Without state interference or any kind of regulation.'

Kalf shook his head.

'And you know the big prize?'

'No.'

'That's won by anyone who flies, within two weeks, in a privately financed spaceship, higher than 100 kilometres, or the edge of outer space.' Gallagher looked excitedly at Kalf. 'There's a prize of ten million dollars.'

'And that's it?' Niklas Kalf asked again.

Gallagher had to think for a moment before he understood what Kalf could mean. He studied his guest closely.

'No,' he said calmly, 'it's about much more than that.'

His fingertips ran over the material as if to reassure himself that it was there, but now he looked carefully at

Kalf. For a moment he seemed to be wondering whether he should say what was really on his mind, and then he did. 'It's about finally doing what Parsons wanted to do: taking white civilization into the universe before it comes to an end here.'

Niklas Kalf didn't immediately understand what Gallagher had said. He thought again of the city, two floors up. The villas in the hills by the sea. The eyes of the coyotes in the night. The illuminated fuselage of a plane coming in to land.

'Love,' he replied quietly, smiling apologetically at Gallagher, 'is not an emotion.'

Gallagher frowned.

Kalf didn't know where that sentence had come from, he just knew that it formed something like the quintessence of that whole long time that he had spent in this country, separated from Liz. And it was suddenly important for him to be understood. He felt dizzy again. But he didn't take his eyes off Gallagher, and tried to concentrate. He was no longer sure which of the two of them was mad. But at the same time he knew precisely what he was trying to say, without having the words to say it.

'You know, Gallagher, animals suffer, too. What distinguishes us from them is not sensation.'

He stopped for a moment, because Gallagher was still staring at him in disbelief, and wondered how he could explain it to him. 'It's like this: you've taken Liz away from me and think that by doing so you have hurt me. Isn't that so?'

Gallagher continued to stare at him.

'And you can give Liz back to me, and with her my happiness.'

The producer nodded.

'A wound that will heal. A trauma that can be resolved.' Kalf smiled. 'But what if I tell you that isn't what's at stake? It isn't a matter of emotions, Gallagher. Love isn't an emotion. I've learned that over the past few months. Love is something quite different.'

But Gallagher didn't understand what he meant. Kalf could tell that from the way he looked at him. There was no point in going on talking. He thought again of how he had killed the black guy. Since then he had avoided remembering the moment of Frank's death so completely that he was almost surprised he had killed someone. It had been something like a reflex. Something you just did.

He slowly started packing the material back into the box.

'What's going on?' Gallagher barked at him, and hurried around the table. 'What are you doing there?'

Kalf nodded. He was now standing so close to the producer that a blow would have maximum force and drive his nasal bone far into his head. He reflected that with such a blow you would have to set your imaginary target behind the boundary of the skin, inside the head, to avoid reeling from the pain of the blow, then concentrated on that very point behind Gallagher's forehead and almost without preparation, but with all his strength, smashed his right fist against his nose.

Before the face exploded in a cloud of red, he saw the expression of complete surprise. At the same time his knuckles felt the blow destroying the nasal cartilage, then it was wet, as the pain of a pointed bone drove into his hand. With a loud groan Phil Gallagher flew backwards, his head hit the marble, a dull crack, and his body fell flat. Blood sprayed a wet, crimson halo around his shattered skull. The producer's body twitched for a moment, mainly his legs, then was still. Kalf's hand, pierced by the nasal bone, was bleeding and starting to hurt.

He sat down on a chair and took long, deep breaths. He knew that silence. It was the same silence in which Frank had lain, as though wrapped in smooth, cool fabric. How elegant it was. The memory of Marvin and Frank paled in the same movement as the red blood seeped from the dead body in front of him, as if condensing the past. It's over, thought Kalf. But what was love if not an emotion? Perhaps love was something like a contract, but a contract that encompassed the whole world because we see the death in our eyes. No animal sees death. Love is what is possible for us beneath the empty sky. At last, he thought again, it's over. And he set off in search of Liz.

Behind the big room was a whole row of kitchens and bathrooms. He followed the sparse wall lamps with their yellowed shades. The floor here was no longer parquet, but a grey-painted jointless surface, and the air was stale and thick. Behind the cold-storage rooms a corridor suddenly opened up, an open service lift that probably led up to the back yard, and just as he was trying to get his bearings he heard the squeak of rubber on concrete.

'Hi, Venus.'

He couldn't tell if she was surprised to see him. Venus Smith slowly rolled along the corridor until she was about ten feet away from him. She put her hands in her lap and just looked at him in silence. Only the fact that she was constantly fumbling with the fabric of her white tracksuit betrayed her unease.

He didn't wait for her to make room for him. Without looking at her, he pushed his way silently past her wheelchair and ran down the dark corridor from which former storerooms led off on either side, with coarse wooden doors, all of them open but one. Niklas Kalf forced himself to breathe calmly and wait for a moment. He looked back once more towards Venus Smith, whose eyes he felt on his back. Then he gently opened the door.

CHAPTER TWENTY-FOUR

Love is not an emotion

Two dirty-brown pelicans flew close side by side, and before they dived they both rose up, silhouettes suddenly jagged, wings pointed, then plunged into the water.

Eyes narrowed, Liz stared into the sun, fragmented white on the sea. A flock of gulls hovered in the air, begging for food that they didn't have, white common gulls and little black-headed gulls, screeching with their beaks wide open and flapping and yet almost motionless in the wind from the sea. The air was fresh and so clear that they could see the sun reflected in the gulls' pupils. Whenever the wind let up for a moment their skin felt warm. Liz breathed deeply in and out again and closed her eyes. Then she looked at him and smiled into the sun.

'I have to sit down.'

They had had to promise the hospital they'd be back in two hours. He took her forearm and helped her sit down slowly in the sand. The *New York Times* had reported that cases of a new kind of illness had appeared in several countries, called Severe Acute Respiratory Syndrome, SARS for short. The WHO had sounded the alarm: '*It seems resistant to antiviral and antibiotic drugs.*' He hadn't told Liz about it. Suddenly everything was simple: nothing is certain but death, and no one can take that away from us. The sky is empty, and we've just got ourselves. That's love. It isn't an emotion. Because if we go, the other one is left alone.

A group of six or seven pelicans approached from the open sea, low over the surf on widespread, unbeating wings. Heads held back and long, massive beaks stretched rigidly forward, the creatures flew past them quickly and resolutely, always close above the ridges of the waves, heading towards Malibu. He pointed at them, and Liz nodded.

The gulls had settled around them and driven away the sandpipers. Two big white petrels flew over the area. Then they saw bottle-nosed dolphins rising from the surf, perhaps fifty yards from the beach. They disappeared and came up again, grey and glistening, also heading north.

'It's beautiful here!'

'Do you like it?'

'Very much! Have you been here often?'

Liz looked at him and their faces nearly touched. They wondered if they should kiss, and were both slightly scared. Then the moment passed.

'No,' he said. 'But I'd always planned to.'

The poem by Heiner Müller came into his mind again. '*Die Bäume verneigen sich*,' he recited quietly,

'*Vor dem Wind vom Pazifik der Bescheid weiß*
Über die Dauer der Millionenstadt
Waiting for doomsday conscious unconscious
Of its fate rising from past and Asia.'

She carefully stroked his face. His skin, which she only knew as light and freckled, was now much darker than before. His lips were chapped and his cheeks still hollow, there were lines around his mouth and his eyelids were unfamiliar to her. The touch of her warm hand made him catch his breath. He wondered how long it had been since he had seen the sun in her blonde curls, and ran his fingers through her hair.

'You've got to tell me everything,' she said quietly as he touched her and turned her face towards the brightness over the sea, the place beyond the bay where aeroplanes rose steeply into the air at regular intervals. She would have to stay here for a while. In hospital at first. Then there would be a trial, in which he would have to give an account of himself.

'What really happened that night in New York?' he asked, and suddenly she was serious and around her mouth he saw again that bitter expression that he didn't think had been there before.

She looked at him as though pleading for help.

'Someone knocked,' she said. 'You were asleep.'

'And then?'

She shrugged. 'I don't know. I opened the door.'

Niklas Kalf nodded. He still thought often of how he had led her from the lower storeys of the cinema. She had hardly been able to walk. The child in the tote bag was asleep, alien and very peaceful. Don't look round, he had murmured repeatedly, and she hid her face under his arm. So she didn't notice that their footsteps were not the only ones on the dully gleaming marble, didn't hear the voices and whispers that he heard without hearing them. Not until they had climbed the stairs, stepped into the hall and the lights of the street forced their way in through the almost opaque, house-high windows, not until then did they leave the murmuring behind. Empty glasses on one of the low tables in the hall, a chair pushed back with a gesture from another world. A cigarette in a glass ashtray smoked itself. Don't look round, Niklas Kalf had murmured again, shoving open the heavy door and pushing Liz and the child outside.

Tired, he closed his eyes against the wind. Last night on the television screen that flickered silently in a corner of the hospital room, the seal of the American President had suddenly appeared, and as he hurried to put on his headphones, the camera showed a speaker's rostrum in a marble-white room with columns and gold chairs.

'*My fellow citizens, events in Iraq have now reached the final days of decision.*'

The memory of that morning when he had discovered Liz had disappeared overwhelmed him at that moment. And as he tried to listen to the President, he had gone on watching Liz's sleeping face for fear that they might take her away from him again. One of her hands rested on the belly of the baby, which was sleeping on its back, its little fists clenched beside its face. Its mouth sucked in sleep. '*Last September I went to the UN General Assembly and urged the nations of the world to unite and bring an end to this danger.*'

Niklas Kalf thought of Marfa and the iron wheel balanced against the silence. The empty expanse. Marvin and Frank. April and her son. *Inner and outer world*, he thought, and finally of Asia, too. He closed his eyes.

'*Saddam Hussein and his sons must leave Iraq within forty-eight hours.*' The way Frank's hands lashed the air as though he could drive away the death that was already in his flesh. And the way he died then. Again and again he saw himself ramming Gallagher's nose into his face.

'We are a peaceful people, yet we're not a fragile people, and we will not be intimidated by thugs and killers. If our enemies dare to strike us, they and all who have aided them will face fearful consequences.'

There could be war tomorrow. He had got up and gone over to Liz. He didn't wake her, but when she turned round and took her hand away, he stroked the baby's belly and felt the spot that was still warm from her touch. It was born in this country. A citizen of Rome, he thought, and couldn't help laughing. This was the centre of the world. Even if that world would soon cease to exist in its present form. *'Goodnight and may God continue to bless America.'*

Niklas Kalf looked down to the bay. We have all the time in the world, he thought. Anyone who thinks otherwise is mad. He tried to imagine what it must have been like for Eugen Meerkaz and his wife, standing here for the first time and looking out at this alien sea. All the time in the world. Close by, a pelican had spotted something in the water. It slowed its flight and straightened in the air, its long, heavy beak already pointing downwards, then plummeted, tipping forward, its wings strangely half tensed, twisted another half-turn as it fell towards the water, and was already plunging into its own nest of white surf.

End Notes

    * Impotent folk, of blind, halt, withered.

   ** For an angel went down at a certain season into the pool, and troubled the water: whosoever then first after the troubling of the water stepped in was made whole of whatsoever disease he had.

  *** 'My wife has been kidnapped. Please help me.'

 **** It's better to use your head than lose it.'

***** 'Always remember, cat, that you will soon be no one and nowhere.'

*****
   * 'Soon you will have forgotten everything, and soon too everyone will have forgotten you.'

*****
  ** The trees bow
To the wind off the Pacific that knows
How long the city of millions will last
Waiting for doomsday conscious unconscious
Of its fate rising from past and Asia

*****
 *** 'What belongs not to you
You must surrender
And what your soul disturbs
Ye may not suffer
Strongly it presses in,
Now we must active be.'

*****
**** 'Love only loving ones
Onward can lead.'

*****
***** He that heareth my word, and believeth on Him that sent me, hath everlasting life and shall not come into condemnation; but is passed from death unto life.

*****
*****
   * Whosoever then first after the troubling of the water stepped in was made whole of whatsoever disease he had.

*****
*****
  ** When Jesus saw him lie, and knew that he had been now a long time in that case, he saith unto him, Wilt thou be made whole? The impotent man answered him: Sir, I have no man, when the water is troubled, to put me into the pool: but while I am coming, another steppeth down before me. Jesus saith unto him, Rise, take up thy bed and walk.

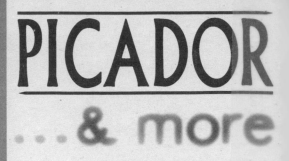